Roadtrip to Redemption

Pawleys Island Paradise series, Book 1

Laurie Larsen,
EPIC Award-winning author of *Preacher Man*

Random Moon Books
A Phase for Every Fancy

This is a work of fiction. Names, characters, places, and incidents are either the product of the author's imagination or are used fictitiously, and any resemblance to actual persons living or dead, business establishments, events, or locales, is entirely coincidental.

All Content by author Laurie Larsen
Cover Art by Steven Novak
Formatting by Polgarus Studio
Published by Random Moon Books
Published in the United States of America

ISBN: 1499347456
ISBN-13: 978-1499347456

A Letter from Laurie …

Dear Reader,

I hope you enjoyed visiting Pawleys Island and meeting Hank, Leslie and the gang as much as I enjoyed writing the book for you!

Did you feel at home in the Old Gray Barn? If so, I did my job. Like Leslie, I spent several childhood summers in Pawleys Island, SC. Like Leslie, I had family members from all over the country migrate to the Old Gray Barn for reunions. Several of the episodes in Leslie's memories come straight from my own memory because they actually happened — even the Portuguese Man o' War episode!

As I started brainstorming on writing my very first series of related stories, I knew I wanted to write about a place that meant a lot to me. It didn't take long before I landed on Pawleys. Just off the coast of Myrtle Beach, Pawleys Island does indeed practice its moniker, "arrogantly shabby" and boasts the world-famous hand-crafted hammocks. And it's a little slice of heaven.

Do you want to go back? Catch up on Leslie and Hank, and find out more about the others you met in *Roadtrip to Redemption*? Good! Because Book 2 in the series is *Tide to Atonement* and it's all about Hank's son Jeremy, his re-acclimation to civilian life after his release from prison, the launch of his wood-working business and his efforts to keep his nose clean. Oh yes, and falling in love. I'll include an excerpt at the end of this e-book. It will be released in early fall (2014).

But first, do me a favor. Please go back to the online retailer where you downloaded *Roadtrip* and leave a review. You can't know how important those reviews are for all authors, but especially independent authors like myself. Short and sweet is fine! It doesn't have to be elaborate, just a few words and a rating, letting readers like yourself know what you thought. Thank you so much.

And now, a small gift for you knitters or people who want to start knitting. In *Roadtrip to Redemption*, Leslie knits a preemie cap for a precious little baby named Carson in Charlotte, North Carolina. The pattern was called "All Around the Square" cap. In real life, that pattern was designed specifically for this book by a very talented friend of mine, Diana Mullins-Atkinson of Oz Dust Designs & The Green Girl Studio. Diana has graciously allowed me to include that pattern as a free gift to readers of *Roadtrip.* I've included Diana's website and info, and if you are a knitter, or just want to be, I know you'll find lots of treasures there.

Happy reading,
Laurie

Chapter One

The manila envelope in her hands grew heavier the longer she stood there, her name – Leslie Malone – printed on the front in black magic marker, blurring as unwanted tears threatened to erupt.

"Lady? Excuse me?"

She jolted at the voice. She gave her head a shake, pulled a brusque hand over her eyes. "Yes. Sorry."

Relief flooding the courier's face was unmistakable. After all, the last thing he needed was a crying woman when he was just trying to do his job. He couldn't really help the fact that he worked for the biggest jerk of a lawyer in town.

He held out a clipboard and a pen and pointed to a line. She signed her name and handed it back. He made a quick escape off her front porch, down her driveway and away in his truck. Were those his tires squealing? Or maybe that was her imagination.

She sighed and returned to her foyer, closing the front door behind her. In all fairness, it wasn't necessarily Tim's lawyer who was the jerk – Tim himself had that honor.

She stepped into her living room and sank onto the sofa. No time like the present. She slipped her finger beneath the sealed flap of the envelope and ripped it open. She pulled out a small stack of papers and flipped through them before turning back to the front page. The contents didn't surprise her. She'd sat through a full day of court, answered the lawyers' questions, shared a mountain of documents she'd gathered at her lawyer's request, and listened to the judge's decisions:

Their marriage was over. Almost twenty years of matrimony — gone.

They'll sell the house and split the profits. And they'd split up all the "stuff" according to the inventory they'd both agreed on.

They'll share Jasmine's college expenses, their contributions proportionate to their incomes.

She'll get half of his 401K when he retires, based on its current balance.

He'll pay child support until Jasmine graduates and gets a job.

She sniffed and tossed the papers on the coffee table. Her lawyer had been pleased with the settlement, especially that last point. Leslie would take her word for it. At this moment, she couldn't care less. But was it possible their lives together had resulted in five neat bullet points? What had once been a loving marriage and family, now was a bunch of legalese.

The phone rang and she jumped. By habit, she rose and glanced at the Caller ID. She puffed out a breath and smiled. "Jaz! How's it going?"

"Fantastic, Mom."

Her daughter's voice always brought a smile to her face. From toddler to teen, and now as a young woman. "Your semester will end before you know it. It'll be nice to have a break from school, huh?"

"Well, yeah."

She caught the slight hesitation but plowed ahead. "It sure will be good to have you home, Jaz. The house is awful quiet these days."

"I bet."

A tone in the softly spoken words made Leslie scurry to find a new topic. She knew Jasmine pitied the state of her parents' marriage. But today was not a day to delve into it. Tears were too close to the surface at any given moment to tempt them.

"Have you checked with the diner? They might need you to waitress this summer, and with me off school, we'll have a lot of time together. I was thinking of some fun things to do – plant our garden, try new recipes, maybe we can even plan a vacation, just the two of us."

Leslie winced at the forced cheer in her tone and bit her lip. Jasmine would recognize it; she was way too sensitive in general, and too close to the subject of Leslie's destroyed marriage, to dismiss the subtlety. The last thing she wanted to do was make Jasmine take sides, or to feel sorry for her at this stage of her life.

Although, with her dad's full-blown mid-life crisis, complete with a toupe, red Corvette and thirty-year-old divorcee girlfriend, the proper side to take was clear. At least in Leslie's opinion.

"Mom, listen. I won't be coming home this summer after all." She cleared her throat and paused.

"What?" Leslie heard music playing behind Jasmine's voice.

"Something really exciting has come up. An opportunity I don't want to turn down because although it's not, um, the best timing … I know I'd regret it later if I didn't go."

A little hand gripped Leslie's heart. She drew a deep breath and forced it out. "Jasmine, spill. What are you talking about?"

Her daughter's words tumbled over themselves. "A few months ago, I applied for a summer abroad program in Paris. I never, ever thought I'd get selected because it's so totally competitive. It's a chance for college students all over the world to work in the Paris fashion scene for three whole months. Go backstage of the runway, work with models, designers, marketers, buyers, retailers. It's an unbelievable internship and only the top fashion students are selected. I really didn't think I'd have a chance but guess what … I was chosen! I found out today!"

A weird buzzing filled her ears. Leslie stood squarely on her two feet and yet, the room was beginning to spin. She slumped into the chair beside the phone as if her spinal column had become a cooked noodle. The pause lengthened into an uncomfortable silence.

"Mom? Are you still there?"

"Yes," she finally spit out. "You never even told me you'd applied for a summer abroad, honey."

"I know. Honestly, Mom, I didn't think I had a chance, so why bother? It's really an honor. It'll be something I'll remember my whole life, and it'll be great for my resume."

"Okay, okay, Jaz. I hate to be the voice of reason here, but have you thought of the logistics?"

"What do you mean?"

Leslie sighed. "The biggest one I can think of is, how much does it cost, and how are we going to pay for it?"

"Oh, that's taken care of, Mom. Don't worry about it."

"You mean, you got a scholarship? It's a no-cost internship?"

Jaz cleared her throat again. "Not exactly. I mean, there's a cost, but it's okay. Dad said he'd pay for it. In fact, he gave me his credit card number and told me to charge the tuition and fees."

A chill crept down Leslie's spine while goose bumps popped on her arm. "You called Dad about this before you called me?"

She winced. Not the most mature of questions to ask – but give her a break: she was new to this divorce stuff. "One day" new, in fact.

"Well, yeah, I mean … before I could accept the internship I knew I had to be able to pay for it, so I, you know …"

Leslie nodded. "Went with your best option." Of course Tim would be able to pay for a summer abroad. His doctor's salary loomed like the Statue of Liberty, her own teacher's salary lingering almost unnoticed in the shadows.

"Well …,"

Leslie detested the uncomfortable silence but couldn't bring herself to say anything cheerful to alleviate it.

"I'm sorry, Mom, but I …"

"No, I understand. I'm not sure I could've helped you anyway. I would've tried, though."

"I know."

For the next few minutes Jasmine chattered about the internship, the work, the classes, the travel. She was excited for her, sure she was. Of course she was! She hoped she showed all the appropriate enthusiasm. But when she hung up, reality hit her upside the head.

She'd be alone all summer.

Leslie closed her eyes and sat still, her mind serving up an image of what her summer break would be like. No husband, no job to go to, no Jasmine to brighten her days. Long days spanning ad infinitum with no plans. Or at least, nothing important to do.

What was the purpose of her life now? What was she put here to do, if it wasn't to be wife, mother and teacher? Prayers helped; she'd learned that time and time again. If nothing else, she usually felt better after verbalizing her requests and getting them out there.

Her spoken words echoed in the empty house. "Lord. I know You're there. Somewhere in all this mess that my life has become. It hasn't been the most stellar of days, and You know that. But come on, how much can one person take? My marriage is over, my daughter will be gone all summer. Not even a job to get up and go to everyday. Nothing, but my new monotone life." She sighed. "Solitude is completely overrated. Give me strength to deal with my new reality. Amen."

She stood and made her way to the kitchen. What on earth was she going to do with herself?

* * *

"Bye, Mrs. Malone!" The echoes of children's voices remained in her memory long after they faded from the room. She stood at the window, waving at the last of her third graders as they ventured forth into their summers. Yet she remained, staring motionless through the pane.

Reluctantly, she turned and faced the empty classroom. A few hours of work, and she'd have the walls stripped of laminated teaching aids and remnant artwork, the desktops scrubbed and her few personal items packed in a box to take along with her. Fifteen times she'd faced the last day of school, always an exciting day. Sad, yes, because she'd miss those little treasures she'd spent the last hundred and eighty-some school days teaching. But new ones came next year to replace the ones she sent on. Summer break was always a welcome reward for all the hard work of the school year.

Never had she felt so reluctant to just … go home.

By 6:00 she loaded her box in the back hatch of her SUV and turned back to gaze at the school. What would she be like when she returned in the fall? Nine months ago, she was confident. She had a husband of twenty years. A lovely home. A daughter excelling in college. A rewarding career she enjoyed.

How life can change.

All that was gone. No husband, no marriage: ruined in the fell swoop of his reckless affair. Jasmine was growing up. The house was going up on the market soon. And she now faced three long, empty months off work.

She climbed into the car and tried to shake off her mood. She'd get home, make some soup and watch television to burn away the evening hours. Then she'd go to bed and wake up tomorrow.

And figure out what to do.

As she approached the house, her stomach twisted. Tim's Mercedes sat unexpected in the driveway. He'd been forced to relinquish his house keys at divorce court so he sat inside the car, awaiting her arrival. She pulled her car beside him and looked over, her heart doing a little twist thing that caused her breath to catch in her chest.

He looked up from some reading and nodded intentionally in her direction. If the nod had words, it would've said, "Oh yes, there you are." For a moment, a sense of guilt for keeping him waiting invaded her. He was a busy man, an important man. Time was money.

Then she smirked. Although there were many things she hated about her new single state, one thing she absolutely loved was she didn't have to feel guilty anymore. It was no longer her worry when she upset Tim, disappointed him, annoyed him. The divorce decree stated that much.

"Hi, Leslie." He got out of his car and walked over to hers, opened her door. He was nothing if not a southern gentleman, raised on the genteel manners of the generations of belles and gentlemen before him. Two decades of living in Pittsburgh had erased his accent, but not those lessons learned long ago.

She supposed those lessons didn't include ditching your wife for a gold-digging tramp a dozen years younger.

"Tim," she acknowledged. "What are you doing here?"

"We need to talk about plans for the house." As he spoke, he headed for the front door, then stopped when she diverted her route and walked toward the back of the car. He followed her and lifted the box, tucking it easily under his arm.

"Okay." She stuck her key in the front door lock and jiggled it. Years of practice made the temperamental thing release the tumblers. She swung the door open and walked in, fighting the inclination to offer him something, treat him like a guest. Because he wasn't.

She turned and looked at him. He had come to a halt uncomfortably in the foyer, gazing into the living room. The occasion marked the first time he'd entered the house since the divorce was final. She wondered if he realized it. For such an intelligent man, sometimes the obvious escaped him.

"Do you mind if I take a look around?"

"What are you looking for?"

He pulled a small notebook and pen out of his shirt pocket. "We need to identify anything that needs fixing before it goes up on the market. We'll agree on the repair, then I'll get estimates and we'll split the costs 50/50."

She frowned. "There's nothing wrong with this house."

She detected a flash of annoyance in his expression before he tamped it down. "I'm not expecting any big repairs. But all houses suffer wear and tear. And the more sparkling and spotless we can make the house look, the better chance we'll sell it quickly. And command a price we like."

Sparkling and spotless. His house wasn't, and his wife wasn't. So he divorced the wife and was selling the house.

She hated the catch in her voice as she said, "Well, go ahead then. But I don't want to have to spend a bunch of money on repairs to a house I'm not even going to live in anymore."

"We'll split the costs."

She rolled her eyes and huffed a stream of air. "Let's face it, Tim, you'll have a lot more disposable income coming out of this divorce than I will. I need to put myself on a budget and stick to it. The last thing I want to spend my hard-earned money on is repairs to this house."

He fixed a long glance on her. "How about I take it out of the child support I owe you? You won't really use it this summer anyway since Jaz won't be home."

Her face burned. "Oh yes, Jasmine's internship in Paris. It was awful nice of you to make the decision to send her overseas without even consulting with me. I believe that's in violation of the custody agreement."

He looked down at his feet. "Okay, you're right. But officially, we weren't divorced when she talked to me about it. I figured you were on the same page as me, supportive of her opportunity."

Water under the bridge. The internship was a unique opportunity. He was financing it so what was she objecting to, really? She shook her head. "You'll keep the home repairs to a minimum, please?"

He nodded. "Nothing crazy. It's a sales strategy. My realtor advised it's the smart thing to do. It'll attract more potential buyers."

"Your realtor?" Irritation crept into her voice.

"Yes, uh …,"

"I believe we were supposed to agree mutually on a realtor. That's what the judge said." Her new life slapped her in the face and she felt the sting of tears in her eyes. To prevent him from detecting it, she turned and headed for the kitchen.

"Leslie."

She ignored the summons and didn't stop till she reached the refrigerator. For something to do, she opened the freezer and stared at its contents.

"Les." He stood so close behind her she could smell his cologne. She'd bought it for him last Christmas. For that matter, she'd bought the shirt he wore, and she'd dragged him out to the mall to pick out and try on the shoes. She was giving her very best effort to hold it together when he squeezed her forearm.

Her tears finally escaped, rolling slowly down both cheeks.

"Ahh, Les. Please don't." His voice softened, tenderized till it was a whisper that caressed her broken heart. He pulled her close and buried his face in her hair, and she went with it. Her body and mind turned to mush as she breathed him in, fitting so naturally against him. He'd held her like this a million times over the lifetime they'd shared.

But now, it was wrong. That stack of papers still sitting on the kitchen table over there declared it, and they'd both signed.

She pushed away and turned her back. She was taking a moment to recover when he said it. "I'm sorry, Leslie. You didn't deserve this."

How many times had she ached to hear those words, that sentiment? How many times had she laid alone in her dark bed, wondering what she'd done to push him away? Had she let herself go, had she let the spark leave their marriage? Was it somehow her fault he'd strayed?

"It's something I'm going through right now. Something . . ., I don't know, something I can't seem to control."

She wanted to scream. Drag her fingers through her hair, grab hold of the ends and pull. Let loose with the worst-sounding shriek of her life.

Instead, she turned to face him. "It's been a long day. I'm going upstairs to take a bath. Please finish up here and leave."

He nodded and she scooted past him up the stairs to soak.

* * *

The next morning, the alarm shrilled at 6:15. She groaned and reached over to silence it, stubbornly refusing to open her eyes. Why oh why had she let her school day alarm awake her? She lay motionless, wondering if her body would allow her to slip back into slumber. Peacefully. Obliviously.

Because if she slept late, it would mean fewer waking hours she'd have to fill.

Twenty minutes later, no luck. Not only had she not drifted back to sleep, she was now wide awake. Where was a yawn when she wanted one? She flipped back the comforter and stalked out of bed.

In the kitchen, she made coffee and sat down with the paper. She marked a few sales she could visit at the mall. That would kill time. She flipped the page and marked a fundraiser walk she could sign up for. Exercise plus feed the hungry – what could be better? Next page, garage sales were advertised. Maybe find a hidden treasure.

She pushed the paper away and sighed. She got up to refill her coffee cup and glanced at the digital clock on the coffee maker. 7:05 AM. She let a frustrated breath escape.

She needed a project. A job that would absorb her for days, maybe a week. Something to take her mind off her empty, lonely summer stretching out interminably in front of her.

Then it hit her: one monstrous task that couldn't be ignored. Giving the house a top-to-bottom cleaning, and throwing out the old stuff she wouldn't want in her new home.

By the end of Day 1, she was comfortably sweaty and slightly sore at the knees. By the end of Day 2, she scanned the pile of stuff and marveled at how much junk had accumulated. On Day 3, as the estate sale service was driving down her street with their truck full of her discarded stuff, she made a conscious effort to control the sensation of panic gathering in her stomach and threatening to erupt into her lungs and throat. She watched the truck disappear around the corner, turned and walked into her nearly empty house.

Who wanted all that old furniture in a perky new condo anyway?

On Day 4, the phone rang. She tiptoed over the newly shampooed carpets, passed the rented shampooer and picked it up.

"Hey, it's me," Tim's deep voice said.

"Hi."

"The realtor's bringing someone over on Monday."

"Who?"

He paused. "Who? I don't know who. A potential buyer."

"Oh." Of course. It didn't really matter who they were as long as they could afford to buy the house.

"Wanted to warn you. Their appointment's at noon. You can be there if you want, but usually it's better if the owner is gone."

"Okay."

So it began. Friends had told her horror stories about having to keep a house in "showcase-ready" condition while still occupying it. Never a dish in the sink, never a piece of clothing on the floor … it could affect a sale.

She made her way to the kitchen and poured herself a diet soda. Carrying it with her, she moved through the rooms of her home, surveying her hard work of the last few days. She'd enjoyed getting absorbed in her task. It was good to keep her mind occupied, work hard and look at the results. Clean, fresh, uncluttered rooms. One last task: a fresh coat of paint in the living and dining rooms, and she'd buy the house herself! Or, she'd want to if she were a buyer.

Instead, she was the seller.

She squeezed her eyes shut over another threat of tears. She inhaled a deep breath and waited for the sadness to pass.

One step at a time. Paint the walls, and then what? Wait for the parade of strangers through her house, disturbing all her family memories? Listen to their whispered comments,

"The closet's too small, the roof will need to be replaced soon," and try like crazy not to be defensive?

Now that her hard work was done, the mystery still remained of how she would fill her days over the whole summer. That's when it dawned on her: take a trip.

Hit the road!

With no destination in mind, get in the car and travel. Who cares how long it took to get there? Just go. Avoid the reality of realtors and buyers. Get away. And come back when it seemed the right thing to do.

The thought lifted her mood, and with her plan made now, she grabbed her purse and headed to the paint store.

Chapter Two

Travel day. Leslie awoke before the alarm, a flutter in her stomach. As she showered, the day outside transformed from early morning darkness to a full-fledged gift from God. She tucked the last of her cosmetics into her suitcase and zipped it up, a solid beam of sunlight penetrating the slats of her window blinds and forming stripes of optimistic daylight on the carpet.

She stared at them, stilling, took a deep breath and closed her eyes. "Lord, be with me on this trip. Guide me along the way. Keep me safe from harm. Help me to find meaning in my new life. Help me to accept my situation. Oh, and let me have some fun along the way."

Her lips curled into an amused smile. Tugging the blinds closed, she dragged her suitcase down the stairs.

Leaving the house and closing it up had a strange sense of finality to it, even though she knew she wouldn't be gone that long. Call it a vacation, similar to the trips she'd taken every summer of her life. But this was nothing like any other trip she'd ever taken. First, she was alone. Because of her marriage in her early twenties and her prompt pregnancy, she'd rarely been alone during her adult life. She was Tim's wife, Jasmine's mother. Period. When she traveled, it was with either or both of them. That was about to change.

Second, she didn't have a travel plan. She didn't know where she was going or when she was coming back. She would open her heart to the direction of God and not worry about the details. It was what it was.

Aimless wandering? Or inspired discovery?

When she pulled the door closed behind her and tugged to make sure it was tight, she headed for her SUV before the anxiety could take hold. She sat in the driver's seat and considered her options. She and Jasmine had talked about a trip to the beach this summer. Why not do it herself? It was early enough in the season, she shouldn't have trouble finding accommodations. If she found a place she liked, she could stay awhile. If not, she'd keep moving.

An initial decision made, she started the car and headed toward highway 79 South outside of town. Maneuvering onto the highway and avoiding the heavy traffic occupied all her thoughts. She must've hit morning suburb rush hour. But as she continued to head away from Pittsburgh, the congestion eventually cleared and she let out a deep breath.

Leslie turned on the radio, jabbed at a few of the pre-programmed radio buttons, but quickly tired of the static and commercials. She switched over to her CD collection and smiled when a familiar song came on. She was a fan of the music collections that included the number one hits of a particular year or decade. Tim had subscribed her in a year-long program one time and she received one CD a month till she owned more music than she could ever listen to in a lifetime. But it was amazing how her memory – so sketchy at remembering other things – allowed her to sing each and every song lyric word for word.

She eased down her window and opened the sunroof and for the next hour, exercised her dormant memory and vocal chords by singing song after song from the 1970's as loud as she wanted.

When the CD ended, she pulled off Route 79 for a cup of coffee at a McDonald's drive-through. Jump back on the road. So far, this trip was a great idea.

Leslie rejoined 79 and drove for another hour. Due to her early start, it was only mid-morning when she crossed over the state line to West Virginia.

"Hip hip! Hooray!" She couldn't help but yell it. It was a family tradition during vacations so ingrained in her that she did it automatically. Every time they crossed over a state line, Tim would yell the hip hip, and she and Jasmine would respond with a hooray. On longer trips they may yell it six or seven times each way. It wasn't quite as satisfying to yell it with only herself to respond. But the sentiment was the same – safe travels, seeing the country. There was good luck and fortune to be had crossing over each state line. She repeated it for the full three repetitions: "Hip hip hooray! Hip hip hooray! We're in West Virginia!"

About a half hour into West Virginia, a car quite a ways in front of her switched lanes, then swerved back again. Curious, Leslie kept an eye on the vehicle as she approached it. Was the driver texting? Falling asleep? It was too early in the day for drowsy drivers, unless this one had stayed up driving all night and desperately needed a break.

As she kept her foot on the gas pedal and maintained an even speed, she was making steady progress catching up with this questionable car. It was losing speed. A brief skyward prayer slipped from her lips, "Lord, help this driver. Keep us both safe."

When she was mere yards away, the car suddenly veered off the highway and came to a stop on the graveled shoulder.

Relief slipped through her. The driver obviously needed a break, and now was taking one. Perfect. Leave the highway safe for those who needed to use it.

She moved to the left lane to give a wide berth. As she passed the car, though, her eyes locked in on the scene and in a few seconds, she knew the last thing she could ever do was continue driving.

The driver sat with his head lolling on the headrest, mouth open. In the passenger seat was a little boy, crying and frantic, looking over at the driver with terror.

Leslie gasped and on instinct, moved back to the right lane and made her way to the shoulder. She came to a gravelly halt, put the car in reverse, flipped around in her seat to look through the rear window, and speeded backwards till she arrived at the car.

She put the car in Park just feet in front of the car. And sat motionless. What did she think she was doing? A woman, traveling by herself, trying to help a stranger. It could all backfire on her if that stranger tried to harm her. Tim would've never stood for it if he were here. Too spontaneous — too unpredictable. Tim stood for self-preservation in this world, never took risks that could put him or the ones he loved in danger.

She jumped out and ran, but even as she did, she could hear Tim's admonishments in her head. When she reached the driver's side, she tugged at the door handle. But it was locked. She peered in through the window. The man's body shook and shook in the driver's seat, uncontrolled convulsions. She pounded on the window with the palms of her hands which did absolutely nothing to help the situation.

The only way she'd get into that car was to appeal to the child. She ran around to the passenger side and tapped on the glass. Instead of looking her way, he set his single-minded focus on his dad, wailing a tortured cry, the tears making wet tracks down his face. The sealed window muffled his terrified weeping.

More tapping couldn't coax him to look her way. Time was of the essence. She ran back to her car and grabbed her cell phone out of her purse. She keyed in 9-1-1. Moments later, a dispatcher asked for her emergency.

"I'm on Highway 79 heading south in West Virginia. There's a man in a car here having some sort of attack. A heart attack or something. He's got a little boy in the car, and they need help."

"Please clarify your location. What exit are you near on 79?"

Leslie felt her heart rate spike. Of course, it would be helpful if she could pinpoint her exact location so the ambulance could come quickly and pick them up. But she had no idea. She hadn't really been paying that much attention. She was just passing through.

"Hello?"

"I'm sorry, I'm trying to think of the last exit I passed but I don't remember."

"Okay."

"Wait! I know." She'd only been in West Virginia a half hour. "I crossed the state line from Pennsylvania about 30 miles ago."

"That'll get us there. I've dispatched the ambulance and rescue squad. They should arrive in … about seven minutes. Meanwhile, can the patient hear you when you speak to him?"

"No! He's locked inside the car with a child. The boy's freaking out and the man is unconscious."

"Please stay on the scene until the rescue squad arrives."

Leslie tucked the cell phone into her pocket and jogged back to the car. The boy had undone his seat belt and was kneeling sideways in his seat. Dad was thrusting and convulsing, a line of spittle trailing down his chin. The boy yelled through his tears, but the words were muffled behind the locked door and she couldn't make out the meaning. But words didn't matter. The boy was traumatized, that much was clear. Leslie's love for children gave her an ache in her heart for this nameless, helpless child.

She stayed, hands on the window, eyes peeled on the poor little guy inside and moments later, she heard sirens. When an ambulance pulled up behind the car, two uniformed men jumped out, quickly assessing the situation. One EMT grabbed a device and made quick work of slipping it into the car window and unlocking the door. The other pulled a stretcher out of the vehicle and rolled it to the driver's side.

As they hoisted the man out of the car, the two lifted him onto the stretcher and strapped him on. The man was moaning, unconscious, blood dripping out the corner of his mouth.

The child stood, hunched over inside the car and hopped onto his dad's now vacated seat. He sobbed, his eyes wide with terror. Leslie held a hand out to him. He startled and gazed up at her, confusion clear on his face.

"They're going to take care of your daddy. Don't you worry about that. They're trained to help in emergencies, and they're going to take him to the hospital."

He stared at her for a second, ignored her outstretched hand, and jumped out of the car, landing on his feet on the gravel. He ran to the stretcher and reached up to put his hands on his dad. "Daddy! Daddy! What's wrong?"

Pain tore through Leslie like a hand squeezing her heart. The EMTs were busy taking the man's vitals and inserting an IV in his arm. They were surely aware of the little tyke desperately trying to get his dad's attention, but the man was in no condition to respond. Instinct took over. She picked up the child and patted his back, murmuring sounds of comfort in his ear. He cried and pulled and twisted, but eventually wore himself out and went limp in her arms.

The men loaded the patient, strapped to the stretcher, into the ambulance and she moved over to the open back door. One of the EMTs motioned her up. "You can ride in here. Bring the boy."

She paused, panic starting to bubble in her throat. "I'm not family. I don't know these people. I happened to be driving by."

The EMT shrugged. "Leave the boy in the ambulance then."

She looked into the terrified eyes of the boy in her arms and knew, more clearly than anything, she couldn't just shove him into the ambulance, close the door and drive away. Although she was a complete stranger, he had settled into her arms and now shifted his eyes from his dad in the truck to her face.

"Do you want me to come with you to the hospital?"

His nod held no hesitation.

She called to the EMT, "I'll come along with you and sit with the boy. Should I leave my car here?"

He nodded and grabbed a couple red flags from a shelf behind him. "Put these in each front windshield, then lock both the cars."

He tossed the flags. She caught them and hurried to the task. Done, she clambered into the back of the emergency vehicle, still holding tight to the boy. They settled onto a bench lining the side. In her silence, she marveled over the uncharacteristic position she found herself in. Had she ever put herself on the line to help strangers in need, in such a personal way? She couldn't think of one other time.

One of the EMTs stayed in the back while the other dashed to the driver's seat, turned on the wailing sirens and took off, the truck bouncing over the rough shoulder terrain before settling into a swift smooth ride on the highway.

"What do you think is wrong with him?" She looked at the medical tech, a kid with broad shoulders, dark hair and a thin layer of stubble above his lip. Funny now that she'd reached a certain age, she thought of people in their twenties and thirties as "kids."

He was holding a clipboard and a pen, hovering over the patient and occasionally marking on a sheet of paper. Although the man was no longer convulsing, he had still not regained consciousness. "Some sort of convulsion – a seizure, maybe? Is he epileptic?"

"I have no idea."

The young man nodded and went back to his work. Leslie turned to the boy on her lap, his face nestled into her neck. "Don't you worry, they're going to take good care of your daddy, okay?"

He nodded, his head pressed into her neck.

"What's your name, sweetie?"

No movement.

"My name's Leslie. I'm a teacher." From the size of him she'd guess him to be about seven, almost the age of the kids she taught every day. The coincidence of the situation made her wonder fleetingly if God's hand was at work here. This family obviously needed a helper, and it was her – someone well equipped to work with kids this age – that happened by at the right moment. She had no idea how this adventure would turn out, but she would stick with it and see it through. If this family needed her … if God needed her here, the least she could do was serve.

"What grade are you in?"

His muffled voice came, "Second."

"What's your teacher's name?"

"Mrs. …" something that sounded like Radcliffe, but Leslie couldn't be sure.

"Well, my last name is Malone. If you'd like to call me Mrs. Malone, that's fine, or if you're comfortable with Leslie, that's fine too."

There was a slight hesitation, then a nodding of his head.

"And what should I call you?"

Again, a pause, and then he pushed back and looked up in her face. "Deakon."

Leslie smiled. Progress. "So nice to meet you, Deakon. And what is your dad's name?"

"Norman."

Leslie nodded. "Okay, well, you and I will help these guys do whatever they can to help your dad recover. Has this kind of thing ever happened to him before?"

He nodded. "There's a note in his wallet."

"A note?"

"Yeah. In case it happens, it tells about what is wrong with him."

"Oh Deakon, thank you so much for telling me that. That's going to really help your daddy." She raised her voice to attract the attention of the EMT. She noticed a nametag pinned to his shirt for the first time that read, "Joe Leon."

"Joe, check his wallet. Deakon here told me there's a note in there about his condition."

Joe nodded and shifted Norman so he could pull the wallet out from his back pocket. Shuffling through it, he found a small piece of folded paper and scanned it quickly. "It's an abnormality of the veins in his brain that can cause a seizure when he's undermedicated. He takes the anticonvulsive, Dilantin. Best to get him some intravenous Dilantin to revive him."

Leslie looked down at Deakon with a reassuring smile. "See? You were a huge help! Now they know exactly what to do to help your daddy."

The little boy gave a small, satisfied smile.

"I don't have any liquid Dilantin onboard but I'll call the ER and tell them to have it on hand. I've initiated an IV so they can administer it as soon as we get there. We're about 3 minutes away." He picked up a phone from a metal suitcase and made the call.

When they reached the hospital parking lot, Norman moaned. His eyes darted desperately until they landed on Deakon. "Buddy."

Deakon yelled, "Daddy!" and jumped off Leslie's lap and hopped to his side. She reached out to guide him by the hips. The ride into the parking lot was bumpy. The last thing the little guy needed now was a bump to the head from losing his balance.

Deakon launched himself onto his dad's chest. Joe gave some cautionary noises but Norman waved his hand, the IV tubes trailing as he made a dismissive gesture. Then he settled both arms around his son. "I'm sorry, buddy. I'm so sorry."

The boy shook his head and sobbed openly.

Joe leaned over the duo and lifted his clipboard. "Welcome back. I have some questions for you. Your name?"

Norman took a deep breath, and holding tight to his son, he replied, "Norman Foster."

"Your address?"

Norman provided it.

"What year is it?"

An odd question, Leslie thought, but Norman didn't bat an eye as he gave the current year, then continued to respond with the state they were in, the day of the week and even the President of the country. Satisfied, Joe put the clipboard away and began to prepare for moving Norman into the ER.

"Buddy, stay close by me and watch out for cars in the parking lot, okay?"

Leslie maneuvered closer to the stretcher. "Norman, I'd be glad to help occupy Deakon until you're more able."

He turned his head, his look of confusion making it clear he hadn't known of her presence before now.

"I'm Leslie Malone. I was driving by on the highway when you went into a seizure. I stopped and called 9-1-1."

His eyes scanned her face and the concerned lines between his eyebrows eased. "Thank you. I can't thank you enough. Although I've had seizures occasionally for the last few years, they're always nocturnal. You don't know how weird it is to go to bed one night, and wake up with a bunch of men dressed in EMT uniforms in your room. Or wake up in an ambulance and wonder how the hell you got there. It's pretty disconcerting."

She nodded. "I can imagine."

"But this … this puts a whole new spin on it. Going into a seizure while driving? I could've killed myself and my son.

This has *never* happened before." He shook his head and let his eyes roll to the ceiling of the vehicle.

"I'm glad it worked out all right. You're going to be fine, Norman."

"This time, yeah. But how can I put Deakon in a car with me ever again? I can't control these things. They come on out of the blue – not very often, mind you. But I had no idea it was going to happen today."

The vehicle stopped and she heard the slam of the driver's door. Soon, the back door swung open and Joe's partner jumped up into the truck, the two of them working together to get Norman out.

"Don't worry about Deakon. I'll stay with him in the waiting room until they're ready for him to come back and visit you."

He locked eyes with her as they carried him backwards out of the vehicle, and brushed his hand against hers as he passed. What was happening to Norman must feel totally out of control. Any man would have trouble dealing with that. Leslie knew he was hesitant to entrust his precious son with a stranger off the street, literally, but she *could* help and that seemed to be what she was supposed to do right now. The purpose of her being here, of all places, at this time.

"We'll be right in the waiting room, don't worry."

She caught his slight nod as they hustled him toward the building. She and Deakon hopped out of the vehicle and followed. Inside the ER, she found a small waiting room with a TV and a basket of toys and books in the corner. At first, Deakon sat quietly on a nearby chair.

"Your dad was talking and awake. He's going to be fine. The doctors are going to put some medicine into his arm which will make him better."

He nodded. "I know."

It dawned on her there might be some relatives who needed a phone call about this unexpected detour. "Deakon, what's your home phone number? Should I call your mommy and let her know you're here?"

Deakon glanced up at her and shook his head, his lower lip poking out. "I don't have a mommy."

Again Leslie's heart wrenched. She had no idea what this boy had been through, but she already knew it was more than any child should have to endure in seven short years. She forced some peppy optimism into her voice. "Okay, how about a grandma or grandpa? A close friend of your dad's maybe?"

"I have a grandma and grandpa but I don't know their number."

"Okay, sweetie, we'll see if your dad wants me to call them later. Meanwhile, do you want to watch TV or play with toys? Do you want me to read you a book maybe?"

He forced his attention to a small stack of books and slid off his chair to study his choices. He picked up a couple, put a few aside, then returned with four short books in his hand, all comic book adaptations – Xmen, Superman, Batman. She patted her lap and he crawled up. She opened the first cover and they both became enthralled in action and adventure.

Thirty minutes passed and a nurse approached them. "You can come back and see Mr. Foster now if you'd like."

Deakon was busy on the floor by now, coloring in a Superman coloring book, bright strokes of red and blue. At the nurse's words, he bounced in place and heaved himself up, his face lit up with a happy smile. He trotted after the nurse, Leslie following along behind.

"Want to push the big round button on the wall?"

Deakon followed the direction the nurse was pointing and pushed his whole palm into it. The double doors whooshed open. Another grin.

Walking behind the nurse, Leslie peeked into each curtained-off makeshift room. So many people receiving care – so many people taking an unexpected pit stop in their day. You can plan and plan, but you are never in control. That's the way life is.

When they reached Norman Foster's cubicle, Deakon screeched his pleasure and broke into a sprint. He tried to jump up onto the hospital bed, but it sat too high, so instead he jumped onto the seat of the guest chair beside the bed, leaned over and laid the entire top half of his body over his dad. Leslie watched father and son, Norman's eyes squeezed shut, his arms wrapped around the little boy.

She looked away, not only because of the prick of tears threatening her eyes, but at the realization that she was an intruder on a poignant family moment. She lingered outside the curtain, her back to the family reunion, but close enough that if they needed her, she would hear. Muffled sounds of joy floated from the room. Then, an uncertain, "Lisa? No, Leslie?"

She circled around and leaned into the room.

"I'm sorry, it's Leslie, isn't it?"

"Yes. Leslie Malone."

"Please, come in."

Leslie took the few steps into the tight space. Deakon now sat on the hospital bed, squeezed up tight against his dad, his legs dangling off the side. "Deakon, looks like your dad's good as new, huh?"

He beamed at her, grabbed his dad's hand and patted it. "Yep."

She grinned at him.

"I can't thank you enough, Leslie. If you weren't driving on that highway at that precise moment ...." He shook his head. "I don't even want to think about what could've happened."

"You're safe and sound, both of you. That's all that matters."

"The doctor came in. They're going to try me on a stronger anti-convulsive for a few months. Unfortunately, I'm not allowed to drive during the trial period. But if I don't have another waking seizure, I'll be back in the saddle."

"That's wonderful news!" Leslie inched into the space and put her hand on top of his where Deakon still grasped it.

"We can make it work. I can't imagine not driving, but I guess under the circumstances, it's what's safest for me, Deakon and the drivers around me."

"As Deakon and I were sitting out there, I was praying for a good outcome for you. I think I got the answer to my prayer."

"Actually, I think you were the answer to my prayer. Thanks for taking such good care of my boy. Now, I have one other favor to ask you."

Leslie nodded.

"Somewhere, they've stashed my clothes. In the pocket of my pants is my cell phone. Could you find it and call someone for me? They won't let me use a cell back here around all the machines."

"Oh, of course. Who is it?"

"When you find the phone, go into the Contact list and look for Mom L. Could you call her, explain what happened and tell her Deak and I need her to come to the hospital right away?"

"Sure. Be right back." Leslie rustled under the hospital bed and found a plastic bag. Inside, she found folded clothes. Rummaging inside the pocket of a pair of blue jeans, she pulled out a phone, then left the cubby. Back through the double doors, she walked through the waiting room and outside.

She located Mom L in the Contacts and placed the call. Foster was his last name. Could Mom L be his mother? Or possibly Deakon's mother's mom?

"Hey." The voice sounded like it knew what voice to be expecting. Time to throw her for a loop.

"Hi, my name is Leslie Malone, and I'm on Norman Foster's cell phone."

"Oh."

"Norman asked me to call you. Please don't be alarmed – everything is okay, but we're at the hospital."

Leslie heard a gasping sound.

"Norman had a seizure while driving."

"A seizure! While driving?"

"Yes. He explained that he has a seizure disorder, but up to this point, they've only been nocturnal. For some reason, this one was waking."

"Is Deakon there?"

"Yes, Deakon is with his dad here in the ER and he's perfectly fine. Please don't worry. But Norman asked that you come right away. They took his driver's license away and they need a ride."

"Absolutely. So, are you a nurse?"

"No. I happened to be driving by when Norman's car started to weave. He pulled over to the shoulder before his seizure, but he was unconscious so I called 9-1-1."

There was a pause and a slow outtake of breath. "You're an angel."

Leslie chuckled. "Not at all."

"Do you believe in God?"

"Oh, yes of course."

"You were there for my grandson. You kept him safe. You were part of God's plan and I thank you for being there."

"Honestly, I didn't do much except read Deakon a few stories. But I was happy to do it."

"I'm going to head over there right now. Could you stick around? I'd love to meet you."

"Sure."

They ended the call and Leslie headed back into the hospital and down the hall to the cubicle. An angel, her? She shook her head, amused. But could it be she'd played a part in God's plan for the Fosters today? So many disastrous things could've happened if she hadn't been there to watch out for Norman, for Deakon.

But of course, if she hadn't called 9-1-1, if she hadn't occupied Deakon, someone else would've. No supernatural miracles here, just what good people do for each other.

When she reached Norman and Deakon, she handed the phone back. "Mission accomplished. She's on her way. She asked me to stick around so she could meet me."

Norman smiled. "She's been a huge part of Deakon's life. Not just a grandmother, but a stand-in mother." He gazed fondly at his son, now lying beside him on the hospital bed. "His mom died delivering him. She never even got to meet the little guy."

"How horrible."

"Yeah. But you know when you've got a little one depending on you, you have to keep going. One foot after another, even if what you really want to do is curl up in a ball."

Gazing at the two, Leslie thought back over the last few months. Tim's mid-life crisis, his affair that ended their marriage. Yes, those were tough to deal with. But this man … look what he'd dealt with in the last seven years. How had he done it, in the face of such sorrow?

One foot after another. Keep moving forward. A motto for herself to live by, born today.

"Oh!" A whoosh of red barreled into the room, a breeze of White Shoulders cologne lingering in its wake.

"Grammy!" Deakon greeted his grandma.

The white-haired woman stilled at the sight of the two of them lying on the hospital bed, holding on to each other on the skinny structure. "Close one today, huh?"

Norman nodded. She leaned over him and placed a kiss on his forehead. Then she turned to her grandson. "You're going to need to help your daddy, you hear?"

Deakon beamed at her.

"He's going to need assistance for a while, and who are the best ones to give it to him?"

"You and me."

The woman stretched over her son-in-law to place a kiss on Deakon's forehead too, and when she did, she started singing, "We get by with a little help from our friends."

Deakon giggled and joined her, "We're gonna try with a little help from our friends."

They launched into a verse and evidently it was a theme song for them, since Deakon knew all the words and stretched his vocal prowess to the max, especially on the high notes. A few lines in, Norman good-naturedly put his fingers in his ears. "Okay, okay, cut, you two."

The singing rambled to a stop, followed by giggling.

"Mom, this is Leslie Malone."

"Of course it is, our guardian angel." The woman turned beautiful eyes on Leslie. She was struck by the woman's mature beauty. The red outfit, only a whir in passing, fit her petite body to a tee, accentuating her trim figure. Her face lacked wrinkles, although Leslie guessed her to be a full decade older than herself. Her makeup was expertly applied and her snow-white hair was stylishly mussy. She would not have looked out of place on the cover of a magazine.

"It is so nice to meet you, Leslie. I'm Joan Lundeen. Deakon's grandmother and all around helper to Norman."

Leslie smiled. She took an instant liking to this woman and found herself wanting everything to go smoothly from here on out for this family so accustomed to trouble.

"Joan, so nice to meet you."

They shook hands and turned back to Norman.

"They're getting my papers ready so I can walk. I'm outta here. I have a prescription for a new med to fill, and we're going to have to figure out my transportation situation for the next few months."

Joan sat in the chair beside the bed and took a firm hold of Norman's hand. "Oh, Norman, why? Why did you have a seizure today?"

He shook his head, confused lines marring his smooth forehead. "I don't know. But I have to wonder if I was over tired from all the overtime lately. I'm going to slow it down for a while here and see if I can keep myself healthy."

The three adults chatted for a few moments while Deakon kept a vice grip on his dad. Shortly, the nurse came in with release papers for Norman to sign. When he'd finished, Leslie stood. "I'll get going now, get out of your hair." She waved away their continued thanks. "Could we exchange email addresses? I'm going on a trip, but when I return I'd love to check up on you and find out how the three of you are making out."

"Excellent idea!" Joan dug into her handbag and pulled out a tiny spiral notebook and pen. She jotted some notes, and handed Leslie the notebook. Leslie wrote her own information down, kept the paper and returned it.

Leslie said her good-byes, happy they were all right, glad she'd been there to help, but suddenly anxious to get on her way. Her roadtrip awaited her.

"Come with us," Norman said. "Joan'll take you …"

"No, no, that's okay. I've got to get going. Thanks anyway."

Norman grinned at her. "Your car's parked on the shoulder of the highway in the middle of nowhere. Just how do you think you're going to get going?"

Leslie stared at him for a moment, then broke out in a laugh. "You're right! I am going to need a ride."

Another chorus broke out of "Help From My Friends" and Leslie joined in as they walked to Joan's car. She slid into the back seat with Deakon. It wasn't a long ride till they reached her car where it sat off the highway, safe and sound. Another round of good-byes and she opened her back door.

"Leslie? I have something for you," Deakon said.

Leslie turned back to him. He pulled a paper out of nowhere, a colorful artistic rendition from the Superman coloring book. "Well, thank you, Deakon. For me?"

He nodded. "It *is* you." He pointed and she saw he'd written her name in block letters above the super hero.

"She was our Superman today, wasn't she, Deak?" Joan smiled from the front seat.

"Well, Superwoman maybe, but I didn't have that picture."

Leslie took the paper and held it to her chest. "I'll treasure it. Thank you, Deakon." She left the car with a final round of waves to this special family, and got into her car, ready to continue her roadtrip.

Chapter Three

Not long after her trip had recommenced, Leslie exited the superhighway 79 and ventured onto a smaller country road called Route 19. A less congested road, she took a long, slow breath and relaxed her shoulders. Gone was the whoosh of high-speed cars passing her by. This road suited her mood fine. After such an eventful day, she wanted to chill out and let the miles drop away underneath her tires. She turned her music back on and progressed from the 70's to the hits of the 80's.

About an hour into the new road, her stomach started making some complaining noises. She glanced at her dashboard clock: 4:10. The whole day had passed by and she hadn't eaten at all since she left home early this morning! Such a contrast to her fear of long, empty summer days with nothing to fill her time. This trip, day one at least, was distracting her effortlessly.

She made a turn and followed the road into a small town called Summersville. She drove by a rustic brick and wood sign proclaiming the entrance to the quaint town sitting on the edge of a gorgeous crystalline lake. The houses displayed the pride their residents took in keeping them clean and neat.

An early dinner was her first priority. As she lowered her speed, she kept a look out for a place to eat. She found one before long – a restored old house, several stories tall and full of personality and charm that now was the home to The Front Porch restaurant. Leslie pulled into a tiny parking lot on the side and started up the eight or so steps to a prominent wooden porch.

Wooden rockers sat in intervals around the roomy porch. Only one was occupied. A young man with long dark hair reclined in the chair, head back, legs outstretched, heels dug into the wooden floor, toes pointing straight up. Shaggy locks almost concealed his closed eyes and a cigarette burned in one hand. As Leslie made her way up the remaining steps, he brought the cigarette to his lips and puffed on it, smoke forming a faint curtain around his face. He was dressed in black pants, a white shirt and a thin black bowtie.

Instinct caused her to step by him quietly, almost on tiptoe. She reached the heavy wooden door but as she pulled the knob, his eyes popped open and he jumped in his seat.

"Oh, hi."

"Hi there," Leslie said.

He let out a puff of smoke. "You here for dinner?"

Leslie nodded.

"You're early. We don't open till five." He pulled his thin, lanky frame out of the chair, lifted his rubber-soled black shoe and rested the foot on his other knee. He squashed the used-up cigarette on the bottom of the shoe, then slipped the extinguished butt into his pants pocket. He quieted, gazing at her with a slightly apologetic smile.

"I can wait."

He nodded, then held up one finger. "Hold on a second. I'll ask if I can seat you. You can at least take a look at the menu and decide what you want. We haven't really started much for the dinner crowd yet."

He pushed past her and took a few steps into the house. Then she heard a "Mom?" from inside. "Hey, Mom?"

"What?" A woman's harried voice came from further inside the house, then the voices reduced to conversational tones, too far away to be overheard.

A minute later, the young man – Leslie guessed him to be a teenager, or a twenty-year-old, at the oldest – returned. "You can come on in. I'll show you your table."

"Thank you." Leslie followed the boy in. They walked through a delightfully decorated room with couches, end tables and a fireplace. Originally, it was most likely the sitting room, morphed into a waiting room for the restaurant. Through another doorway was a sizeable room with a variety of dining tables. The boy pointed to a small table for two and she sat down, placing her purse on the facing chair.

He stepped away and returned with a menu. "Like I said, we're not quite open yet, and we've got a limited staff, but if you decide what you want, let me know and I'll see if it's ready yet, or if you'll have to wait."

Leslie smiled and nodded her thanks. She scanned the menu and saw a good number of simple but hearty home cooked selections. Truth be told, she didn't really care what she ate. Most of it sounded good and she wasn't picky. Just darn hungry.

The boy returned with a water pitcher and as he filled up her glass she said, "What's made and ready to be served?"

He looked at her, considering. "Probably the meat loaf. The mac and cheese dinner. Club sandwich. And any of the salads."

She handed the menu back to him. "Sold. I'll take the meat loaf, mashed potatoes and side salad." He jotted it down on a pad and she noticed his nametag pinned to his shirtfront. "Thank you, Nathan."

His face blushed pink into his cheeks. "Oops, sorry. I was supposed to introduce myself and welcome you to The Front Porch."

She shook her head. "That's okay. I threw you off, coming so early."

He headed away toward the kitchen. Leslie glanced around the dining room. It was stock full of knick-knacks. Quilts of different color schemes and designs hung, displayed on the walls. Alone in the dining room, she got up and walked closer to get a look. Running her hand over the sewn handiwork, she admired the beautiful colors and patterns chosen to complete each unique creation. Although she'd never had the talent or interest to create quilts, she had always been a fan. An art form steeped in Americana, yet useful as well.

She'd almost made her way around the entire room, studying the gorgeous quilts on each wall when she heard a yell from the kitchen, "Nathan! Order up!"

With a last glance, Leslie made her way back to her seat. She pulled her napkin off the table, shook it open and placed it on her lap. Another summons for her waiter hung in the quiet of the restaurant. Moments later, the door to the kitchen swung open and a woman who appeared to be about her own age, with dark curly hair and an apron tied over her jeans and tee shirt came her way, holding a plate steaming with her dinner. The woman slid the plate onto her spot and pointed at her water glass. "Would you like more water? Anything else to drink? Did he even ask you?"

The woman's face showed a smudge of darkness under each eye, and her unruly hair gave her a frazzled look.

"Oh, water's fine. Thank you."

The woman grabbed a pitcher from a nearby station and filled up her glass. "How can he disappear every time I need him? He has one customer, one! And when it's time to deliver the order, he's … gone!" The woman puffed out an exasperated breath and shook her head.

"He's your son, right?"

"Yeah." The resemblance was obvious in the hair and lankiness both their bodies boasted. "I can't even fire the kid, because he belongs to me!" The woman shook her head and rolled her eyes, amused now, less annoyed.

"I have a daughter I bet is about his age."

"He's twenty."

"Yep, I thought so. They were probably born around the same time." The aroma of the meat loaf in such close proximity caused her stomach to announce its intention with a distinct growl.

Both women laughed. "Oh my, you better start eating. Would you like anything else?"

Leslie shook her head and picked up her fork.

"Okay. Save room for dessert. I make them all from scratch. Today I've got apple and peach pies, and a delicious peanut butter/chocolate pie. Oh, and my name's Rita, if you need me."

Rita headed back to the kitchen and Leslie dug in. She suppressed a verbal "Mmmmm" at the first bite. The meat loaf was heavenly. Her empty stomach wanted to stand up and cheer. Halfway through the delicious meal, she heard a disruption in the back. Muffled shouts made Leslie look up from her food.

A mix of Nathan's and his mother's voices emanated from the kitchen. She could make out anger in both voices, but not the words. They yelled over each other, and the swinging door from the dining room to the kitchen did little to filter them. Then, a distinct order in Rita's voice, "Give it! Give it to me, now."

"It's mine. You always want to take over my life!"

"Well, you're doing a hell of a job running it yourself, son. Hand it over. You're done."

"No."

A metallic thud followed, then another one.

"Stop it, Nathan. I can't have you here when you're out of control. Go walk it off. You're not driving the car. It's not safe."

Leslie put her fork down, mesmerized by the unfortunate family drama not far away. A slight pause, and then Nathan's voice again, "I hate this! I hate it here. I hate you, Mom."

A shuddering door slam followed. Then, complete silence. Leslie sat there, blinking. She glanced down at her half-eaten dinner and she didn't feel so hungry anymore. She pushed it away and sipped her water.

She sat a few minutes and wondered what to do next. She wanted nothing more than her bill so she could pay and flee. But that would be the height of awkwardness, tracking down Rita now, asking for her bill. She supposed she could stick a ten-dollar bill on the table and sneak out. That should more than cover the meal.

Leslie was no stranger to fights between parents and children. Especially grown children who weren't quite independent, but hated the fact they still relied on Mom and Dad. Of course, she and Jasmine had their disagreements. Not that loud usually, and never had it ended in "I hate you." That was a pronouncement rarely said in the heat of the argument, but always apologized for later. It was hurtful, and how could a child flinging that at them and then storming out the door not affect a parent?

An unmistakable sob came from the kitchen, making her in less of a rush to leave. Sure, she didn't know Rita at all. But she was a fellow mother. Maybe she could help. Maybe Rita needed a shoulder to cry on – literally.

She pushed back from the table, her solid chair making a scraping sound on the wood floor. She made her way to the kitchen, saying a quick prayer, "Lord, help me to help this mother. Give me the words to say to provide comfort."

She tiptoed across the dining room and pushed slowly on the swinging door leading to the kitchen. At first she didn't see Rita, and wondered if she'd followed Nathan out. But another sob came from around the corner of a waist-high counter, and Leslie followed the sound. There, crumpled on the floor next to the workspace, was Rita, her head in her hands.

Leslie joined her on the floor. She put her hand tentatively on her shoulder, and Rita looked up, startled. Rita mopped her eyes with the palms of both hands, and ran them through her hair, moistening the tips with her own tears.

"I'm sorry …"

"Don't be. I figured you'd maybe need a hug and an ear. Us moms have to stick together."

Rita stared intently for a few moments, then nodded. Her shoulders relaxed and she cried some more, Leslie patting her on the back, shushing her like she used to do to Jasmine during a crying spell. It's odd how comforting those gestures are, and how universal. Over five minutes passed and Rita started to pull herself together. Leslie saw a stack of napkins close by and reached for them, handing a few to Rita, who used one to wipe her eyes and nose.

She stood shakily. "Thanks. I'm sure you're very sorry you stopped in here for dinner today. Obviously I won't charge you for your meal."

Leslie smiled. "Don't be ridiculous. Of course I'm paying. It's the best meat loaf I've had in years."

Rita choked out a short laugh. "Too bad I can't raise kids as well as I bake meat loaf."

Leslie knew it was intended to be a lighthearted comment, but it brought on more tears. Rita wiped her face and drew a deep breath into her lungs.

"Sometimes kids make decisions we don't approve of, no matter how well we've raised them. Especially kids Nathan's age." Leslie leaned against the counter, giving Rita some space. "Would it help to talk about it? I know I'm a complete stranger but I'd be happy to listen if you want to talk."

Rita gave her a sideways glance. "You know, maybe you can put a fresh eye on it and give me some advice I haven't thought of before."

Leslie nodded. "I'll sure try."

Rita reached for something nearby on the floor, then tossed it onto the counter. Leslie studied it. It was a zip locked plastic sandwich bag filled with what looked like Italian spices – parsley, oregano, basil. But of course they weren't spices. Leslie had never been this up close and personal to marijuana before, but she could recognize it when she saw it. She looked at Rita and sighed. "Drugs."

"Yes. He had his *dealer* deliver it here. To my business." She picked it up and carried it over to the industrial sized stainless steel sink, turned on the water. Opening the bag, she dumped the contents down the drain. The distinct odor of the herb met Leslie's nostrils.

"How long's he been using?"

"Since about a month after his dad left."

Leslie nodded her sympathy. A boy needed his father, and this one evidently left his family and his responsibilities. "Does Nathan still see his dad?"

Rita shook her head. "Neither of us do. At least, not since he deployed to Afghanistan."

"Oh, he's military?"

"Yep." Rita picked up a peach pie and a chocolate peanut butter delicious-looking dessert. "Want a piece while we talk?" She motioned with the pies.

"Oh my, I'd love a piece of that chocolate."

Rita grinned and set them down. Grabbing a knife, she sliced a piece for Leslie and one for herself. She walked back out to the dining room with them and Leslie followed. When they'd settled in with their desserts and forks, Rita continued, "I guess I should start at the beginning. Nathan's my only child. He's a sweetheart, he really is."

Leslie nodded. "I could tell that, from the brief interaction I had with him."

"He was always a little bit of a mama's boy. And I have to say I never minded. But my husband, Gary, is on the rough and tough side. He was a football player when I met him. Later, he joined the reserves and went into infantry. He's been deployed several times. When he's home, he's in construction."

Leslie took a forkful of the dessert and placed it in her mouth. She fought the urge to moan her pleasure at the explosion of flavor.

"He is a good dad, always was. But he and Nathan never really bonded. They had totally separate interests. But Gary tried. He'd take Nathan to music lessons, listen to him sing.

When Nathan was in a play in high school, Gary not only went, but invited some of his friends.

"Before, when Gary deployed and it was just me and Nathan at home, we could manage. I mean, we missed him, me especially. But Nathan seemed largely unaffected. But this time was different. Gary left about a month after Nathan started college. He didn't do well his first semester, and I wondered if Nathan was worried about me being home alone. Nathan called me in October. He was flunking all his classes."

Rita ran a hand through her hair again, and scrubbed her face with her hands. "I encouraged him to stick it out for a whole semester. Work with a tutor, get some help. He agreed to try, but he never turned his grades around. When he came home for Thanksgiving, he never went back. One whole semester's tuition down the drain."

Leslie frowned. She'd never had to worry about grades with Jasmine. If anything, she worried her daughter was too much of a studier – her nose always in a book, never noticing life was passing her by. Which is why, if she were honest with herself, she was pleased Jaz was going to Paris, despite the fact it meant a summer away from Leslie.

"Once he was home, I noticed some problem areas. He wasn't the same kid as he was in high school. He kept to himself more, never opened up or confided in me. My friends told me that's typical for a young man who is developing independence. But more things. He stayed up till all hours of the night, and slept in past noon every day. Never left his room, other than to shower and eat. Never saw his friends. And he had no purpose in life – no school, no job, no means to support himself. No longer a kid, but not yet a man, living in his mother's house."

Leslie pushed her empty dish away. Rita hadn't started hers yet.

"When I suggested he go look for a job, it started World War III. Granted, it's not like job opportunities abound in Summersville. But he could've at least looked for something. He refused. Finally, I gave him a job here. I didn't give him a choice. I told him if he wasn't going to school, he'd have to work, period.

"That's when I started noticing strange kids dropping by. Kids I'd never seen before, and they'd only stay a few minutes and leave. He uses his earnings from the restaurant — money I pay him — for drugs."

Her voice trembled. The weight of her story was taking its toll. Leslie reached over and placed her hand on top of Rita's.

"I think he picked up the habit while he was away at school. Which explains why he flunked out. For all I know, marijuana is just the beginning. What if he's ventured into more addictive drugs and he's letting the addiction run his life? Or ruin his life." She smirked.

"What does your husband say about it?"

Rita lifted her head and looked into Leslie's eyes. "I haven't told him," she whispered.

Leslie was shocked. "Why?"

Rita shook her head and looked down. "It's sort of the military wife's code. You don't tell your man any bad news. He's got it bad enough over there. He faces danger and loss of life every day. I either need to fix this on my own, or it'll have to wait till he comes back."

Leslie's head was reeling. She couldn't imagine Rita's reality. Military wives staying so strong on the home front to protect their men on the battlefield. She doubted if she herself would have the strength. But it was obviously nearly killing Rita.

"But Rita, you can't fix this on your own. This is Nathan's problem. He needs to fix it."

Rita blinked.

"You can encourage and urge him. But you can't overcome a drug addiction for him. He needs to come to the conclusion his life stinks the way it is, and he needs to do something about it."

Rita sat still, her eyes widening. "Oh, my gosh."

"What?"

"You just said something that gave me a whole new perspective."

"I did?"

"Yes. He needs to come to the conclusion that his life stinks so much, he needs to do something to change it."

"Uh huh." Leslie watched her new friend, her face shedding its dread and beaming a little.

"But guess what: his life doesn't stink. I take care of everything for him." Rita grabbed her fork and dug it into her slice of peach pie. "He doesn't go to school because he flunked out of college. He doesn't have a job, so I give him one and a paycheck. He has no bills so he spends his money on drugs. He doesn't pay rent – he lives with me scot-free."

She stuck the sugary treat in her mouth and chewed on it, smiling. Leslie looked at her expectantly. From Rita's tone of voice you'd think she was happy about these revelations. Or maybe she was happy she'd finally figured out the problem.

Rita dropped her fork, got up and took steps back and forth in front of the table while she worked this out. "It's a mother's job to love her child. To do all she can for her child. To make life as good as possible for said child. That's what I thought I was doing. But …!" She twirled around and faced Leslie, sticking her pointed finger in Leslie's face, "I'm not doing him any favors, now am I?"

Leslie smiled at her enthusiasm and shook her head.

"He has no consequences to his actions. He has no incentive to do better. Because ta-dah! Mom's always there to pick up the pieces." She froze on the spot and gasped. "You could even say I'm ruining his life by handling it this way."

Leslie stood and joined her. "No. He's ruining his life, not you. He's old enough to go away to college, work hard and do well. He's old enough to get a job and support himself. But I can see how, in your attempts to take care of things for him, and protect him from the bad things in life, you've taken away any need or desire for him to take care of business himself."

Rita stared, eyebrows raised. "I did it because I loved him."

"I know. Maybe it's time for a new kind of love now."

After a moment of silence, Rita walked back to the chair and sat. "How? I can't just push him out of the house. He needs me. Now more than ever."

"Yes. But what he needs from you might be different than what you're currently giving him."

Rita nodded. "I have to change my approach. But how?"

Leslie reached over the tabletop and took one of Rita's hands, squeezed it between hers. "Could it be he needs some medical help?"

Unhappiness took over the lines of her face. "Maybe," she whispered. A shudder rippled through her shoulders. She flopped back in her chair and scanned the ceiling. "I don't have the first clue how to start. What to do. Where to go."

"You don't have to go through it alone. Who can help you? Are your parents around?"

Rita shrugged. "They're still alive – not local, though."

"Call your mom. She'll help. She can listen and give advice, that is, if you want to take it."

Rita nodded. The front door opened and closed, and soon, two couples walked into the dining room. Rita wiped her arm over face, pushed back her hair from her eyes. She forced a smile. "Be right with you, folks. Sit anywhere you like." Rita collected the dessert plates and pie. "Well, the show must go on."

"Do you have any other help coming in?"

Rita shook her head. "No. Mondays are usually slow, and I figured I could handle the crowd myself with Nathan waiting tables." She smirked. "So much for that plan." She started back to the kitchen.

Leslie followed her. "Well, you're looking at Plan B."

Rita frowned at her over her shoulder. "Huh?"

"I'll cover for Nathan tonight. At least till he comes back."

"I doubt he'll be back. He's so ticked off at me it wouldn't bother him in the least if I have a rough night here by myself."

"All the better reason for me to help. Give me a pad, a pen. Do I need anything else?" Leslie grabbed a nearby menu and scanned its contents. "Any specials tonight?"

She was familiarizing herself with the fare and didn't realize silent moments were ticking away without a response from Rita, until she finished reading all the selections and looked up at her new friend. Rita was staring at her with something close to amazement in her eyes.

"Who are you? Who sent you here when I needed you the most?"

Leslie chuckled.

"Seriously, are you an angel? Can I pinch you?"

"Hey, like I said before, us moms need to stick together. It's not an easy job. Believe me, I've been through my ups and downs with Jasmine too. This too will pass." Leslie spied an apron with two front pockets lying nearby and put it on. Rita handed her a pad and pen and she slipped them into the left pocket.

"I can't thank you enough. For everything."

"Shush. I've got customers waiting." Leslie shot her a beaming smile and pushed through the swinging doors.

The next two hours passed quickly. Although there was never a large crowd, there was a constant trickle of customers and the pace was enough to keep the newbie waitress hopping. She greeted and seated customers, made small talk, poured water, took orders, then delivered the meals when Rita had whipped them up. By seven PM, Leslie had earned thirty dollars in tips. When the last customers left, she pushed through the kitchen doors using her fistful of bills to fan herself.

"Well, excu-u-use me!"

Rita looked over and laughed. "You made a haul!"

"Hey, I think I've found a new talent."

"You're a fantastic waitress. I sure could use you every night."

Leslie laughed and quieted. It had been a long, eventful day and the weariness was beginning to seep into her bones. But as far as first days went, this vacation had gotten off to the most memorable and unique start ever.

"How much longer are you open?"

"I close at 8 on weeknights, 10 on weekends. But don't worry, the worst of the crowd has come and gone. It'll be slow from here on out, if we even get more customers at all."

Leslie nodded. "Can you suggest a hotel? I'm passing through and need to find somewhere to stay. I definitely don't want to drive anymore tonight."

Rita smiled. "I can suggest a perfect place. It's comfortable, homey and really close by. And for that matter, the price is right."

"Sounds perfect. Where is it?"

"Right here."

"What?"

"Stay here. Seriously. I have an extra room and it's all made up. I once had the notion of offering my spare rooms for rent on a nightly basis. Sort of like a bed and breakfast. I did it for a year, then decided to convert the main floor to the restaurant instead. But I still have the guest room. You can stay there."

The thought of a bed in such close proximity was tempting. Heavenly, in fact. "I wouldn't want to impose."

"Impose? Don't be crazy. I insist. You're looking for a room, and I've got one. You were there when I needed you, now I can do something to help you. Please."

Leslie hesitated only a second more. "Do you have a bathtub?"

Rita laughed. "Yes I do. And bubble bath."

"Sold."

She went out to her car, got her suitcase and carried it back to the house. Rita led her up the wide staircase, gleaming with polished wood. The second door on the right after they hit the landing, Rita opened and stood back. Leslie rolled her suitcase in and looked around. The room was immaculate and delightful – all blue walls, wooden floors, braided throw rugs and white eyelet fabric.

"It's adorable." Leslie twirled around and beamed at Rita. "It's the best way I can imagine to end my day."

Rita grinned and marched into the room, pulling the blinds down, plumping the pillows and pulling back the soft, white comforter. "Make yourself at home. There's an adjoining bathroom with a tub and shower. There's a tiny TV in here, but you're welcome to come down to the living room if you want a big one. If you find yourself hungry or thirsty, come to the restaurant kitchen. I'll probably be down there for another hour and a half."

Leslie shook her head. "I can't think of a thing I want to do other than get out of these clothes, soak in a hot tub, then hit the hay."

Rita squeezed her arm as she walked back to the door. "Then sleep well, my friend."

Sleep came easily in the quiet old house, and before she knew it, the sun was peeking in through the slats of the wooden blinds. Leslie stretched lazily and glanced at the bedside table. The alarm clock read 8:10. She closed her eyes again. Could she convince herself to slip back into slumber? But she was looking forward to continuing her roadtrip.

She rose and made the bed, slipped into the bathroom and freshened herself, then dressed in clean clothes. A sheet of paper had been slid under the door. "Ready for breakfast? Come down to the restaurant whenever you want."

Leslie chuckled. That woman must love to cook. She wondered if Rita served breakfast in The Front Porch. Making her way down the gorgeous old stairway, she made a right through the business's waiting room, through the dining room and into the kitchen. Rita was there, hard at work, a strip of flour on her cheek. "Good morning."

Rita looked up from frosting a delicious-looking vanilla cake with chocolate cream icing. "Hey! There she is! Are you a coffee drinker? I have a pot made."

Leslie laughed. "You better believe it. I make my living teaching eight-year-olds. I take my coffee strong and black."

Rita grabbed a mug and filled it. "You're a teacher, huh? Doesn't surprise me in the least. You sure taught me something last night. And I want to thank you for it."

Leslie took a long sip and the hot liquid eased languorously through her body. She shrugged. "What'd I do?"

"You opened my eyes to a new approach with Nathan. In my attempts to love him, I was babying him. Not only does a young man not flourish under those conditions, I wasn't making him accountable for his own actions. But with God's help, I'm going to change that."

Leslie bobbed her head in agreement. "Good for you, Rita. Where is Nathan, by the way? Did he make it home last night?"

"No. But I did get a text from him. He spent the night with an old high school friend. Brad's a good guy, so I was happy to hear it, and relieved to get the text."

Leslie sat on a tall barstool facing the counter where Rita was working. She held the mug in both hands and enjoyed another long, leisurely sip.

"I'm going to make breakfast for you. What would you like? Eggs? Bacon? Toast?"

Leslie laughed. "You're going to spoil me. You already made dinner for me, and put me up for the night."

"A good breakfast will start your day out right. Are you hitting the road?"

Leslie nodded. "Yeah, I guess I'll keep moving. It's kind of an odd trip for me because, well, I'm alone, for one thing. And I have no particular destination. Other than the beach."

Rita stared. "Now, that does sound intriguing. Tell me all about it while I whip us up some eggs."

Leslie gave Rita a condensed version of her recent life, leading up to the impromptu decision to take a solo roadtrip. When their breakfast was ready, Rita pulled up a second barstool and joined Leslie with two heaping plates of breakfast favorites.

"So how far do you want to get today?"

"I have no idea. I'm going to follow my whim and who knows what excitement is in store? I mean, my first day was a doozy."

"Well, I admire you for what you're doing, and truth be told, I envy you too. I wouldn't mind getting away from my normal life for an undetermined amount of time. Driving wherever I feel like it, stopping whenever I want. Sounds heavenly."

Leslie gazed at her new friend. "You have important work to do here, though, don't you?"

Rita quieted, then turned her attention to Leslie. "You're right. I do."

"Do you mind if I ask you one other thing?"

Rita shrugged. "Why not? Go for it."

"Don't you think you should talk to your husband about this?"

Rita started to protest but Leslie forged ahead. "It's none of my business, Rita, and tell me to butt out and I'll understand. I get the whole 'keep your soldier safe by keeping it light and happy' philosophy. But on the other hand, Nathan is his son too. And I think he'd want to have some input. Maybe he'd want to talk to Nathan himself and take some of the burden off you. Or, he might have ideas for treatment that aren't evident to you because you live with it day in and day out."

Rita was looking down at her empty plate, frowning, nodding.

"You two are still a team in raising Nathan, even though he's on the other side of the world. You don't have to do this alone, you know."

Rita reached up and flicked a tear from her eye. She turned to Leslie. "I'll think about it. I really will."

Leslie cleared the dishes and took them to the sink. They walked back to the guest room and retrieved Leslie's suitcase. When she'd locked it in her SUV outside, she turned to face Rita. Surprisingly, she realized she was going to miss this woman she'd only known a few hours.

Rita extended her hand and Leslie saw a business card tucked between her index and middle fingers. "Keep in touch. My phone number and email address are on there."

Leslie grinned. "It won't be so hard to leave knowing we'll talk again soon." She stepped forward and wrapped her arms around Rita. The hug was warm. "Thanks for everything."

"Thank *you*. And have a safe trip."

Leslie drove down the long driveway, waving out the window till she could no longer see the big homey house in the rearview mirror. She wondered what Day 2 would bring.

Chapter Four

As Leslie drove, the sun grew bigger and brighter in the sky. Her left arm, resting on the ledge of her open window, tingled. It was going to be a hot one, but that was all right. She had always loved summer. Hot weather was her friend. She made her way onto a big highway, I-77 South. Eventually reaching the ocean meant going east and south. This road was as good as any.

About an hour into the drive, her cell phone rang. She pushed the speaker option and tossed it back onto the passenger seat. "Hello?"

"Mom!"

"Sweetheart!" A wave of joy exploded through her, starting in her heart and putting a huge smile on her face. "How's Paris?"

"Oh, my gosh, Mom, it's incredible." Jasmine launched into a ten-minute monologue of the people she was meeting, the work she was doing, the sights she was seeing. Leslie grinned at the excitement in her voice.

"Well, you're having a summer of a lifetime, darling. Enjoy every minute."

"I am, believe me. And how about you? Where are you, by the way?"

"Ummm." Leslie glanced around for a hint of her location. Beautiful green mountains decorated the landscape. "The Appalachian Mountains."

Jasmine laughed. "That covers a broad range, Mom. Are you getting along okay on your crazy, carefree road trip?"

Leslie smiled. "I'm getting along like a champ. Don't worry about me. Eventually I'm going to make my way to the ocean, but for now, I'm heading south through Virginia. I've met some very memorable people already."

Leslie told Jasmine about meeting Norman and Deakon Foster, and Joan Lundeen, Deakon's grandmother. Then she described her evening with Nathan and Rita. She chatted happily and when she'd finished, Jasmine said, "Wow Mom, that's quite a trip already. You sound so happy and content."

"Do I?"

"Yeah, and I have to tell you, I'm glad to hear it. I was worried about leaving you this summer. I thought you'd be depressed because of the divorce and all."

"Sure. The whole reason I took this trip was because the long, empty summer was stretching out in front of me, looking miserable. Teachers always associate summer with freedom and fun, and this summer was looking like anything but. Now, I'm having some fun and getting out of my comfort zone at the same time."

"God always knows what we need, right Mom?"

Leslie smiled. It was one of those childhood phrases she'd repeated as a mantra to her daughter whenever things got rough. Why had it taken Jaz repeating it now for her to remember this nugget?

"You're right Jaz, He sure does."

Jasmine wrapped up the conversation because she was due to run an errand for her designer boss. Leslie disconnected the call, but kept the happiness in her heart.

Early in the afternoon, she passed signs for Charlotte, North Carolina. She was about ready for some lunch, and maybe Charlotte would offer something of interest to pass the time today. She followed the signs into the city and looked around. On her right was a charming park that reminded her of an old-fashioned town square. Sidewalks crisscrossed through a patch of grass about a city block in diameter. Stone benches sat randomly by, providing a leisurely resting spot.

After her large breakfast with Rita, a simple cold cut sandwich sounded great, and the chance to sit in the park and soak in some early summer sunshine sounded even better. She drove a block or two and noticed a grocery store. Pulling into the lot, she headed to the store's deli and joined a short line of customers. She peeked around the older woman in front of her to check out her selections.

"May I help you?"

The woman in front of her moved forward and began placing her order. "The honey ham there, yes. Two pounds. The roasted turkey. No, that one's on sale, isn't it? Two pounds. The smoked roast beef, two pounds of that also."

Leslie's stomach let out an unbidden growl. The woman ordering turned. "Sorry about that. Sounds like my stomach wants to go wherever you're taking all that delicious food."

"Well, let your stomach, and the rest of you know you're welcome."

Leslie smiled and shook her head. She continued to wait while the woman ordered a variety of cheeses, potato salad and cole slaw. It sounded like a feast.

When the deli worker gave the total amount, the older woman pulled out an envelope and started counting bills.

"The ladies working this morning, Evelyn?"

The woman finished shuffling through the bills and handed over a stack. "We sure are. We're on deadline now, and there's no time to waste. Full stomachs will keep those sticks flying."

Sticks? What was this lady organizing? She couldn't imagine. She peered at the older woman, who, seemed friendly enough. She decided to ask. "I'm sorry to be nosy, but I have to ask: what work are you leading that involves ladies throwing sticks in the air?"

Evelyn let out a laugh. "Well, I guess that's what it sounded like, didn't it? No, they're not throwing sticks in the air, but the sticks are flying nonetheless." She leaned over her grocery cart, moving around the various elements of her feast. "But I tell you what, if you want to satisfy your curiosity, why don't you follow me and see for yourself? You'll get your answer, and you'll also get a nice hearty lunch. Eh?"

Leslie shook her head. "Actually, I don't live in the area. I'm on a trip and only stopped for some lunch."

"All the better! You'll have a good lunch to set you on your way."

The woman stopped poking around in her cart and looked up at Leslie with a beaming smile. She reached maybe to Leslie's chin, and her face boasted lines sure to have been formed from a lifetime of smiling. She had a headful of bright graying hair, fashionably styled and a fresh manicure on slightly arthritic fingers. "I could use your help getting this stuff delivered anyway."

Leslie smiled. The woman exuded charm. "Well then, I'm at your service."

"Lovely!"

Leslie pushed the cart outside and helped load the groceries into the trunk of Evelyn's car. With a squeeze to Leslie's forearm, she leaned close. "God bless you, young lady." Leslie chuckled. When was the last time she'd been called a young lady? Youth was relative, she guessed.

Walking to her car, her smile lingered, remembering Evelyn's choice of words, and not just the 'young lady' part. She had felt blessed these last few days. God had led her to meet people and contribute. He'd used her unique skillset to help others. If she could continue to keep her heart open to God's direction, what else could she do?

Leslie steered her SUV through the parking lot and followed Evelyn's sedan onto the street. Her heart raced with the uncertainty of the moment. She not only didn't know where she was going, but who she was going with, or why. She sent a quick silent prayer heavenward, "God, keep me safe and use me to do your will, today and always," and felt like she must have her bases covered. After a few turns, she drove into a church parking lot and let out a laugh. She rolled her eyes up to the sky and shook her head. "Wow, a church. How could I guess?"

After parking, she hurried over to Evelyn's car and helped her carry the bulging grocery bags inside. Evelyn, hoisting several of them, strolled down a main hallway and ducked into a small kitchenette.

"Here you go, lay everything on this counter." Evelyn was slightly winded but got right to work, pulling groceries out of bags.

The women worked side by side and when they were done, they had lunch meat and cheeses spread out on round plastic trays, bread in a straw basket and salads in bowls. Evelyn's eyes twinkled along with her grin. "Thank you for your help, uh, …? Mercy me, I never introduced myself! I'm Evelyn Fletcher. Lived here my whole life, and been a member of Cross Pointe Church since I was a teen."

Leslie squeezed her hand. "Nice to meet you, Evelyn. I'm Leslie Malone from Pittsburgh and I'm glad I was in the right place today to meet you and give you a hand." She lingered in the warmth of Evelyn's gaze. "Now, are you going to reveal the mystery? Who is all this delicious food for, and what are they all doing here on a weekday afternoon?"

Evelyn laughed. "Come with me and find out."

They grabbed as much as they could carry and Leslie followed Evelyn to a room off the main hallway, across from the office. The room doubled as a library, boasting shelves of books on three walls, floor to ceiling. Tables stood back to back in a square, seating at least twenty women, all busy with sticks and yarn … knitting.

"A knitting group!" Leslie exclaimed. "That's what you meant by sticks flying. I won't tell you where my imagination went with that one."

They returned to the kitchen, picked up the remaining food and delivered it to the knitting room. Evelyn clapped her hands. "Attention, ladies! Attention, everyone. I have two announcements. First, your lunch is here. You've all worked so hard this morning, and your donations have bought us all a delicious meal. So, please feel free to take a break to eat.

"Secondly, we have a new friend. Leslie is here visiting from Pittsburgh and she kindly reached out a helping hand to an old lady at the grocery store. So I invited her to stay for lunch."

A wave of elderly voices flowed to her with audible wishes of welcome. Leslie waved. As the ladies got up and moved to the makeshift buffet line, several patted her shoulder and started a short conversation.

"So what are you knitting? Are you working on a group project?"

"Oh my, yes. We've joined in a partnership with Levine Children's Hospital here in Charlotte. We provide a hand-knit blanket for each newborn, and the parents take it home with them when they leave. Pink ones and blue ones, of course. We've done that for several years and it's a delightful project. So nice knowing our knitted blankets go to good use, starting a new baby out right."

Leslie scanned the ladies in the room, some stopping for lunch, others continuing their knitting of beautiful pink and blue blankets. Her gaze rested on one lady in the corner using not two long, straight knitting needles, but four. "What's that lady making, Evelyn? That doesn't look like a blanket."

Evelyn followed the direction of her gaze. "Oh yes, Carla's working on our new project, starting this month. The hospital asked us if we could start providing knitted baby caps for the preemies born each month. A nice warm cap helps their temperature control. So I asked the ladies if they wanted to take on this additional request. We prayed about it, and felt we could."

Leslie smiled. Carla was probably half done with her preemie cap and looked like she didn't want to stop for nourishment. "That cap pattern looks pretty intricate. Is it hard?"

Evelyn put an arm on her shoulder and guided her in Carla's direction. "Are you a knitter yourself?"

Leslie shrugged. "Not in years. I'm a teacher so I'm always on the lookout for fun things to do and learn in the summer months. I took a weekly knitting class one summer at a craft shop near my house. But that must've been, oh, ten years ago?"

They reached Carla's chair. Evelyn pointed to a couple sheets of paper with printed instructions and a color photo of a cap, setting on the table in front of her. The pattern title was 'All Around the Square Hat.' "Can we take a peek at that?"

Carla glanced up and shook her head. "I'm working."

Evelyn nodded. "But sweetie, you need to give yourself a break. You've been at this for five hours straight." Evelyn motioned to Leslie to take a look at a short stack of pink caps on the table.

"You made all of these today? I'm impressed."

At the unrecognized voice, Carla dragged her attention off her cap creation and looked over her shoulder, her hands still knitting away, using the four needles in a square. "Yes, well, if you get in a rhythm, you can whip these things out. I average one per hour. Without breaks."

Evelyn reached over Carla's shoulder and commandeered the half-made cap, tugging it out of Carla's hands. "Stop for a sandwich and a drink." The firmness in her voice had Carla hesitating, running her gaze over Evelyn's hands, then sighing.

"All right. A quick one. Then back at it. Those are due tonight, you know. I promised."

Evelyn squeezed her shoulder with her free hand. "I know, sweetie, and you won't let them down. You never do."

Carla nodded and rose, stretching her spine as she shambled over to the food table. As she did, Leslie noticed something else sitting on the table beside the pattern. She picked up a color print of a tiny baby in an incubator, wires and tubes connected in multiple places around the scrawny body, a pink knitted preemie cap on her head. Leslie studied the photo, an overwhelming sense of sadness filling her heart, bringing the sting of tears to her eyes. She blinked and looked over to Evelyn.

"Her inspiration. Her granddaughter, Anna Rose. This is why we agreed to do the preemie caps for Levine."

Leslie peered closer at the picture. In the shady background she could make out a woman sitting beside the incubator, separated from the precious baby by the thick plastic wall. But a hand rested on the barrier, as if the little life inside could sense her presence, cheering her on, praying for her safety and recovery. She pointed to the hand, although the upper body and head had not made it into the picture. "Is that Carla there?"

Evelyn nodded, a grim set to her lips. "Yes, she never left that baby's side. Carla's daughter, the mama, was sick for the first few days, and needed bed rest herself. Carla took it upon herself to make sure Anna Rose had a family member present day and night, every minute. She about made herself sick as well."

Leslie stared at the flushed pink skin, the tiny features of the baby. It nearly broke her heart to ask the question. "Did she …?" She turned to Evelyn, scanned her eyes. "Did she make it?"

Evelyn shook her head, her face taut with the incomparable trauma of the loss of a child. Leslie heaved a deep breath in her chest, let it out, and said a silent prayer for

Anna Rose, now a tiny angel, and her family who loved her, who she left behind.

"This was taken about two months ago. Carla came up with the idea of the cap project for the hospital, and brought it to our knitting group. Of course, we couldn't say no."

Leslie glanced over to the food table where Carla held a plate and was constructing a sandwich. "She sure is dedicated."

"Almost too much so. It's great to have a project to throw yourself into after a loss. But you can see what she's like. It's almost like she has to singlehandedly make every cap herself. But it's impossible. The need is too great."

Leslie set the picture down. "I can't imagine."

"The Neonatal Intensive Care Unit at Levines is the best in the area, maybe the state. They have something like eighty five beds, and treat nearly a thousand babies a year."

"And your group knits blankets and caps for all of them?"

Evelyn chuckled. "Not all of them. I imagine there are several knitting groups that make up the total. But we commit to a dozen blankets a month and a dozen caps. For a group our size, that's a lot of knitting." Evelyn motioned across the room. "Time for us to have some nourishment. But first, a question for you: would you like to take those ten-year-old knitting skills, dust them off and make something for a premature baby to use?"

A case of nerves stabbed her heart. "Oh gosh, I couldn't."

"Why not?"

"It's been too long. You all are on a tight deadline. No one has time to tutor me and teach me how to do this again. It's not a good time."

They made their way around the tables. Evelyn said, "No time like the present. How about starting with a cap? It should only take a couple hours for a beginning knitter. And imagine the goodness you'll feel when you pack it in with all the rest of them."

Leslie considered. "We'll see."

Later, after a belly-filling lunch, Evelyn gathered the supplies Leslie would need to produce a preemie cap: a printed pattern, the needles, a pencil, scissors. "Pink or blue?"

Leslie shook her head. She hadn't actually agreed to making a cap, but what the heck? If it came out horribly, she could always unravel it. "Give me blue."

Evelyn's smile beamed and she grabbed a skein of baby blue wool. "I'll join you." With supplies in hand, Evelyn led Leslie to a few empty seats at Carla's table. Carla looked up. She was settling back in after her own lunch. "You got company, Carla. The cap-makers."

Carla smiled. "Great. I'd like to have three more done by five."

"Put each of us in for one. Carla, meet Leslie."

The two women murmured their greetings and got down to the business of knitting. Leslie picked up the yarn. Its softness sent a familiar rush of pleasure through her. She pulled the pattern closer. There had to be a way to get the wool on the four needles and get it started, but it had been too long since she'd knitted to know the specifics. She didn't have the first clue. The pattern instructed, "Ten (10) stitches using a long tail cast on." Yeah, right.

"Um…" she looked up and found Evelyn smiling at her.

"Give them to me and I'll cast you on."

Leslie nodded. The term was familiar but she had no memory of how to do it. Evelyn reached out and Leslie put the wonderful blue wool in her hand. Evelyn pulled out a strand till it was the length of her arm, and looped the yarn onto the needles. She knit the ten stitches and when the cap was ready to begin, she handed it back.

"Okay, thanks." It was a starting point, but where to go next? Leslie studied the pattern again. Terms floated out to her, once part of her vocabulary – purl stitch, knit stitch, bind-off.

"The good thing about us both following the same pattern at the same table, is I can mentor you while I go. Watch what I do, and I'll explain it as I go along. And if you have any questions, don't hesitate to ask. Think of the precious tiny baby who is going to wear your creation, and it'll be fuel to keep you going."

Evelyn's pep talk did the trick. There was no need to feel frustrated or overwhelmed. These women were all there for the same purpose, helping newborn babies stay warm and feel loved. Leslie could help, even if her skills weren't current. Eventually she'd knitted enough stitches to have all four needles involved, knitted yarn on each, in a square. She moved from one needle to the next as the pattern called for, moved on to what could probably pass as a purl stitch and heard Evelyn's encouragement, "That's the way."

Twenty minutes into the adventure, Leslie found that certain basics about knitting were coming back to her, and she remembered why she enjoyed this hobby, a decade past. Although she needed to concentrate, eventually she could chat with Carla or Evelyn. If she made a mistake, she unraveled the last few stitches.

Late afternoon, the ladies were beginning to wrap up. Conversational noises increased as they put the finishing touches on their projects, rolled up the remaining wool and began packing their tools away into bags. Evelyn got up and made her way through the crowded room. Another lady moved to the corner of the room and positioned herself next to a large silver bell, a string hanging down beneath the clapper.

Evelyn located the first of the completed blankets, gathered it in her arms and yelled, "One!" The bell tolled. All the ladies cheered, and the creator of the first blanket beamed her delight. On Evelyn went to the next table and another finished blanket was added to her arms. "Two!" More bell-tolling, more cheering.

Leslie laughed, enjoying the obvious joy and pleasure of everyone in the room. The ladies were exuberant in camaraderie, togetherness and productivity. They had used their talents to create useful, wonderful, hand-made treasures, with the certainty that they would be put to use very soon by a group of precious babies in need of warmth and comfort. Knowing this would be enough, but the ladies piled on the celebration with a monthly ceremony of bell-ringing and cheering. The joy in the room was palpable and Leslie wished she'd be around a month from now for the next gathering.

Moments later, Evelyn held such a large stack of blankets, her face was barely visible over the top. "Ten!" "Eleven!" There was a collective holding of breath by almost every woman in the room. The goal was twelve. Would they meet it?

"We have eleven blankets, friends. Is one more done?" Every head swiveled silently, searching for the last blanket to donate. Leslie's heart dropped. They couldn't be one short. This group deserved the victory of donating exactly their committed number. They'd worked so hard.

One woman held a pink blanket up in the air. "It's not quite done, but I'll work on it tonight and deliver it in the morning."

Applause broke out around the room. It wasn't quite perfect, but then again, nothing in life ever was. Those premature babies who hung onto life at Levine Children's Hospital weren't starting life with perfection. And yet, everyone working together did their best to give their shaky lives a fighting start.

"Thank you, Ruth. That will be perfect," Evelyn said. "Now, Carla? Would you gather the caps, please?"

Carla stood and picked up her stack of caps in front of her. "Seven!"

The ladies laughed and clapped as the bell ringer counted out seven chimes of the bell. Carla smiled as she waited. Then, she picked up Evelyn's single blue cap and piled it on. "Eight." Then Carla reached for Leslie's cap.

Leslie reached out and grabbed her hand, a flood of nervousness attacking her heart. "Let's wait and see how many we get. This one isn't exactly right. If I have more time, I'd like to work on it a little more."

Carla nodded and moved to the next table. Leslie saw Evelyn gaze at them from across the room, her eyebrows raised in curiosity.

By the time Carla made her way through the room, she'd collected fourteen caps. Chairs pushed back from tables made whooshing sounds on the carpeted floor as women stood and stretched their backs and fingers after a sedentary day of creation.

Leslie gathered her things and hastily stuffed the blue cap into her purse. They had more than met their cap goal without her raggedy one. Although it wasn't needed for the hospital donation, Leslie was glad she did it. It brought back a pleasure she'd previously developed for knitting. Maybe she'd do some more of it when she reached her destination at the beach.

She made her way over to Evelyn. "Thank you so much for pulling me in today. I never thought I could knit anything after ten years away, but it was fun."

Evelyn put an arm on her shoulder. "You want to feel really good? Come with Carla and me to the hospital to do the delivery."

Leslie didn't hesitate. "Sure."

They headed for Evelyn's car and traveled the short distance to the hospital. They parked in a garage and loaded up their arms with knitted creations. They entered the main lobby and Leslie swooned at the beauty of the modern atrium. "This looks more like a children's museum than a hospital."

Evelyn and Carla grinned and continued on their way to the receptionist, but Leslie took a moment to savor the stunning sight. It was truly a room that would take a child's sting out of a trip to the hospital. The open, sunny area was welcoming and fun, the furniture modern and clean. Tilting her head back, she soaked in the tall spaciousness. Stationary kites decorated the open air between the first and third floors. A huge net hung down, and sparkling glass tubes dangled from the knitted strands, catching the light and casting enchanted reflections on the floor.

Not wanting to miss out on the chance to deliver the blankets, Leslie tore herself away when Evelyn led the way to the elevators. The doors opened on the seventh floor to a traditional hospital ward, the walls painted a muted grayish blue. Leslie followed the others to a nurse's station.

"There they are! We were looking forward to your visit today, ladies."

A nurse dressed in scrubs held her arms out and the ladies piled the blankets on. Leslie followed suit with the caps.

"We're one blanket short, but we brought extra caps," Carla explained.

"The blanket will be delivered tomorrow, though," said Evelyn.

The nurse nodded, her head barely visible in the midst of knitted cotton yarn. "We have a rash of babies being released today and tomorrow so we'll need the blankets to send home with them. And unfortunately we have about a dozen new babies born and admitted into the NICU, so the caps will help keep the tiny angels warm while they're here."

The nurse headed down a hallway and directly into a large nursery full of babies, each in their own tiny crib marked with their name and identifying information. Leslie stood with Evelyn and Carla on the outside of a wall-to-floor glass window, watching as the nurse placed a new blanket inside each crib, either under the infant, to the side or covering the baby. Then she covered each baby's head with a cap from the church ladies' stash. Leslie could tell from the nurse's sureness of hand, she was an experienced professional, and those precious children were in good hands at Levine.

A quiet sniff to her left made Leslie turn her head. Carla watched the distribution of the caps and blankets with tears streaming down her cheeks. Compassion for the woman made Leslie move closer and put an arm around her. "This must be so difficult for you to watch."

Carla nodded, her mouth set in grim determination. "My beautiful Anna Rose couldn't be saved. But I do my best to make sure other families don't have to experience the same loss we did. In my small way, this is what God says I can do." She turned and gazed at Leslie. "So, I do it."

Leslie squeezed her tight and Carla gripped her hand. "We do what we can, don't we?"

The nurse finished with the deliveries and joined the three of them in the hallway. "You have no idea how welcome these gifts are. You see that mother?"

They turned back to the window. A young woman sat in a chair beside an incubator. Inside was a tiny little baby, resembling Anna Rose in all manner of tubes and cords leaving its body. The mother's hand was extended into the container, resting lightly on the baby's clothed tummy.

"She had a terrible case of toxemia. She wasn't even due for another two months, but her doctor was concerned that if they didn't take the baby, she could die. So, they did a c-section, and the poor thing weighed only two pounds. Much of his bodily systems aren't developed yet. It's still touch and go for him."

A hitch in Leslie's throat made it hard to breathe. She bowed her head and said a silent prayer, "Please be with this young mother and her tiny baby. Please shelter them from further pain and disappointment, and lead them both to a life of health and recovery."

"It's a baby boy?" Evelyn asked.

"Yes."

"He doesn't have a cap," Carla noticed.

The nurse nodded. "He's so premature, it's hard for him to be touched. Even a cap may cause him discomfort on his scalp. Do you see how Mom's making a connection, very faintly on top of his onesie?"

Leslie saw. "Is it painful for him?"

"We're not sure if it's painful, or more tingly. It's a condition that generally improves the more days he's alive. As he gets older, we'll be able to let Mom touch him directly skin to skin. Speaking of Mom, her time's up. She's only allowed in there for thirty minutes every two hours." The nurse slipped into the nursery and patted the young woman on the shoulder. She jolted at the contact, her eyes sad as she looked up at the nurse and nodded. With a last furtive glance at her baby, she stood and turned away.

Leslie watched her walk down the hallway. "I'll just be a moment," she whispered to Evelyn.

She took off after the young mom. She turned into a vending machine room and Leslie followed her in. "Excuse me."

The young mom turned to her. "Yes?"

Leslie dug in her purse and pulled out the cap, held it out to her. "Hi. I made this cap today, but I thought it wasn't quite accomplished enough to donate. I haven't knitted in years."

"It's beautiful, don't be silly."

"It's not as perfect as the ones made by the expert knitters. But feel how soft it is."

The woman gave a small smile and ran a hand over it, nodding at Leslie. "Wonderful."

"I'd like you to keep it. Maybe wash it with Downy. Realize that it was made with love, and I want your boy to have it. What's his name?"

"Carson." The woman took the cap. "Thank you very much. That's so sweet of you."

"Please keep the faith. Carson's going to make it. You will carry him out of here someday, even if you can't imagine it now."

The woman stilled and stared into Leslie's eyes. She reached up and grabbed both Leslie's hands in her own. "Thank you for saying that. I so needed to hear it."

They stood without movement and then the woman dropped her hands, held up the hat and walked away.

When they returned to the church, Leslie got out of the back seat and circled around to the driver side window. She leaned in and thanked Evelyn again for a wonderful day. "You know, Carla said something I'll always remember. God tells us what we can do to help. So we do it."

Evelyn nodded.

"It's a good way to lead our lives isn't it, that simple theology."

"It sure is. I'm glad God put you in the grocery store at the same moment he put me there. You enjoy the rest of your day, now, all right?"

Leslie turned on her engine and looked around. It was time to find a hotel for the night.

Chapter Five

The next morning dawned bright and sunny, a veritable gift from a God trying hard to bestow a most perfect day. Leslie rolled her suitcase to her car and tossed it into the hatch. Despite the choppiness of her trip – the stop and go and her flexibility to take her time – she was making progress. Her current location, Charlotte, NC was probably two-thirds of the way toward her destination. And she'd met some wonderful people and had some extraordinary adventures so far. But she was anxious to arrive.

Today. This was the day she'd get to the beach.

Hopping into the front seat, she pulled out her GPS and frowned at the display screen. How did it work? Tim always took care of the directions when they drove. He detested the GPS, always used the old-fashioned method of researching his route with the atlas. Well, he wasn't here, and one of the very good things about that was, she could do things her way now. And she was just tech-savvy enough to figure out this little helpful gadget if she put her mind to it. She suspected they'd become good partners.

Now, first things first: where should she tell the GPS to go? The early morning became a still backdrop to summer sounds – a bird chirp in a nearby tree, a cicada hum, a bee buzzing outside her window. In the quietness, a memory emerged.

When she was a child, her family visited the same vacation spot at least eight years in a row. Her family members dotted across the US map, with cousins living in Tennessee, Ohio, California, Illinois. Difficult as it was to stay in touch in the era before convenient electronic gadgets, the adults of the families made an annual pledge to gather at the beach, spending memorable, happy days co-habitating a house in Pawleys Island, South Carolina.

Some families could stay a week, some two. Some came later, some overlapped by only a few days. But for eight glorious summers as a child, Leslie was one member of a large clan who didn't watch the clock, didn't set the alarm, had very few rules. Four or five moms, dads, a grandparent or two, and an army of kids all connected through DNA, got reacquainted after twelve months apart, on the shore of the most beautiful ocean nature offered in the world: the Atlantic.

Somehow by fate, the adults of the family located a house that accommodated this crazy, come-as-you-are vacation. A large gray wooden plank house sitting on stilts over a sandy-floored garage, the back covered porch overlooking its own little slice of beach and ocean. Out the front door and across a narrow gravel road, a long wooden fishing dock led out over a saltwater creek where the patient cousin could hold a fishing pole or a crabbing string with bait, hoping to score a catch to hand off to the moms to transform in the kitchen into something tasty. The house, christened "The Old Gray Barn" was homey but not luxurious, not in the least. Wooden floors with space between the slats to sweep the sand through, left there by children's feet fresh from the beach. A cramped but functional kitchen, a dining area and spacious open living room with a multitude of couches shared the first floor with two or three bedrooms. Up the short flight of stairs were two dormitory-style bedrooms containing eight or so beds apiece. The kids quickly deemed one the girls' room and the other, the boys'.

Leslie smiled at the memories of those long-ago vacations as they flooded her imagination. They hadn't ever returned, not through all their summer vacations as a family of three. Tim always preferred Hilton Head, or somewhere on the Gulf in Florida. They'd sampled Maui and the Caribbean. But this trip was all about following where her whim led her. Why not set the GPS to Pawleys Island and try to find the Old Gray Barn? Was it still there? Had a hurricane swept it away? Had developers leveled it and built modern condominiums?

It was now her mission to find out. She typed in the destination and was thrilled to learn it was four and a half hours away. She'd be there by lunchtime. Happily, she buckled herself in, set her music and took off.

The GPS kept her busy, keeping up with all the road changes. There didn't seem to be a straight path from Charlotte to Pawleys. But it kept the trip interesting, staying on one road for twelve miles or so, then merging onto another. Two and a half hours in, she crossed over the South Carolina border, cheering as she did. As the beach got closer, the air streaming in through her open window grew heavier. The tangy smell of salt tickled her nostrils, and the density of ocean air filled her lungs. Along with it, she could barely contain her glee.

In the early afternoon, she arrived. She had no clear childhood memory of the town itself, so she didn't have a clue how to locate The Old Gray Barn. Her GPS wouldn't help her with that dilemma either. She'd have to stop for lunch and hope someone could help.

A few minutes later, she pulled into a restaurant, a shabby small building with an inlet water view, its marquis boasting the best fried shrimp in town. Leslie went in and was seated. A young woman placed a napkin rolled with silverware and a menu on the table.

"What would you like to drink?"

"Pepsi, thanks."

She pushed the menu aside because the shrimp had caught her fancy, then reached for it again. Maybe she'd come back here, if the food was good. The locale was fine, the view was terrific, and glancing at the menu, she saw the prices were affordable.

The waitress brought the icy drink. "Know what you want?"

"I'll take the fried shrimp dinner."

The woman smiled and nodded. "Excellent choice. Sides?" She pointed at a list on the menu.

To celebrate being in the south, Leslie chose cole slaw, hush puppies and collard greens. The waitress bounced off to place the order.

As she waited, she glanced around the dining room. White painted walls were covered with framed prints and photographs of the ocean, sunsets or fishing boats. The place reminded her of every single beach town cheap seafood joint she'd ever been to, and she reveled in its familiarity. Being at the beach just made her happy, it always had.

Her meal came, along with a fragrant rush of fried goodness. "This looks delicious. But I have a question for you. I'm looking for an old rental house called The Old Gray

Barn. I stayed there when I was a kid. Are you familiar with it?"

"No, ma'am. We have quite a few rentals around here. Is it oceanfront?"

"Yep."

"In Pawleys?"

"I believe so, yes."

"That narrows it down some. Let me get you some flyers that might be helpful." She walked towards the door and surveyed a library of brochures offering dining, shopping and entertainment options. She pulled a few out and brought them over. "Here's a few of our more prominent real estate companies. I believe they all manage vacation rentals. If you have a computer with you, you can look up their websites and search for the house. If not, there's phone numbers and their offices should all be open."

Leslie smiled. "You've been so helpful, thanks."

She devoured the meal and asked for a refill of Pepsi. Pushing her plate away, she flipped through the brochures and pulled out her cell phone. After three calls, she hit success on her fourth.

"You manage the rentals of The Old Gray Barn?"

"Yes, we do. When were you interested in it, and how big is your group?"

She laughed. "I don't think I'll be renting it – I'm traveling alone."

"Oh my, no," the woman on the phone said. "It sleeps twenty one. You don't want to stay there alone, I'd guess."

"Twenty one! Well, I believe it. We used to rent it every summer when I was a kid, and we had loads of people in there. In fact, that's why I'm calling. I'm in the area for the first time since I was a child, and wanted a trip down memory lane. I'd like to drive by, maybe stop in and see it. Is that all right?"

"Sure. In fact, it's not rented this week. We're doing some light renovations." She gave the address and Leslie jotted it down on the brochure. She left a few dollars on the table, then jumped up to pay her bill. She made her way to her car with an unmistakable sense of excitement in her heart.

The GPS led her directly to it. Fuzzy memories over thirty years old sharpened little by little as she approached. When the machine announced, "You have reached your destination," Leslie had no doubt. It had hardly changed with the passage of time. She slowed to a stop, sat on the thin road and gazed at the house where so many pleasant family memories originated, as well as a few unpleasant ones. Her hands tingled as her heart raced with her glee at finding it, unharmed by the many years that had passed.

She pulled into the driveway – still sand mixed with tiny broken seashells. She remembered sitting cross-legged with her cousins on the tiny patches of driveway not occupied by cars, lifting handfuls of sand and tossing them into colanders borrowed from the kitchen, watching the soft, white sand fall through, capturing the seashell remnants in the Tupperware device. Occasionally among the broken pieces, a perfect miniature conch shell rested there, a treasure to be saved in the dormitory bedroom, and hauled back to Pittsburgh at summer's end.

She left the car and climbed the rustic wooden stairway that led to a wide front porch, now home to a half dozen wooden rocking chairs, and the front door. Not finding a doorbell, she knocked on the old door with her knuckles, waited, then tried again with her open palm. No one answered, but it didn't deter her. Now that she knew where the house was, she could come back with a request to tour the inside. But the least she could do was walk around to the back and enjoy the gorgeous ocean view.

Back down the stairs, she walked around the left side. There was the outdoor shower, complete with a wooden stall built to provide privacy. As kids, she and her cousins would always use it to hose off sand and salt from their bathing suits and skin before going into the house, but a person could actually take a nude shower with soap and shampoo without fear of being seen. In fact, one of her older cousins, Joshua, did just that – claiming the shower as his own. She remembered his mother, her Aunt Patty remarking that if it weren't for the novelty of an outdoor heated shower, and the audacity of her teenage son taking a nude shower outside, she didn't believe he'd bathe all week.

A smile played on her lips as she rounded the side of the house and took in the view she'd been aching to see: the direct access to the ocean. Her heart exploded with joy and she broke into a run toward the water. A path led through a patch of waving sea oats, an oasis of green growth before reaching the clean tan sand. She leaned down to untie her shoes, then kicking them off helter-skelter, and her socks after, she continued her trek to the ocean. When her toes hit the waves, she shivered. June was early for this part of the Atlantic, and it would continue to warm over the coming months of summer. But it was still delicious.

She waded into the water until it reached her knees, then turned to her right and walked the length of two more houses till she reached a twenty-foot line of stacked rocks, a breakwater jetty that on this private beach, had been built every three house-lengths or so, to protect the shoreline from erosion by redirecting the water currents. As children, the adults lectured her and her cousins to stay clear of the jetty. When the waves got big, their small bodies could be thrown uncontrollably against the rocks, causing disaster. Now, as an adult, she stood gazing before turning back.

She strode through the water till she returned to the patch of ocean in front of The Old Gray Barn. Her skin had adjusted to the chill of the water, and she stood still and soaked in the beauty and thrill of returning to such a treasured childhood spot. She closed her eyes and let her most vivid memory of this vacation locale flow through her head.

Leslie and her cousin Margaret had taken a long inflatable raft and made their way out beyond the white water break of the waves. They rested comfortably, Margaret lying on top of the raft with a big toe sticking luxuriously in the water, Leslie's bottom half completely submerged, leaning her arms and upper body on the raft beside her cousin. They chatted. Leslie didn't remember the topic of conversation, but she did remember that at that age, she idolized her cousin Margaret with her long, shiny straight black hair, her easy smile and laugh. She was probably trying to impress Margaret with her knowledge of some topic, either real or made up, when suddenly, an electric sear of pain ripped through her leg, around the circumference of her knee. She screamed and kicked her legs frantically. The fire of the pain shifted to her other leg, and she shrieked with shock before breaking into sobs.

Margaret alerted, tried awkwardly to sit up in the plastic raft to help. But soon, Margaret screamed too. Leslie's and Margaret's moms, sitting on towels on the beach, stood, gazing out at the mishap in the waves. Leslie's memory of how exactly she made it in out of the ocean to the sand was unclear, but between Margaret, her mother and her aunt, she made it to the beach, wailing in pain.

When her mom saw Leslie's leg, her eyes grew wide and her mouth dropped open. "What happened? What did you do?"

Leslie's tears and sobs continued as her mother took her by the shoulders and dragged her over to the towel. Margaret tried to offer an explanation but no one had any idea what had caused angry red strips of swelled, burnt skin around her knee and down the front of her shins. The same phenomenon appeared on Margaret's big toe.

She remembered the attention and tender loving care she received later from all the moms and aunts, as well as most of her cousins. Everyone felt terrible about the unknown, unseen sea creature that had attacked Leslie and taken away her innocent joy of swimming in the ocean, oblivious to the dangers lurking there. Although she would return to swim in the waves again, many times, she would never again do it without recalling the searing pain of what was determined by the adults to be the electric sting of a Portuguese Man O' War the girls had ventured upon in their aimless floating. Leslie's mother consulted with other vacationers and created a soothing poultice which Leslie wore wrapped around her legs for three straight days. No ocean, sand or sun for her – her vacation took on a completely different tone while she was in her enforced recovery, staying in the shady safety of the house, reading stacks of books she selected from the local library.

"Hello?"

Leslie shook her head, dispensing the vivid memory, and turned her attention toward the beach. A man stood on the sand, a dark ball cap on his head, waving a hand at her. Leslie waved and strode toward him. As she approached, she saw he was middle-aged, most likely in his early 50's. By the looks of him, he'd taken good care of himself. Fit and fluid, she imagined he loved the outdoors and had spent a lot of time there. The bill of his cap shaded a handsome face lined naturally from the sun and a lifetime of smiles. His body was tall and sturdy and she thought there probably wasn't a job he couldn't do if it involved physical labor and he put his mind to it.

He brought his other hand up to shield his eyes from the sun and she caught the tightening of his bicep peeking from his tee shirt sleeve. His skin, in early June, was already the color she strived for after a summer full of careful trips to the pool with a bottle of SPF 25. "Hi," she called.

He nodded at her. "I saw your car in the drive, then I saw you in the ocean. I wanted to tell you, in case you didn't know, uh, this is a private beach." He dropped his gaze to his feet, then looked back at her face.

His tone was gravelly and masculine.

"My name is Leslie Malone." She stuck her hand out. He shook it. "I'm visiting here from Pittsburgh. I used to come to this house every summer when I was a kid. I thought it would be fun to stop by and see if it's changed." She turned and looked back at the house. "It hasn't. Not at all."

His lips curled in a lazy grin. "My name's Hank. And I'll take that as a compliment. It's my job to work on these old beach homes to make sure they stay in good shape."

"Oh, how interesting. Then thank you for keeping my childhood vacation memories intact."

His easy expression made her imagine the same attractive smile on a younger face by thirty years. "You're welcome."

They stood in the sand for a moment of silence, then Leslie turned to find her discarded shoes and socks. "Do you mind if I come inside for a quick tour? I called the management company and they told me it was fine, since there are no renters this week."

He shrugged. "Help yourself. I'm working on the back porch. You're welcome to slip inside and take a look around."

She followed him up the wooden stairs onto the back porch. He picked up a hammer and resumed his work, reinforcing the porch boards with new nails. She walked through the back screen door and as it slammed shut behind her, she laughed out loud. How many times had her mom or one of her aunts yelled out, "Don't slam the door!" when she or one of her cousins had entered the house from the beach?

The back door led directly into the great room. It had been refurnished, of course, and a modern flat screen TV sat along one wall, but the room materialized unscathed right out of her memory. On one wall hung four photographs combined into one wooden frame, showing the effect Hurricane Hugo had on the house back in 1989. While surrounding houses were damaged or downright destroyed, the Old Gray Barn stayed intact. The stilts the house sat on saved it from massive flooding, as the ocean waters devoured the beach and rolled heavily under the house. Somehow the jarring winds didn't destroy the gray frame house. It held its ground, and survived.

Leslie ran her hand over the photos and said a word of thanks to God. She peeked into the parents' bedrooms off the great room, then into the kitchen where many a simple summer meal was prepared. Then, up the stairs and into each of the dormitory-style bedrooms. Funny, they seemed so much larger in her childhood memory than gazing at them now as an adult.

She sighed and returned to the back porch. Hank was pounding a new nail into one of the floorboards. He stopped when she approached.

"Thanks for letting me in. It really brings back a lot of memories. We had such good times here."

He nodded. "I'm glad. Pretty cool to meet someone who knew of this house – how long ago?"

She laughed. "Oh my. Thirty five years? Long time ago. And being here brings back so many wonderful memories. Oh, and some not so wonderful ones." She told him the story of the Portuguese Man O' War.

"Ouch. Do you have a scar?"

Leslie looked down at her knees, ran a finger across the back side of them. "No, not that I've ever noticed."

"That poultice did the trick, then."

"Yeah." She stood, looking down at him as he kneeled. His eyes were the azure color of the ocean, she saw, now that she was close to him. A vivid, amazing blue she could lose herself in, if she stared much longer. Maybe he reminded her of someone. A celebrity? Which one?

Well, now she was making him uncomfortable because he came to his feet and stood there in an awkward silence. She gave herself a mental shake.

"I'll leave you to your work. I'm sorry for the interruption." She held her hand out to shake again.

"Actually, I was going to stop for an iced tea. Care to join me?"

"Sure!" She was sure her reply was too quick and too enthusiastic for such a casual invitation, but the thought of staying here with him and sharing a drink made her happy.

And being happy around a handsome man was one of life's pleasures she hadn't experienced too often lately.

"Have a seat. It's sweet tea, I should add. It's the south, you know."

"Sounds delicious, thank you."

She sat in one of the wooden rockers occupying the porch and he soon returned with two big chunky glasses full of tea and ice. He removed the ball cap and wiped a strong hand over his face, then back through his hair, damp with sweat. He took a series of gulps and she admired the bobbing of his Adam's apple as he swallowed. She took a sip of hers, and the tea was so sweet she felt her teeth floating in sugar. "It doesn't disappoint. Delicious. Did you make it?"

His laughter came out in a self-derisive snort. "No. I do a lot of work in kitchens, but not the kind of work that produces food. Or drink."

She smiled and sipped again. "So you work for the realty company?"

He shrugged. "Indirectly. I'm an all-around handyman. Had my own business for as long as I can remember. I work on houses mainly, but I'll do commercial, too. Restaurants, offices. Wherever the work is."

"It's great to be so handy. I wish I had some skills."

He leaned back in the wooden chair beside her and set it to rocking. The wood on wood scraping sounded like it could be a percussion section in a country anthem. "I've always been pretty good with stuff like that. You know, putting things together, fixing what's broken."

"I cringe when I have to assemble something. I pull out the instructions, read them through, but it's like reading Greek."

He laughed. "With experience, you find there's a certain rhythm to that stuff. A pattern. Once you've done one, they all tend to follow the same logic."

She turned her head toward him. He squinted toward the ocean, making his cheeks ball up in rosy bumps. "Let me guess, you don't even read the directions, do you?"

He looked her way, his raised eyebrows teasing her with the answer. He shook his head. "Only as a last resort." He took a long drag from the tea and drained his glass. "These vacation homes are good jobs. They're generally older, like this one here, so they need a lot of upkeep. And there's plenty of them."

"Job security."

"Yep."

Leslie stretched her legs out in front of her and crossed them at the ankles. "How big is your company?"

He shook his head. "Just me."

Something about his clipped response made her look his direction. Frown lines creased his forehead. His glass set on the porch beside him. "Would you like a refill?" she asked. "I'll get it for you."

His gaze paused on her face. "Sure, why not?"

She retrieved the glass, bringing it back a few minutes later with fresh ice and tea. As they sat in companionable silence, he took a deep breath. "My son used to work with me. He was more interested in the business side, and he had plenty of ideas of how to grow and expand. But . . . ."

She waited, the calmness of the ocean waves carrying a familiar, beloved sound to her ears. "It didn't work out?" Seagulls cawing in the distance filled the gap in conversation. "Sometimes bringing a child into a family business works, and sometimes it doesn't."

He nodded. "It worked for a good while. Jeremy was my office manager, promoter, client-getter. He even hired a few more workers so I could be the crew boss, leading the bigger jobs."

"That's great."

He stood and wiped his hands on his jeans legs. "Well, I guess this porch won't get done by itself, huh? I'm here all week. Long list of jobs to do on this old house. Better stay on schedule."

Leslie came to her feet. "I can't thank you enough for the opportunity to look through the house. And for keeping it in such great shape. It looks like it walked right out of my memories. Oh, and for the iced tea." She lifted her glass, then reached for his. "I'll drop these off in the sink on my way out."

As she headed into the kitchen, she added in her head one more thing to thank him for, the first nudging of physical attraction she'd felt for a man in more years than she could count. Although she had absolutely no intention of acting on the urge, it felt somehow reassuring to know she was capable of noticing hormones when they were dancing through her body.

She walked toward the front door and turned to take one last look at the main floor. She startled when she saw he'd followed her to the door.

"Drive safe now. Nice to meet you." He frowned a moment, then smiled. "Leslie."

"Yes, you too, Hank." She stepped onto the front porch and made her way toward the stairway.

"Where are you staying, by the way?"

She shrugged. "Haven't decided yet. I made it to town and had lunch, then headed straight over here." She squinted up at him. "Do you have any recommendations?"

"How long are you staying?"

"I know it sounds crazy, but I have no idea. Just following my whim on this trip. Wherever God leads me."

He nodded, considering. "You'd be missing out if you didn't stay at the Seaside Inn. It's quaint and homey, nothing fancy. But it's comfortable and they'll take real good care of you over there. Tell them I sent you."

"Okay, sure, I'll do that. Hank … I don't believe I know your last name."

"It's Harrison. My daughter is the innkeeper. She and her husband live there, along with my granddaughter." He pulled a small notepad from his shirt pocket, jotted down the address and handed it to her.

"Thank you. I'll take a look."

"You, uh, traveling alone?"

"Yep." She watched him mull her answer over, then she trotted down the wooden stairs. Then an idea hit her. She turned back. "It just dawned on me who you remind me of. Harrison Ford!"

He scratched his head. "The Star Wars fella?"

"Yes! You really resemble him, and what a coincidence your last name is Harrison."

He chuckled and shrugged. She waved and got in her car.

She reached for her GPS, expertly typed in the inn's address. Ten minutes later, she was pulling into a small, packed-dirt parking lot in front of the inn. Aptly named, it sat, similar to the Old Gray Barn, with the ocean behind it and the salt-water creek across the street in front. She climbed a wooden stairway that led to a broad white wooden inn with green shutters.

She walked through the front door and into an adorable living room. Bleached wood paneling covered the walls and floors and the cotton coziness of the furniture made Leslie want to plop down with a book and read with the soothing sound of waves behind her. A wooden counter stood at one side of the room, a young woman sat behind it, flipping through a ledger.

"Hi."

She popped up and smiled. "May I help you?"

"Yes, I'd like a room."

She tapped into a computer. "How many nights?"

Leslie paused. "Can we take it on a night by night basis? My plans aren't entirely set in stone."

"Sure. It's early in the season and we actually have several vacancies." She took down information and Leslie handed her a credit card.

"Are you the innkeeper?"

She held out a hand. "Yes, Marianne Mueller. My husband Tom and I own the place."

Leslie took her hand. "It's lovely. I met your father today and he sent me over."

A smile bloomed on her face, wiping away any trace of fatigue or stress that may have been present before. "You don't say! In that case, I'll give you the family discount." She went back into the account and tapped away on her keyboard.

"Family discount? I appreciate it, but I did say, I met your father today, right?"

Marianne snickered. "A friend of my dad's is a friend of mine … and the Seaside Inn. You just got fifteen percent off your bill."

"Thank you very much."

Marianne handed her a key – the old fashioned kind, not a plastic card. "Your price includes three meals a day. 8:30, 1:15 and 6:15. You'll need to call for a reservation for the evening meal, though. Oh, and coffee on the back porch starting at 7:30, if you happen to get up that early. Follow me and I'll take you to your room."

Leslie hustled to keep up with the younger woman. "You feed all your guests three meals a day?" She was astounded.

"Yes, if they want. Of course, they can go out, but there's no discount for skipped meals."

Leslie laughed. They climbed stairs to the second floor and started down a long hallway. At the third door on the left, Marianne motioned to the lock and Leslie got to work with the key. She opened the door into a cute room with wooden floors and two open windows facing the ocean. A salt-tinted breeze made the white curtains whoosh against the light wood paneling. Two double beds separated by an antique nightstand were finished with handmade quilts. A wooden rocker with a straw braided seat sat nearby.

"You have a half bath here – a toilet and a sink," Marianne stood in a small doorway inside the room, "but for showers, you have a couple choices. We have several hot water showers outside if you want to wear a swimsuit, or we have three showers for guests in this main house. There generally aren't too many problems with everyone wanting them at the same time."

In the tiny bathroom, she opened the door of a cabinet. "Towels and toiletries in here. Of course, you're welcome to utilize the entire inn. The living room is for everyone, as well as the back porch. A boardwalk leads to the beach that's private for inn guests. There's a circular deck if you want to stay off the sand." She stopped for a moment and looked around. "Any questions?"

Leslie smiled and shook her head. "Not a one. It's adorable. So much personality. I'm glad I'm here."

"Most of our guests prefer this over a stay at a Holiday Inn. More homey. Feel free to make friends with the other guests. Usually makes a great vacation even better." She moved to the door. "If you need anything, Tom and I are always around. Just come find us."

Leslie closed the door behind her and turned in a slow circle, taking in her new surroundings. This place was perfect. No way would Tim ever vacation in such a rustic place as this. He always went for the ultra-modern, luxurious vacation spots. And of course, she'd enjoyed those too. But staying at a place like this on her roadtrip seemed appropriate. She was mixing it up – doing things differently. Her life had changed and this trip was unlike anything she'd ever done before.

She pocketed the key, and left the room for exploration. She walked through the entire inn, familiarizing herself with her new home away from home. Walking through the back screened-in porch, she made her way down the long wooden boardwalk that led to the beach. The white sand was beautiful and fine and she took off her shoes to enjoy a barefoot walk. Comfy cushioned beach chairs dotted the sand behind the inn, and she looked forward to returning later to relax with a book, a drink and a bathing suit. But for now, she was elated to stretch her legs. She picked a direction and walked.

All the beachfront homes were old but well kept. She remembered a phrase from the realtor brochures, "arrogantly shabby," the island's catch phrase. She smiled and realized her heart was full of joy. She sent a prayer of thanks skyward.

An hour or so later, she returned to her room. She dug her car keys out of her purse, and retrieved her suitcase. Huffing from dragging it up the steep wooden steps, she stopped to rest for a minute in the comfortable living room.

"Oh, there she is!"

She looked up and saw Marianne smiling at her from behind the counter. Standing next to her, holding his cap in his hands, was a newly showered and laundered Hank.

Chapter Six

The grin that jumped on her face at the sight of him was one of those natural, God-given pleasures she couldn't have prevented, even if she'd wanted to. And if she'd detected the slightest hesitation on his part at the sight of her, the grin was evidently the invitation he'd been waiting for. He took a few steps toward her, stopping inches away. "I thought I'd make sure you found it okay."

"Yes, I did. Thanks for the recommendation. This place is perfect for me."

He glanced down at her suitcase. "Why don't I help you carry this upstairs?"

She nodded. "After dragging it up from the car, I'd be happy for the help."

He hoisted it without much effort and headed for the stairs. "You know, my son-in-law would've carried this for you from your car to your room. You didn't need to struggle yourself."

She shook her head. "Not necessary. I got it. And got in my cardio workout at the same time. So, a win-win."

He chuckled. "You sound like a self-sufficient lady."

The observation pleased her. "I guess I am." She beamed at him.

When they reached the top floor, he paused and she passed him, walked to her door and used her key to open it.

He handed the suitcase to her. Curious, she glimpsed over her shoulder at him while she entered the room and threw the luggage on her extra bed. He remained determinedly in the hallway.

Hmmm, a true southern gentleman. She turned to thank him when he said, "Care to meet my granddaughter?"

She laughed. "Absolutely!"

They headed down the hall, down the stairs and out the back. They crossed the long boardwalk and emerged onto the sand. A little girl wearing shorts, a pink tee shirt and a Myrtle Beach Pelicans ball cap sat digging with a plastic shovel. As they approached, she filled a small bucket, picked it up and trotted to the water's edge. She splashed a couple shovel-fulls of salt water in the bucket and headed back to her spot. The single-minded mission, however, was happily interrupted when she caught sight of her grandpa.

"Paw Paw!" she yelled and ran toward him, water-logged bucket of sand still in tow. He took a few long strides and when she thrust her body in the air at him, he was there with open arms to catch her. He twirled her around in a close-bodied circle. "Hi, beautiful."

She gave him kisses on his neck, and then it was back to business. She squirmed to look at the ground. "That's my sand castle there. Don't step on it, Paw Paw."

"I saw it." He deposited her on the sand and she ran over to inspect it. "Looks like a good one, too."

He kneeled on the sand beside her creation. Plastic molds of architectural options littered the space around the castle. He turned his head and threw a wink in Leslie's direction.

"Stella, this pretty lady wants to meet you. She's staying at the inn for a while."

Stella nodded and looked up a second or two before returning to repairing a turret.

Leslie got on her knees near the other two. "Hi Stella, nice to meet you."

"Hi," she threw over her shoulder.

"Darlin', mind your manners. I want you to greet Miss Leslie the proper way, now."

Leslie was about to object. The little girl was busy and focused, and not interested in meeting a stranger. Let her play. But she bit her tongue on her objection. Teaching manners to children was a tenuous job that required consistent expectations. She looked over at Hank and smiled, admiring his resolve.

The girl responded by standing and turning her back to the castle for a moment. She stepped closer to Leslie, held her hand out and said, "Nice to meet you, Miss Leslie. Welcome to the Inn."

Delighted, Leslie took her hand. "Thank you. You're so lucky to live here all the time."

"Yes, ma'am." She peeked over at her granddad, who was a picture of pride.

Leslie dropped her hand and gave her a break. "So, let's see this creation of yours. It's very impressive, isn't it?"

Stella returned to her castle and got absorbed in repairs to the tower, then the new additions to the structure. Leslie and Hank sat back on the sand, watching her.

"I guess her to be about five."

He gave her a look. "You're close. She'll be five in two weeks."

"I teach eight-year-olds."

He smiled. "Do you, now? Do you like it?"

"I love spending my days with kids. Tiring. But rewarding. She's a sweetie, and so smart, too."

"She sure is. One of God's gifts to my life. Healthy grandchildren."

"How many do you have?"

"Three. But she's my only local one. The others live in Colorado so I don't get to see them grow up. I visit as often as I can, but it's still no more than once or twice a year."

Grandchildren – one of life's joys she hadn't experienced yet, but looked forward to. "Is that your son you mentioned, who used to be in business with you? Are those his children?"

"No."

She glanced over at him when the explanation didn't continue. He must have felt her gaze because he looked over. "I have two daughters. Marianne and my other one, Sadie, have the children. Jeremy doesn't have any."

The sun started its slow descent and the feel of the day evolved from hot and sunny, to cooler and twilight. Eventually, Leslie heard Marianne calling to Stella from the inn. Time for cleaning up, then dinner. Hank helped her gather her tools and wipe the sand off her feet and clothes. They began the trek back to the inn, Stella talking about her hunger for dinner.

Hank said, "Care to join Stella and I for dinner tonight? You haven't tasted shrimp scampi till you taste the Inn's."

"Oh, darn. I never made a reservation."

Stella dropped Hank's hand and ran ahead of them. "A benefit of eating with the innkeeper's daughter and father. We can squeeze you in without a reservation."

Despite her late lunch, Leslie realized she was hungry and could definitely eat shrimp scampi. "I'd love to join you.

Thanks for asking me. In fact, knowing you has had several benefits. Marianne gave me the family discount because of you."

He looked at her a second, then ducked his head. He cleared his throat as they walked. She glanced his way. Was that a flush of pink on his neck?

When they reached the living room, Marianne took Stella for a clean-up. Hank said, "I'll wait for my two dinner dates here. Take your time."

Back in her room, Leslie took a chance on the shower and was pleased to find it was available. Warm water washed away the sweat, sand and sunscreen of the afternoon and soon she was staring into her suitcase, wondering what type of wardrobe a dinner with a grandpa/granddaughter duo warranted. Most of her clothes contained wrinkles from spending several days folded in a suitcase. She pulled out a sundress, flipped it in the air a couple times, and laid it on her bed, brushing out the wrinkles as best she could. A peek into the closet confirmed there was no iron. But she supposed that was consistent with the "arrogantly shabby" moniker. She quickly did her hair and her makeup, and after slipping the dress on, she stopped before the full-length mirror.

The thought of being so fussy about her appearance amused her because it was so uncharacteristic of her. In long-term relationships, looks became secondary to the function you fulfilled. In her marriage, she had become the housekeeper, the cook, the mom and the secondary income earner. Did it even matter how she looked? Tim must've thought so, judging from his choice of a younger woman after he left her. But would pretty new clothes and makeup shades have prevented him from straying? She doubted it.

On closer inspection, she noticed the afternoon in the sun had given her cheeks a nice pink color, and her light brown hair had a few highlights that hadn't been there before. The ocean had always been the place she was her happiest, and maybe that transcended to her personal appearance, as well. The dress was wrinkled, but who cares?

She made her way back to the living room where Hank sat on a couch, watching Stella play with some blocks on the floor. He came to his feet at her arrival, and in his soft southern drawl he said, "Don't you look pretty now?"

She smiled and darn if she didn't feel pretty at that moment. With him staring at her in admiration on Day 1 of her beach vacation after such an extraordinary road trip, she felt beautiful. And right where she was meant to be.

"Thank you." Hank gathered Stella and they went into the dining room. They sat at a small table in the middle of the room, and as she was settling into her seat, Leslie glanced around. There was a good crowd. Must be why reservations were needed, and she made a point of remembering from now on. The meal evolved gradually, first a big glass of sweet tea, then a basket of homemade rolls with sweet butter. A salad doused with Italian dressing followed, then the aromatic scampi served over a bed of rice. When she thought she was as full as possible, a delicious-looking slice of key lime pie arrived. She made a deal with Hank to share hers, and he could take his full slice home for later.

"I'm going to dedicate my walk on the beach tomorrow to burning off all these calories," she said with a laugh.

He nodded. "Marianne hired a cook with skills, I gotta give her that. The shrimp he used was caught this morning. He picks out the freshest food possible."

"You mean, one cook produces all this food? There isn't a staff?"

"One takes care of dinner. A second one covers breakfast and lunch. Speaking of breakfast, you need to make sure you're up. There's a made-to-order omelet bar."

How different her evening would be sitting in a typical chain hotel, wondering what she could find for dinner, probably going to a hamburger joint out of convenience.

Marianne stepped up to the table. "Time for Miss Stella to go back to her room and think about settling in for the night."

Hank rose and picked her up, squeezing her in a tight hug. "Love ya, darlin'." She rested her head on his shoulder and her eyes drifted shut.

"Looks like she's worn out from her day on the beach." Leslie patted her back. "Night night, Stella."

When Marianne took her away, Hank watched their departure and lingered on the spot for a few seconds. He pulled his eyes away and looked at Leslie. "I love that little girl."

Leslie nodded. She could tell he did, from the way they interacted and the obvious joy each one felt when together. "You're a great grandpa."

"Could I interest you in a walk on the beach?"

"Sure."

The sun had set on the day, bathing the beach in darkness, but the pristine white sand in contrast seemed to provide a light source of its own for two casual strollers. Leslie slipped out of her sandals when they reached the end of the boardwalk and left them there for retrieval when they returned. The sand under her feet felt deliciously cool and an inadvertent shiver ran through her. Hank's arm immediately came up around her shoulders, and with it, the warmth of his solid body.

"Cold? I should've suggested you run and get a sweater."

"No, I'm fine. The sand was chilly on my bare feet."

His arm stayed in place and it pleased her, despite the fact a strange man's hand on her bare shoulder seemed oddly intimate. In fact, her conflicting emotions threw her for such a loop that the first few minutes of their walk, she was so preoccupied with whether or not she should encourage the physical contact, she was unable to speak with him. Fortunately, he seemed to be interested in a silent stroll as well.

She was sure he was only being polite, trying to keep her warm because she'd shivered, not for any reason having to do with physical attraction. That whole southern gentleman thing. He'd do it for anyone, she was quite certain.

Although, she'd picked up on several clues throughout the day that seemed to indicate he was interested in getting to know her. That he even thought she was attractive. He'd complimented her several times, hadn't he?

Or was that part of southern courtesy as well? Darn, she was out of her league!

"Thank you for the body warmth. I think the walking has warmed me up now."

He immediately dropped his arm and continued walking, keeping a respectable distance. She looked over at him and although darkness prevented her from seeing him clearly, she detected a grin on his face.

Maybe it was the darkness that gave her courage that bright sunlight wouldn't have. Maybe it was the fact she was so inexperienced as a newly single woman. Maybe it was being so many miles away from home. But that split second, she made up her mind. She'd be totally honest with him and let the repercussions fall where they may. Or come crashing down, as it were.

"Hank."

"Yep?"

"I have no idea what I'm doing."

He chuckled. "You want to narrow that down for me?"

She looked straight ahead and concentrated on lifting one foot after another from the sand. "I'm recently divorced."

"Mmmm. I wondered. I mean, what your status is."

"You did?" She darted a glance at him but he chose that moment to look toward the houses they were passing. She made out a glimpse of his left ear.

"Yeah, you know, just curious. You're traveling alone and all."

"Oh."

"And you don't wear a wedding ring." He said it as though hesitant to reveal his observation, however if she was being completely honest, he must have figured, why not follow suit?

"You noticed that?"

"Sure."

Leslie nodded and walked, the waves pounding in and out provided a powerful sound as a backdrop. "I was married for twenty years. Until a few weeks ago. It's over."

He didn't speak for a moment. Then, "I'm sorry." A few steps later, "The man's a fool."

Leslie chuckled. She had to admit it felt good. With the strength of the darkness providing uninhibitedness she wouldn't normally possess, Leslie came out with it. She talked about the bleak, empty summer stretching out in front of her.

She told Hank about her decision to turn her back on her life temporarily, to let God send her where He wanted her to go.

And she told him about the adventures God had sent her on already, about Deakon and Norman Foster and Joan Lundeen. About Rita and Nathan and the struggles of a family adjusting to life without Dad around to share the burdens. And about Evelyn Fletcher and Carla and the rest of the church ladies who met every month to make and deliver warm blankets and caps to the babies born at Levine Children's Hospital. She told him about Carson, the preemie baby who would wear her own imperfect creation when he was up to it.

As she spoke, the waves provided a soundtrack and the lights in the houses along the beach went out, one by one. Hank took her hand and pulled her over to a log to sit. After a rest, they wandered back in the direction of the inn. By the time they reached it, Leslie was done. Without hesitation, she'd shared so much with this man she'd known since this afternoon. She felt vaguely exhausted.

As they approached the inn's back porch still brightly lit inside, her natural inhibition returned. What had she put this poor man through? Long minutes – she caught sight of a clock hanging on the wall inside the porch and was amazed to learn it was close to midnight – no, *hours* of revelation. Had she bored him? Made him want to turn tail and run as fast as possible, but was too polite to do it? Would he deposit her in the inn and be glad for his escape route, never to return?

Before she could apologize, he brought her to a stop outside the porch, her face lit by the glow of the distant light as it penetrated the dark. Placing his hands on her shoulders, he turned her till she faced him, then he lowered his head and placed a kiss on her forehead. And he lingered there. Leslie let her eyes close and she soaked in the heat shimmering off his body, warming her in their closeness. She inhaled his scent, some kind of masculine combination of soap and musk cologne. He pulled away and she looked up to meet his eyes, happy that he seemed to want to be there.

"I'm glad our paths crossed today," he said. "I can't even begin to tell you how much."

She let her eyes rest on his face. He was a picture of contentment.

"Just so you know, it was uncharacteristic of me to reveal all that personal stuff to someone I barely know. I can't imagine what came over me. I apologize for keeping you so late."

His lips pushed out a nonverbal objection to her apology. "I enjoyed it, every minute. You needed to talk about it, and I was happy to listen."

"You're a good listener."

"And you're an amazing woman." The volume of his voice reduced almost to a whisper, enough that she wondered if she'd understood him correctly. But his normal tone returned and he went on, "I'm going to say good night, sleep well, and I will see you again soon."

"Good night, Hank."

He slipped into the screened porch and through the doorway that led to the front of the inn. She watched him go, trying to recall the feel of his lips on her forehead and his scent in her nostrils.

Back in her room, she undressed and prepared for bed. Under the sheets, she said a silent prayer of gratitude for the events of the day, for her safe arrival at the beach, for her discovery of The Old Gray Barn and the Seaside Inn. She said a special thank you for meeting Hank. After she'd said amen and started to drift off, a revelation floated through her mind. She needed people too. Not only had God used her to help others when they needed her, He also knew what she needed and was watching out for her.

Chapter Seven

As far as Leslie was concerned, her vacation officially began today. So, she slid into her favorite vacation behavior.

She slept without setting the alarm. Leslie peeked at the clock once, and seeing it was 6:19, she sighed in unhurried relief and slipped back to sleep, waking again at 8:24. A very respectable time to wake on a leisurely beach vacation.

She fluffed her hair with her fingers, brushed her teeth, rubbed some lotion on her face and dressed in shorts and a tee shirt. No shower or makeup required. Leslie made her way to the back sunroom and helped herself to coffee and a muffin. Then she tiptoed barefoot down the wooden boardwalk to the chairs facing the ocean. The day had dawned sunny and clear, and although the sun hadn't reached full strength yet, she predicted it would be a beautiful beach day.

She enjoyed her small breakfast with her toes dug in the cool sand, her eyes soaking in the scenery and her ears taking in the sounds of the surf and the seagulls overhead. Her thoughts wandered to the day before. Unbidden, she replayed in her mind her meeting Hank at the Barn, and sure enough, her heart rate increased during the reminiscence just like it had in real time. She shook her head, and berated herself for acting and feeling like a young woman. She had no business getting giddy about a man, particularly at this stage of her life.

She stood, shaking her arms and legs out, and rested her empty mug in the seat of the chair. She needed a little exercise to give her mind something else to focus on. Loosened up, she headed down to the water's edge for a walk.

The first ten minutes or so, she luxuriated in a slow stroll, then picked up the pace. She flexed her leg muscles, working her feet in and out of the sand and pushed herself to move. She'd never been a runner but she understood the value of exercise, both from a physical and mental health perspective. As she pumped her arms and motored her legs through the sand, her heart pounded and her breathing came heavier.

When she'd gone as far as she thought she possibly could, she set a target two house lengths away, and kept going. Her leg muscles screaming, her chest heaving, she reached the targeted spot, and plopped into the sand on her back, arms and legs out, eyes closed, a big smile of achievement covering her face. Her huffing slowed as her heart rate regulated and eventually returned to normal.

She pushed to her feet, wiping off the sand and strolled back to the Inn. Grabbing her cup, she deposited it on the porch and headed for her room. After a shower, she applied sunscreen, put on a swimsuit and cover up and returned to the beach. She spent the better part of the day lying in a lounge chair under an umbrella, reading a book and occasionally dipping in the ocean. This stretch of beach wasn't known for big, crashing waves. Its softer rolling waves were a perfect fit for Leslie and she could float on her back, rolling gently with the surf.

When she called it a day, the sun was deep in the west. She yawned, relaxing hours causing the illusion of exhaustion. On her way back through the living room, she added her name to the dinner reservation list.

At 6:15, she entered the dining room, famished for the delicious dinner she knew would follow. Marianne sat her with a family of three and Leslie enjoyed her conversation while eating the most delicious barbequed spare ribs, cornbread and greens she'd ever had. Topped off by a peach cobbler with ice cream, she rolled back to her room and spent the remaining evening hours watching a few sit coms on television. She turned the light off at nine thirty and sank into a dark, restful sleep.

The next morning, she called Jasmine. She caught her daughter as she was entering a Parisian underground metro station.

"Hi Mom. I'm rushing off to an appointment and I'm not sure how the reception will be under here."

"Oh, that's okay, honey. You can always call me back later. I wanted to hear your voice. You doing good?"

Her tinny voice echoed and Leslie could picture her walking down cement steps into an enclosed station. "Better than good, Mom. I love it here. I'm learning so much, it's insane."

Leslie smiled. "I'm glad to hear it. I'm sure you're doing great."

"Good stuff for the resume. How about you? Where are you now?"

"I'm in Pawleys Island, South Carolina. I'm staying in a cute place called the Seaside Inn. It's just what the doctor ordered. Beautiful beach, great weather."

"It's – hear you are so – deserve to be –"

Leslie pressed her cell phone closer to her ear. "Jaz? Can you hear me? You're breaking up."

A crackling followed, then she heard, "—have to go, but did you hear from Dad?"

"Your dad? No, why?"

Crackle, crackle, " – wants you to call him. – has something to tell you."

The connection died and the reception went silent. Leslie mused over the limited conversation. Her baby was deliriously happy living her dream, and that filled Leslie with joy. But Tim was trying to get a hold of her, and that filled her with dread. What did he want? It had to be about the house, what else would it be? Despite the fact she didn't want Tim's voice to interrupt her idyllic vacation getaway, now that she knew he wanted to talk, her thoughts would be monopolized with wondering why. So she bucked it up and called him.

"Dr. Malone."

"Hi Tim. It's Leslie." She smirked at his hesitation. By design, she'd identified herself by name even though it wasn't necessary. Because of their long history together, she had no doubt she could give him a single syllable – "hi" – and he'd know exactly who was calling. But that was a deeper level of intimacy than this man deserved now. She was no longer intimate with him or his life. Therefore, she'd treat him like she would any other business partner. Because that's exactly what he was now – a partner in two things – getting Jasmine through college, and selling the house. And that was all.

"Oh, hi. How are you?"

Did it matter how she was? No, she decided. Again, strictly business. She avoided his question. "I spoke with

Jasmine and she told me you were trying to get a hold of me."

"Oh, uh, yes. I got some feedback from the realtor. Several potential buyers have been through the house, and nobody's placed an offer yet. The realtor asks why, and it always comes down to the same few items."

"Mm hmm."

"Don't worry, they're not major items. The carpet's old and worn out. A new flat carpet in a neutral color would do wonders in helping people envision themselves in the house. Oh, and the blinds."

"What's wrong with the blinds?"

"They're white and they're aluminum. They should be wood."

Leslie rolled her eyes. "Why?"

"Because it's an upgrade that everyone expects now as standard."

They had lived with white aluminum blinds for over a dozen years and nothing bad had come of it. Just because everyone was getting the upgrade didn't mean they had to.

"The realtor advised we make those replacements and try another month. If no sales at that point, we should consider replacing the kitchen counter with marble."

"That's ridiculous. There's nothing wrong with my Formica countertop."

She heard his irritated sigh. "Work with me here, Leslie. Don't you want to sell the house?"

She paused. Did she? No, in truth she didn't. She didn't particularly want to rip her family apart either, but he'd made it impossible for her to go back to the way things were.

"I guess. Go ahead and arrange the carpet. Let's wait on the blinds and definitely hold on the marble."

He paused, she was sure debating whether he should fight it, but eventually knew when to fold. "Okay, fine. Would you like to pick out the carpet?"

"Why would I want to do that? I'm perfectly happy with my old carpet. Besides, I'm out of town and won't be able to arrange it. You'll have to do it." Or have your mistress do it.

"Where are you?" His tone seemed hesitant, knowing it really was none of his business, but curious anyway.

"On vacation." His next question was a silent one, but she knew he was wondering nonetheless. "I'm in a seaside inn at the beach for a while."

He paused and she knew him well enough to know what thoughts were going through his mind, all objections. "How did you get there? Did you fly?"

"No, I drove."

"By yourself?" He'd always discouraged her from driving longer distances alone when they were together. Although she thought at the time, it was because he didn't want anything to happen to her, now she suspected it was because he didn't trust her to handle the drive on her own. He never gave her credit for her potential.

"Yes, all by myself, Tim, and I made it fine. Safe and sound."

"Ah, that's great, Les. You always have loved the ocean."

"Yep. Okay, so if there's nothing else …?"

"You said you spoke to Jasmine. How did she sound?" The man couldn't seem to take a hint.

"Well, she sounded busy, on her way to something, so we couldn't talk long. She's going to call me back later when she has time. But overall, she seemed very happy."

"Great. I'm glad she's having such a good summer."

"Good-bye, Tim." She didn't wait for him to respond because his voice was getting that nostalgic, soft tone to it that had always made her melt, and even though he'd destroyed their marriage and their family, and she knew their divorce was the right thing under the circumstances, she couldn't trust herself to listen to that tone without remembering all the hundreds of times she'd heard it before. Happy times while lying in bed, sleeping in on a weekend morning, sharing the Sunday paper amidst the blankets. Hearing it over the phone while he was on a business trip, miles away, doing important work, but knowing her voice was the last thing he wanted and needed to hear before turning out the light.

It was different now. And she had to be ruthless with cutting the ties. Or else she'd never get on with the business of rebuilding her life.

She left her room and headed downstairs. Marianne and Tom were in the middle of attaching a colorful, long "Happy Anniversary" banner to the living room wall. Tom stood on a three-step ladder in one corner, reaching behind the couch to attach the sign with thumb tacks. Marianne stood on the opposite side on the floor, trying to hold up the other end of the banner while casting glances at Stella. The neglected girl was emitting a full-out wail.

"Stella, stop it, sweetie. I can't help you right now. You'll have to wait."

"No!" The wails stopped long enough for the girl to throw out that favorite syllable, then started again. As Leslie walked into the room, Marianne tossed her an apologetic glance.

"Sorry for all the craziness in here," she said, raising her voice over Stella's cries. "We're hosting a party for some guests tonight and Miss Stella does not like having to share us at the moment."

Leslie gazed at the pre-schooler, a coloring book and box of crayons missing the mark at grasping her attention. "Would you mind if I take her into the dining room? I have a sudden urge for a beautiful picture and I know of only one little girl who can color one for me."

Marianne looked hopeful, but replied, "Oh, don't worry about us. Don't change any plans you have."

"No trouble at all. Why don't we let you finish your decorating and you can find us in there?" She held an open hand out to Stella. The girl was keeping up the pretense of crying, but the thought of coloring with Leslie had piqued her interest. Minimal additional prompting from Leslie, and Stella jumped to her feet, accepted her hand and trotted into the dining room. They settled in at a table.

"What is your favorite picture? Will you pick your favorite to color and then give it to me? I'll hang it in my room." Leslie grinned at her. Stella got busy flipping through the book, wiping tears from her cheeks. Her decision made, she got to work, head down and knuckles white, gripping the fat crayon.

A fleeting memory of Jasmine at that age made Leslie focus on the child. Same concentration level, same love of the dramatic. Give them each a job and they won't stop till they're done.

"There they are. Two of my favorite ladies."

"Paw Paw!" A conflict of desires played across Stella's face – her determination to finish her coloring, along with her longing to jump down and hug her grandpa. Leslie chuckled. Stella compromised by staying in her seat, crayon in one hand, while reaching for him with her free hand, squirming and squealing in delight. He wrapped an arm around her and kneeled behind her, his head even with hers.

"Well now, isn't that a work of art?"

"It's going to be featured in my prestigious collection," Leslie said.

"Is that right? Now you're making me jealous."

Stella peeked behind her at her grandpa. "Don't you worry, Paw Paw. I'll color you one next!" The word came out like "n-ay-xt" with her southern accent.

"You've got yourself a deal." Hank stood and moved to the vacant chair next to Leslie. As the artistic effort continued, he leaned in close. "How are you doing today?"

"Great. I had a wonderfully relaxing beach day yesterday. Perfect." She grinned.

"Just what the doc ordered, huh?"

"A day at the beach always does me good."

He stood and slipped away, returning with two glasses of iced water. She took a hearty sip and felt the coolness saturate her system.

"What are you doing for dinner tonight?" he asked.

"I hadn't thought about it. Of course, I can eat here, but after the feast the last two nights, I think I might want something light like a can of soup."

He reached toward her hand and gave her middle knuckle a casual caress. "You bring the can, I'll throw in a cold cut sandwich."

What was he talking about?

"I'm sorry, let me ask a lady properly." He lifted her hand and placed it in his own. "Leslie, would you come over to my house for supper tonight? I'll treat you to a lunchmeat sandwich and canned soup." He laughed. "I believe I told you I don't cook."

"I'd love to," she said through a smile.

He reached for a red crayon and ripped a stray page out of Stella's coloring book. She barely noticed. He wrote an address and handed it to her. "What time?"

"Um. 6:30?"

"You got it." He wrapped his hand around hers and gave it a squeeze. He stood and placed a kiss on Stella's head. "Bye, cupcake." The little girl waved. He tossed Leslie a wink.

The day passed pleasantly with the slow pace inherent to a beach vacation day. She spent some time with Stella and was rewarded with a completed coloring, which she took upstairs and hung in her room next to Deakon's masterpiece. She took a barefoot walk on the beach, working up enough of an appetite to enjoy the dining room lunch of salad, clam chowder (homemade, she suspected), big hard rolls and butter. She enjoyed a few hours of reading time while sitting on the deck outside.

Nerves loomed over her leisurely afternoon, though. Dismayed by the feeling of apprehension that had taken root in her chest, she scoffed at herself. Why on earth would she be nervous about picking up a can of soup and joining a new friend for a sandwich? Ridiculous for a woman her age. You'd think she was a teenage girl facing her first date with a cute boy.

Shaking her head, she tried to concentrate on page 57 of her new paperback, since she'd finished her first one yesterday. But when she read the same paragraph three times without remembering the words, she flipped the book shut and dropped it in her lap. She could so relate to that teenage girl; she was more like her than she cared to admit. She'd spent enough time with Hank over the last few days to realize two things: one, she liked him, and two, he appeared to like her, too. And that elevated this simple evening of canned soup and sandwiches to something past friendship.

And she had absolutely no idea how to deal with that possibility.

She dragged herself out of the chair and went back to her room to shower. About six, she walked out to her car dressed in denim shorts, heeled sandals and freshly painted toenails. She'd chosen a sleeveless top, floral-printed, with a scooped neckline. The days she'd spent in the sun had given her chest, arms and legs the healthy glow of a mild suntan.

At the grocery store, she picked out a small selection of soups: beef and vegetable, chicken and noodle, tomato. Back in her car, she typed Hank's address into her GPS and drove the short distance to his house.

She pulled into his driveway and took in the sight of his house. It was what would generously be called a "fixer-upper." Tiny-looking, she supposed it met the needs of a single person. Literally a square wooden house with a door and two windows in the front and an attached porch, she could see a few windows along the side. Gray paint chipped off the house's exterior. The porch's lattice finish had slats missing, giving it a neglected look. She pushed the gearshift into Park and gathered her things. Walking across the yard, she added another item to her mental list of items this house needed. The yard needed a mow and probably hours' worth of trimming.

She climbed the steps but before she could push the doorbell, the door swung open and Hank was standing behind the screen, his smile causing her heart to pound a few beats faster.

"Hi, you found it." He held the screen door open and reached a hand out for the bag. "Don't you look pretty as a picture?"

She chuckled.

"Something funny?" he asked with a grin.

"I tell ya, I could get spoiled being around you. I'm not used to so many compliments." She supposed it was his southern upbringing, but she had to admit she liked it.

"How could a beautiful lady like you not get flooded with compliments? Good thing you dumped that ole man of yours. He didn't deserve you."

She waited for a bite of pain at the thought of her failed marriage, but it didn't come. He'd meant it good naturedly, and she accepted it that way.

They walked into the tiny house, and as she expected from looking at the outside, the floor plan was very simple. The front door led into a great room and behind it, the kitchen. A short hall to the left led to two bedrooms in the back of the house, one on each side, and a single bathroom. The impromptu tour took all of two minutes. But she puzzled over the abundance of furniture crammed into the little place. And good stuff too. Rich leather couch and loveseat, an oak table that looked to be hand crafted. In the bedroom, a full suite of matching furniture. It didn't add up. Why would he have such a ratty house, yet fill it with showcase-quality furniture?

When the tour was done, he took her to the kitchen. "What would you like to drink?"

He showed her the choices, and she opted for a diet cola. He handed her the drink on ice, and busied himself opening the soup cans and pouring the contents into three separate pots, warming up the burners on the stove.

"Can I help you with anything?" she asked.

"No, no. You relax. You're on vacation."

She laughed and sat at the table in the main room, where she could still keep an eye on him in the small kitchen. "Yes, I am. And I haven't felt this pampered in years."

The soups taken care of, Hank set out slices of bread on a cutting board, then went to the refrigerator, returning holding a variety of deli bags of meats and cheeses. He laid the options out, creating a smorgasbord. Soon, he poured the soups into bowls and they helped themselves to hearty deli sandwiches and soup.

"How was your day today? Are you still at the Old Gray Barn?"

"Nah," he said, swallowing his bite. "Finished up there for now, but I get a lot of work from that management company. I'm down the street now, working on one of their other old properties."

"Guess it keeps you busy."

"Sure does."

A question formed in her mind but she kept it unasked. Something about this man had her wondering. What was his story? He was obviously capable of refurbishing an old house to its former glory. But why didn't he use those skills on this place?

And why was a man his age, after successfully raising a family of his own, living in this sort of ramshackle hut anyway?

And how would she even tackle these personal questions with a man she'd only known a few days, without him telling her (rightfully) to mind her own business?

She picked up the second half of her sandwich and dipped it into the broth of chicken noodle soup. "So, tell me about this place. How long have you been here? Do you have any plans for it?"

He smiled, but a shadow of an uncomfortable expression crossed his face. She'd hoped the questions sounded like general conversation topics. Were they threatening somehow?

He finished chewing his bite of sandwich, then leaned back in his chair to size her up. "Long story, there."

"If you don't want to talk about it, that's fine."

He took in a breath, pushed it out with some effort. "In fact, I do. That's one of the reasons I invited you over here tonight."

"What do you mean?"

"Do you believe in the power of prayer, Leslie?"

His question took her by surprise because it seemed like a complete change of topic. They were talking about his house, now they were talking about prayer.

"Why, yes. Yes, I do."

He nodded, grinned. "I thought so. I really did." He stood and held a hand out to her. She took it and he led her to the great room, where they settled on the sofa she'd seen earlier. The leather was highly shined and comfortable as she sank into it with him.

"I'm taking a chance here, Leslie. I'm hoping you won't think I'm crazy for saying this, but here I go. I've been praying for a long time, and I really believe you're the answer to my prayers."

He stopped and looked into her eyes, undoubtedly waiting for some reaction. Some discouragement to continuing. But he wasn't going to find it here. After all she'd experienced on this trip, one thing she was sure of: God utilized people who believed in Him to help other people on this earth. All people needed to do was believe, and be willing to help out where needed. God does great things through those with a willing heart.

"I don't think you're crazy. Go on."

An audible sigh of relief left his lips and a smile played there. "I didn't think God had led me astray. First He introduces this beautiful lady into my life, then when you told me those amazing stories about your roadtrip, how you were able to help people just by being in the right place at the right time, and keeping your eyes and ears open, I knew it was the Creator giving me the nudge I needed."

"An answer to prayer?"

"Yes, but for someone as stubborn as me, it takes something more than subtle. It takes something like a bang over the head with a hammer."

Leslie laughed at the image. "Ouch. So tell me, what is it you've been praying about? And how do you think I can help?"

He squeezed her hand, which was still lodged in his. He looked down at their hands, then up into her eyes. "Do you remember me telling you I had a son named Jeremy?"

"Yes, two daughters and one son. And Jeremy used to work with you in your family business."

"Right. Jeremy was my shadow when he was a kid. He enjoyed going along on my jobs with me, whenever he could. He got real handy with tools at a young age, and when he came onto a job site with me, I'd give him jobs to do. By the time he was a teenager, I swear he was about as good at handyman stuff as I was. He tried a lot of different jobs, and with me looking over his shoulder, checking his work, we became quite a team.

"After high school, Jeremy went to college and got a degree in business. He had big plans for the handyman business. I'd always kept it small. Just me in the winter months, add some seasonal help in the summer when the jobs picked up. It was enough to support my family. We weren't rich but we certainly had enough to live on. Plus, Jeremy and I had built our home."

He looked around the tiny bungalow. "Not this place, no. At the peak of the business's success, Jeremy and I designed and built a big, beautiful home right off Pawleys, inland about a mile from the coast. He was the site manager and his dream was to use the house as a spec home to build a home construction business. He wanted to expand to where the big money was. Move away from doing smaller jobs, and only take on the bigger."

He turned his head and the tension around his eyes proved how difficult the telling of this story was for him.

"As Jeremy got more and more involved in the business, I let him take over more and more responsibility. Heck, I didn't want no part of it. I went along with his business plan, but I personally wanted to stay with the handyman stuff. It's what I'd always done, and I didn't want to break out of my comfort zone. Let the young turk run with the big, expensive jobs. That's what I sent him to college for.

"So, before you know it, Jeremy was in charge of all the finances – paying all the bills, investing all the income, making the purchase decisions. He was taking on bigger projects and hiring help to get them done. Before I knew it, he had twenty full time employees, taking on enough work to keep them all busy. It worried me, because we'd always been such a small operation. But I knew he was young and energetic and educated, and this was his vision, his dream. I wanted to get out eventually and leave the business to the next generation. So I kept doing what I'd always done. I stayed on the side doing handyman jobs, and I put my head down and closed my eyes to what was going on."

A shudder slipped down Leslie's spine.

"I knew there was trouble, but it was way too late to turn it around. I noticed Jeremy was getting touchy. You know, tense, grumpy, rude. I tried to ask questions, but he brushed me off. We both knew I'd put my head in the sand, and now that he was evidently in over his head, his attitude was, I couldn't help. We struggled with that for a while. But the bomb hit a few months later.

"My wife, Ruthie, hadn't been feeling well. She went to the doctor and we discovered the worst. Ruthie had leukemia."

Leslie gasped. "I'm so sorry!"

He gave her a comforting smile. "It's okay, darling. It's been ten years ago now." He turned to face her on the couch. "Don't get me wrong. Not a day goes by I don't think of her, but the sting of loss has passed."

Leslie knew the feeling. She'd lost both her parents and still thought of them frequently.

Hank continued, "She started treatment and a few weeks in, I got a rejection letter from the insurance company. It came to the house, but since our insurance has always been a business expense and Jeremy was the one paying the bills, I went to him, thinking there must be some mistake. Maybe he'd missed a payment and could send it in, and we'd get the doctor's bill paid." He shook his head. "Unfortunately, this was the tip of the iceberg. And over the next few years, we chipped away at that thing till the whole ugly story came out in the open."

He shifted in his seat and went on. "Long story short, Jeremy was in over his head and had made some bad business decisions. A lot of them. He'd taken on too much work and bid way too low to get the jobs. His first few construction projects, he operated at a loss. Unbeknownst to me, he wiped out the company's savings, accumulated over my lifetime, and still couldn't pay his employees and his suppliers. Then he started cutting corners on the projects. Eventually, he had several lawsuits on his hands. People suing him because he hadn't paid them, because the houses weren't good quality. How he kept this from me for so long, I have no idea. I was a fool going merrily along my way, thinking everything was fine."

Leslie leaned in close. "You can't blame yourself for this. Jeremy was a grown man, making business decisions. Those were his mistakes, not yours."

Hank's voice softened with grief. "Yeah, but he was my boy. And it was my business he was destroying. My life's work I'd built up for over twenty years." He shook his head. "I was so naïve."

He pulled a shaky hand over his chin. "When Jeremy realized what deep crap he was in, he took out a huge loan and the loaner was, shall we say, not the most reputable. But any bank or loaning institution would come in and do a check of the business to see what kind of shape the books were in. And Jeremy figured, probably rightfully, we would be turned down."

"Because he'd spent all your money," Leslie murmured.

"Right. So he went with some guy he found in Atlantic City. I never found out who this guy was exactly, but you can imagine. He gave Jeremy a big wad of cash and demanded a huge interest rate of return. Jeremy took it, thinking if he could pay off his current debts, he could apply what he'd learned and start pricing his jobs properly, and go legitimate – earn some good profit moving forward."

Leslie looked down at her lap. "But it didn't work out that way."

"No. He used the money to pay off the lawsuits, had a little left over to pay off some unpaid bills. But the construction company's reputation was destroyed by then. There are a lot of outfits around here that want your business to build houses. And word travels fast. News of Jeremy's problems spread and he didn't win any bids with his new pricing model. Nobody would hire him. Not to say I blamed them."

Leslie sighed. "And I suppose the insurance was cancelled?"

Hank nodded. "That was one of the bills that went unpaid. By the time Jeremy had the loan money to pay it off, our policy had already cancelled. And now that Ruthie had a serious medical condition, we couldn't get it back. We were all uninsured."

Leslie shook her head in disbelief. What a horrible story. What a disaster this family had been through. Yet Hank had said she was an answer to his prayers. So he hadn't lost his faith through this catastrophe. That was good. But what could *she* possibly do to help him?

"Obviously, once I found out about all this, I couldn't ignore it anymore. I took over the business side and dug into all the financial issues. As much as it killed me, I fired Jeremy and all his employees, those who hadn't already quit. I had to. There was no way around it. And I declared bankruptcy for the company. The company eventually dissolved, and I took on the responsibility of paying off all those outstanding debts."

"You!"

"Sure. I was the owner of the company, so I was responsible."

"Doesn't seem fair. You had no knowledge of the wrongdoing."

Hank nodded. "But I should've. The court took everything I had that was worth anything, including the spec home. That went a long way in paying off debt. And I went back to what I do best – small handyman jobs. Honest, sweaty work."

"What about your wife?"

"Ruthie died about a year after her diagnosis." He turned to take in Leslie's eyes, her face. "Since we were uninsured at that time, we had to go on Medicaid for all her treatment. It killed me to sacrifice top quality care, and you should've seen some of the places we had to go to. So if you look at it that way, it was a blessing for her to go so fast. She went home to her Father."

On impulse, Leslie wrapped her arms around him, embracing him. He'd been through so much. How had he survived? Where had he found the strength?

"And Jeremy?"

Hank shook his head. She felt it against her shoulder as they hugged. "Jeremy's in prison, Leslie."

Leslie pulled back. "Prison?"

Hank nodded. "When the pieces fell, Jeremy was charged with two counts of tax evasion and a few charges related to loan sharking and predatory lending. That's against the law, you know." He gave her a half-hearted grin.

"Where is he?"

"Oh, he's over in Columbia. He's made it to what they call a pre-release center. He'll be getting out soon. He's about served his sentence."

Chapter Eight

A phone rang, a shrill ring cutting through the quiet room, causing Leslie to jump in her seat. Hank chuckled, uttered an "Excuse me a moment," and went to answer it. She watched him go, her mind stuck on the unspeakable story he'd told her. Would she have come out of that same set of events unscathed? She was sure he had his scars. On his mind, on his heart. How could he not?

But scarred or not, she had met the man he was now. And that man caused her heart to skitter a bit. She looked around the room. Now, his unkempt cottage made a whole lot of sense. He worked hard to earn money, most of which went towards paying off his son's debts. His son's mistakes. What a father this man was. She already knew it, based on his interactions with Marianne and Stella. But it was easy to be a good parent to a good child. Anyone could do that. It took a truly remarkable person to be a good and loyal parent to a child who'd made so many mistakes.

She heard his voice from the other room, wrapping up the conversation. Then he popped back into the great room.

"Hey, you want to get out of here a bit? Go on a drive?"

"Sure." She stood up, smoothing out her shorts with her palms.

"That was someone I've done some work for. He wants to show me something else I can do for him. I hope you don't mind."

"Not at all. Or, I could go home. I don't want to interrupt your business."

He put an arm around her shoulder. "I'd be honored if you went with me. And it should only take a few minutes."

"Let's go, then."

They locked the house and climbed into Hank's pickup. It was a short drive through residential streets and they pulled up in front of a moderate house that looked about forty years old. Hank slipped his hand into hers as they walked to the front door and Leslie realized she was coming to love how comfortable it felt when he did things like that.

A man in his late thirties answered the door. "Talk about customer service. You didn't need to drop everything the minute I called, Hank." But his smile said he was glad he had.

"Not a problem at all. I had plans this evening, but I brought them along with me." He planted a happy smile on Leslie. "This is my friend Leslie. Leslie, this is Bob."

Leslie murmured a greeting, then they went into the house. It was in pristine shape inside. The living room was welcoming and friendly, decorated in a beach cottage theme. The walls blue, the wooden furniture painted a shabby-chic white, the walls covered with beach-themed paintings and paraphernalia. An adjoining dining room was more formal, an oak table, chairs and china cabinet, the walls displaying portraits of Bob with a striking blond woman posing in front of various travel destinations: the Eiffel Tower, the Grand Canyon, Times Square.

Bob said, "Next on Martha's list is the hallway bathroom. This way."

They followed him. The bathroom was cramped and in need of modernization. The sink and vanity, as well as the commode, appeared original to the house. Bob showed Hank some pictures cut out of a catalog. "She likes this countertop, and this ceramic sink. Does that go together?"

"Sure. Martha's got excellent taste. She makes my job easy."

Bob laughed. "I'm relieved to hear you say that. She's out buying the stuff now. If she knew I invited you over, she would want to be here. Once she's on the hunt for home design, you can barely stop her."

Hank studied some paint color and ceramic tile samples and nodded. "This'll work. What's your timeline?"

"Flexible to your schedule. When can you fit us in?"

Hank tilted his head back, his mind moving. "I've got about two weeks left on Springs Avenue. How about I start the Monday after that? I could fit this bathroom remodel in before I start the next batch with Beach Management."

Bob pulled out a handheld device and typed with his thumbs. "Perfect. Martha will be so happy to get it started."

"Shouldn't take a full week. Three days, maybe? I'll write up an estimate and get it to you."

"Okay, but I know it'll be reasonable. It always is." He turned to Leslie. "Do you know how talented this guy is?"

She smiled tentatively.

"He's done this entire house almost, room by room. The living room, dining room, kitchen, family room. We bought it knowing we had to fix it up, but didn't realize how sadly lacking we were in the skills to do it. Martha has the vision, but I didn't have the know-how to carry her vision through. We were lucky the day we found Hank."

She looked over at him and thought she detected a faint blush. "Your home is beautiful."

"Okay, see you in a few weeks." Hank ushered her out and back to the truck.

"You don't like taking compliments, do you?"

He laughed. "No, it's not that. It's just, this is business. This is work. Lots of people can do this stuff. Nothing to get cocky about."

"You do wonderful work. You have a ton of skills. You can really do all that – tile, paint, installing countertops?"

"Oh, sure. Whatever it takes. Laying carpet, some electrical, carpentry. It's not hard. Takes some time and patience. Oh, and direction from the client. That's why I love working at their house. Martha tells me exactly what she wants. That's helpful."

Instead of heading back to his house, Hank drove in the direction of the coastline and pulled into the parking lot of a public beach. They left their shoes in the truck and joined hands as they maneuvered the short incline to the beach. Leslie was pleased when he didn't drop her hand as they reached level ground.

They walked leisurely and although she glanced at him several times, he didn't meet her eyes, instead he studied the ocean skyline.

"Thank you for sharing your story with me, Hank."

His eyebrows shot up, then relaxed with a smile. "A lot there, huh?

Leslie laughed. "What is it about us, anyway? I had 'diarrhea of the mouth' with you the other night, and it must have been a contagious condition for you tonight."

"I'm sure you could guess, I don't share that story with many folks," Hank said.

She nodded.

"But there is a reason why I shared it with you." He stopped walking and faced her, capturing her other hand in the process. "You, of all people, know God sometimes answers prayers by sending people who can help."

"I've certainly learned that lesson on my short roadtrip. Being willing to help where needed sometimes opens doors to miracles."

"Right. When you told me your story the other night on the beach, I felt like God was taking a hammer and pounding my brain with it. 'Listen, dummy. This is important.'" He wiped a hand across his forehead and joined with hers again. "I mean, I've been praying for years about Jeremy. Asking for God's help on his behalf, to get him through his prison sentence without too much damage. Prayers for a normal life when he gets released."

She squeezed his hands. "Of course you have. You love him. I can tell that you're a very good father."

He shook his head, sighed. "But there's a prayer I've been ignoring, Leslie. There's a prayer I've been neglecting for almost ten years now that I should've been saying. But I couldn't bring myself to do it."

His voice was strained with pain under the surface. This man, this traditional southern gentleman, was close to tears and she had no idea what to do to help him. She glanced around, looking for a place to sit, but not finding anything, she said, "Do you want to sit, Hank? Here, in the sand?"

They sank into the sand and she pretended not to notice when he scrubbed both his eyes. In a moment, he'd pulled himself together and he cleared his throat.

"I'm a simple man, Leslie. I've always followed God, always tried to live a good life. But this thing with Jeremy really threw me for a loop."

"Of course it has. He did some terrible things. It would throw anyone for a loop." She put her hand on the soft denim covering his leg, trying to offer some comfort.

He studied her hand. "You say you think I'm a good dad. I'll tell you something you might find hard to believe." He lifted his head and looked straight at her. "Jeremy's been in jail for close to a decade and I've never visited him. Not once."

He was right. She did find that hard to believe. If Jasmine had, God forbid, gone to jail, for whatever reason, her first impulse would be to chase her there and make her life as easy as possible. It was implausible, probably impossible. But that's what she'd want to do. To stay away from her daughter for a decade, to write her off completely, was unthinkable.

"I don't know what to say, Hank. I'm sure you had your reasons," she ended lamely. Knowing it sounded as inadequate to him as it did to her, she tried again. "I mean, like I said, he did some really horrible things."

Hank lifted his hand and used his fingers to count. "He lied to me. He stole from me. He destroyed my life's work and my reputation. He took away everything I worked for and my financial stability for my family, my future."

"Yes."

Hank gave a harsh shake of his head. "But that's not why I can't forgive the boy. Those are all mistakes, sure. All things I've struggled with over the years, wondering why on earth he did those things. Why he couldn't confide in me when he was in over his head. Where had I failed him? The boy I raised couldn't be responsible for those acts of betrayal. And yet, he was."

The sound of the surf behind them came into her awareness, and a few isolated gulls cried overhead. Darkness was starting to sink in and it was getting more difficult to see him clearly. He stood and took a few steps away from her. She didn't follow, and when he spoke again she had to concentrate to hear him.

"What I find unforgiveable is what he did to his mother. My Ruthie had to live her last months with sub-par medical care because of him. She was dying, and she deserved the best I could give her. But I couldn't give her the best. I couldn't pay for it."

"Oh, Hank …" She had no idea what to say. What could possibly comfort this man with such a heavy burden on his heart?

"That's why I've never stepped foot in the jail to visit him, why I've never called him or even sent a letter. I can't get past what he did to his mom."

Leslie cleared her throat, her mind racing. "Did he know about her leukemia when he neglected to pay the insurance bill?"

He flipped around to face her. "No, but it doesn't matter. He let our insurance lapse and when we needed it, it was gone. Because of his bad judgment."

She nodded. "You loved her," she said softly.

"I sure did. Ruthie was my everything." He looked down at his feet and Leslie gave in to a strong urge to go to him, put her arms around him, stroke his hair and rub his back. The love and devotion Hank had for his wife, gone a decade now, was another item in a growing list she admired and respected him for.

They stood together, her arms around him, for long moments. Then he sniffed and pulled away. "I need you to pray with me. For me. God's put a burden on my heart about this. Probably because Jeremy's being released soon. I need to come to terms with this. I can't live with this the rest of my days."

She nodded. Never the one to pray out loud with others like many of her church friends, she pushed aside her apprehension. Hank needed her help, and God had placed her here. It was time for action.

She gripped both his hands, and connecting eyes with him, she shut hers, bowed her head and prayed, "Dear God, I want to thank you for this man, one of your very faithful servants. He is hurting, Father. He's had a decade of hurt surrounding his son Jeremy and his wife Ruthie. Please lift this burden now, God. We know you want us to lead praiseful, unencumbered lives. Please follow through with your promise now, and flood Hank with a sense of forgiveness for Jeremy. He's paid the price for his mistakes, now let his father experience that wonderful peace of forgiveness. Please help me help him with this transformation, and we thank You for Your love for us. In Jesus' name we pray, amen."

She started to pull her hands away but Hank squeezed them. She stayed standing, facing him in the sand, holding onto his hands. She closed her eyes and listened to the constant pounding of the waves coming in. In a few moments, Hank took a deep breath and released her hands.

"Thank you."

"It'll help. I'm sure of it."

He nodded, looked around and motioned to where he'd left the truck parked. "Shall we?"

"Sure."

They ambled back to the truck and got in. Although they didn't speak, it wasn't an uncomfortable silence. More like an amiable silence between two people where words weren't always necessary. They drove back to his house. Leslie walked to her car and he followed her.

"You know, this is a great first step. But it may not happen overnight." She felt like she needed to say something in case he was expecting miraculous results.

He grinned sadly. "You don't have to tell me that, darlin'. It ain't my first rodeo."

She laughed.

He continued, "I know God's capable of washing my heart clean of bad feelings, but I also know I have work to do. As you said, getting you to pray with me about it is a first step. First of many."

She patted him on the shoulder. "I'm honored you asked me."

They said their good-byes and she got in her car. As she drove down the street and turned, he was on her mind long after he was out of her sight.

* * *

As Leslie was slipping off to sleep that night, her cell phone rang. It was sitting beside her on the bedside table so she reached over and picked it up. Jasmine's picture lit up the dark room.

"Hello, sweetie!"

"Hi, Mom. Did I wake you up?"

"No, I hadn't fallen asleep yet. But my goodness, you're up awful late. It's what, 4:30 in the morning there?"

"I'm not up late, I'm up early. I'm actually sitting in a train station. Several of us are going to a fashion show in Monaco."

Leslie sat up in bed. "How exciting!"

"Yeah, not so much. I mean, it'll be great to get out of the city and see the countryside. It's our first chance to do that since we got here. But we'll be working like dogs. We're the gophers backstage, helping the designers and the models get dressed, running errands. We won't actually get to watch the show."

"Hmmm. Still a good experience. I mean, you're going to the French Riviera."

"Yeah." Her daughter sighed. "I'm getting a little homesick. I miss you and Dad and God forbid, Pittsburgh. I miss good ole American cheeseburgers and catching a baseball game every once in a while."

"Are you okay?"

"Yeah, I'm fine. It's so different from what I'm used to. Just weepy this week, that's all, Mom. Nothing to worry about. So, tell me about your vacation. Are you having a good time?"

Leslie began telling Jasmine about her trip and after she'd talked for about four straight minutes, Jasmine interrupted her. "Mom, you sound so happy."

Leslie smiled. "Yes, I suppose I am." Amazing, considering the circumstances.

"It sounds like this Hank is a pretty special man."

"Oh …"

"Sounds like you're seeing a lot of him."

Leslie squinted in the dark. What had she revealed about Hank that had led Jasmine to that conclusion? "No, not at all, sweetie."

"Are you falling in love?" Jasmine's voice was playful and joking, but Leslie put the squash on that right away.

"Of course not! I've only known him a few days. Really, Jasmine!"

Jasmine giggled. "If you find a man who appreciates you for the wonderful woman you are, who you enjoy being with, hey, what's wrong with that? Go for it, I say."

Leslie brushed off the advice and changed the subject, but later, after she'd wished her daughter well with the French fashion show in the south of France and they'd broken the line between them, she went back to thinking about Hank. Was she interested in him as a potential love interest? Would he be interested in her? And even if those answers were yes, what was the point? They lived hours away in different states. Would she be ready to fall in love again so soon after her divorce? Would it be foolish to give her heart away again?

Endless questions swirled around her brain and she finally fell to sleep with Hank on her mind.

Chapter Nine

The next morning, Leslie sat on a cushioned wicker couch on the screened-in porch, her feet resting on the coffee table, facing the ocean. A mug of coffee rested in her hand, steam rising from its freshly poured heat. Although she expected sunshine later in the day, right now the morning was overcast and drizzly. Perfect morning to relax on the porch and watch the waves. Better than any TV show or movie she knew of.

Marianne brought a tray of muffins and assorted danish and placed them on the serving table in the corner. She smiled her greeting. "Hungry?"

Leslie nodded. "In fact, I am. And those look delicious."

She got up and went to the table, surveying her choices. She picked a decadent chocolate brownie-type muffin with huge chocolate chips poking out. "On what planet do we actually call this a breakfast item?" she chuckled. But she'd chosen it, so she was committed. She took it back to her seat. "I guess I'll have to take an extra-long walk on the beach today and burn off calories."

Marianne said, "Like you need to worry about that. You're so petite." She busied herself straightening the table, throwing away waste from the early morning coffee drinkers. To Leslie, it seemed a decent time to broach what could be an uncomfortable subject. Looking around to make sure they were alone, she spoke.

"Marianne, do you have a moment?"

"Absolutely."

"I have something I want to talk to you about."

Marianne nodded. "In that case, I'll take this opportunity to sample one of these baked goods myself." She selected a peach danish and joined Leslie on the couch.

Leslie took in a breath. "I hope I won't upset you with this topic. But your dad told me about your brother Jeremy last night."

Marianne's eyes went wide, then narrowed, creases of confusion forming between her brows. "What? I mean, what did he tell you?"

Leslie understood the hesitancy and placed what she hoped was a reassuring hand on Marianne's forearm. "I believe he told me the whole story, not leaving anything out. How Jeremy took over the family business with hopes of expansion and growth, but how he moved into illegal activity to cover bad decisions. And the consequences of those actions. And the punishment he's serving now."

As she spoke, Marianne went white and her eyes widened and glazed.

"And the fact that Jeremy's going to be released soon."

Marianne sat motionless. Then, "Wow. I don't know what to say. Other than, you must be very special to my father. He's never, and I mean *never*, spoken to anyone about this before. The fact that he told you all that personal family stuff must mean he trusts you, and thinks very highly of you."

Her words floored Leslie. Of course she'd suspected this topic hadn't come flowing from Hank's lips easily. Being an old-fashioned man, she imagined he didn't dig deep and speak of his problems or feelings often. But why had he chosen her to tell the story? And what did that mean to their future relationship? If there was one. A worm of apprehension crawled down her esophagus.

"I don't know what to say to that."

Marianne shook her head, came out of her fog. "I'm sorry. I didn't mean to place a burden on you. Maybe you don't realize how unusual it is for my dad to open up. And this subject of my brother has been a sore subject, and that's putting it mildly, for almost a decade now. You have no idea how it has torn our family apart."

Leslie looked into her coffee mug. "Actually, I think I do. He told me about your mom and her illness. And the loss of the insurance coverage."

Marianne made a low whistle. She looked up at Leslie and studied her as if seeing her through new eyes. "You have no idea how huge this is. And as crazy as it sounds, I now have to ask you a very unorthodox question."

Leslie raised her eyebrows.

"What are your intentions toward my father?"

They both broke into a chuckle. They ended and Marianne continued, "But seriously…"

Leslie shrugged. "He's a very nice man. I enjoy spending time with him. But for God's sake, I've known him, what, a week? And things aren't exactly peachy in my own life. I'm here in Pawleys basically escaping a bad divorce. I'm newly single, and I have to say, not because I want to be. I thought I had a solid, loving marriage. We were empty nesters, and I thought we'd move towards our new life together. But my husband had other plans. He decided he wanted to spend his later life with someone other than me."

She rubbed her thumb absently on the mug handle. "I'm having a real hard time with that. My family, small though it is, is torn apart. I'm on refuge here, but eventually I do have to go back and face reality. Sell my house, find somewhere else to live, go back to school in the fall in a completely different place than when the last school year ended. How am I going to deal with that?"

Marianne put a hand over hers.

"Starting a new relationship with a man is the last thing on my mind, or my priority list." Leslie let out a sigh of pent up air and looked into Marianne's kind face.

Marianne squeezed. "It's not easy, is it? Life, in general?"

Leslie shook her head sadly. "No, it isn't. But I know two things. One is, be open to where God leads you, and you can't go wrong. Your father believes God has put the two of us together to help each other, and I'm willing to believe that too. I don't know why, but I'm willing to follow where He leads. And two, I enjoy spending time with your father. So it's not like it's a hardship." She smiled.

Marianne nodded, thinking. "I hope my father doesn't get a broken heart out of all this. No offense. But he's been through hell and back with my mother and brother. I don't know how much more he can take."

A flash of apprehension encircled Leslie's heart. She understood exactly why Marianne was concerned, but she had no idea what to do about it. Prayer was probably the best course. She shook off the feeling. "Can I ask you something personal?"

Marianne laughed. "Seems appropriate."

Leslie nodded. "I know your dad's anger at Jeremy has kept him from visiting or staying in touch. How about you and your sister? Is Jeremy alienated from the whole family?"

"No. I personally visit him once a month. I'm not sure about Sadie. It'd be a much farther drive for her. Jeremy's been in several prisons over his sentence, but all within South Carolina. Usually a few hours' drive or less." She shook her head. "I know what he did was horrible, but he's my brother, you know? And he's paying the price with his sentence. I don't know."

"So you've forgiven him for what he did."

Marianne looked away, a few tears sprouting in her eyes. "I don't know. I guess. The fact that my dad won't forgive him almost seems like he loved our mother more than we did. And that makes me feel like I'm not being loyal to her. But Jeremy is rehabilitated, I know he is. He feels horrible about what he did. He feels horrible Dad has given up on him, but he also feels like Dad's totally justified." She sighed. "It's a mess."

Leslie wrapped an arm around her shoulders. "Families are messy, aren't they?"

* * *

Later that afternoon, the grayness had swept away and the sunshine had returned. Leslie sat on a reclining chair on the beach, her arms and legs glistening with sunscreen, a floppy hat and sunglasses covering her face. She watched a child have the time of her life digging in the sand, forming a sand castle, adding water as needed, running back and forth from the water's edge, seemingly never tiring.

Her fattening breakfast was moving to the forefront of her mind, and she was starting the chore of convincing herself to get up and move, when someone stepped up, blocking the sun from her face. She put a hand over her eyes and looked up. It was Hank.

He was dressed in work clothes. His comfortably faded jeans looked like he'd worn them so many times, the loose knees were perfectly formed from kneeling. Long forgotten paint spatters decorated his thighs. A faded tee shirt, once maroon, hugged his chest. Leslie caught herself staring at his form. She thought she knew him well enough to know he didn't maintain his physical fitness in a gym. Tim had spent all day in an office or hospital, then had to pay a high priced membership fee to exercise at a gym with a personal trainer instructing him on how to build muscles. But for Hank, it came along with his activities every day. Hard physical work, day in and day out, chiseled the muscles in his arms, chest and abdomen and he probably never gave it a second thought.

"Uh, good afternoon."

Leslie flushed as she realized he'd probably been standing there long moments as she examined him without a word. "Hello!" She glanced around and pointed at a nearby beach chair. "Would you like to sit awhile?"

He shook his head. "I'm on a job. I stopped by for a lemonade with Stella and I figured I'd do myself a favor and come see you."

Leslie smiled at his compliment. The man was sweet.

"Also, I feel like I have to make up for the measly supper last night."

"Not at all! It was delicious and just what the doctor ordered after so many heavy meals in a row."

He squatted easily so their faces were more on the level. "Well, I happen to have it on good source that tonight is salmon night. Do you like salmon?"

Leslie moaned. "Who doesn't? And I bet it's delicious here."

"It sure is. On my way out I'll make a reservation for the two of us. What time?"

Eating later would give them a chance for a romantic walk on the dark beach afterward. "How about seven?"

"Perfect. I'll meet you in the great room a few minutes before. Have a nice day, now." He reached for her hand, gave it a squeeze, then trekked through the sand out of her vision.

She had a dinner date.

A few minutes before seven, she went downstairs and caught sight of him chuckling with Marianne near the entrance to the dining room. As she approached, Hank stood with his back to her but Marianne caught eyes with her over his shoulder. She winked, which caused Hank to spin around, and a grin to brighten a dark night covered his face.

"Well, don't you look beautiful?" He reached out, gripped her hands and took in an eyeful. She was pleased she'd spent time on her hair and makeup, and chose a white cotton mini skirt paired with a pink tee shirt. This man was so good for her ego.

She giggled. "Thank you, and you got all cleaned up too. Very handsome." It wasn't just an empty return to his compliment. He really did look like a picture of health and vitality in his khaki shorts, Hawaiian shirt and leather sandals. His suntan complemented his white grin.

"Well, don't we make a pair?" He winked at Marianne. "Give us the best seat in the house, please."

"Coming right up. This way, please." She led them to a table for two by the window.

As they settled in, excitement welled inside Leslie. She had a surprise for Hank and she wasn't exactly sure how to break it to him without ruining the suspense. This afternoon, after he'd left her to her spot on the beach, an idea had popped into her head. Maybe it was God-inspired, considering their prayer of the previous evening, but regardless, it was a good idea. She'd gone inside, done some internet research and made a phone call, and now she was ready to execute.

"Question for you, Hank. What are you doing tomorrow?"

"Tomorrow? Working. I work every day. Why?"

A bubble of disappointment dampened her high spirits. "Oh, bummer. Any way you can take a day off?"

He studied her and smiled. "For a good enough reason, I suppose I could be convinced."

"You work so hard. You deserve to take a day away from work."

"Well, I'm working on one of those old beach houses over by your old vacation home. Then I'll start the Hinthorns' bathroom project."

"Would one day throw you off schedule?" She smiled. "I've planned a surprise for you."

His face lit up and her heart jumped along with it. "Well now, I'd be hard pressed to turn down an invitation like that. A surprise for me planned by a beautiful lady. Yes, I'd say it's time for a day off. You tell me when and where you want me."

He looked so happy, it touched her heart with joy for him. "Meet me here at ten AM, and I'll drive. Casual clothes."

With the novelty of a surprise hanging over them, the rest of their evening seemed frosted in anticipation. Conversation came easily. The salmon was delicious, of course, as was the

Caesar salad, green beans soaked in butter and bacon, and the ice cream with blueberries for dessert. By the time they took their after-dinner walk, the sun had set and a beautiful deepness settled over the ocean.

Comfortable now, Hank reached for her hand and tucked it into his. A few minutes down the beach with bare feet, she involuntarily shivered. Always in tune to her, he put an arm around her as they strolled.

"Chilly?"

"It has gotten sort of brisk out, hasn't it?"

"Let me help." He stopped walking and faced her, put his hands on her arms and rubbed up and down. The friction from his hands did result in warmth, but he didn't stop there. After half a minute, he wrapped his arms around her and pulled her in to his chest. She closed her eyes, tucked her head in and breathed. The man smelled delicious. Her mouth curled into its own smile because of her contentment at being at that place at that moment. She felt safe and appreciated, right where God wanted her to be.

When he pulled back, she felt the chill start to creep back in, but she knew all she had to do was ask for another embrace if she wanted it. She beamed at him and he responded with a hand on her cheek. He drew closer, his eyes connected with hers and his lips a breath away. He made a moan in the back of his throat and then his lips covered hers and the warmth was hers again, this time his mouth its enchanting source. She closed her eyes and tipped her head back to receive the fullness of his kiss. She reached for his arms, then his shoulders, pulling him closer until their bodies were pressed against one another's.

It had been ages since she'd kissed a man like this and what was most surprising were the feelings that must have been hiding under the surface, emerged with Hank's urging. She was a mature woman, long past the time for being giddy in love. And yet, he brought those feelings out in her.

What would her daughter think?

She chuckled at that thought, and Hank pulled back momentarily, giving her a puzzled look. "If something strikes you as funny, I don't think I'm doing this right."

She tipped her head back, still in his arms and laughed. "No, no, that's not it. You're definitely doing it right."

He smiled. "Then what …?"

She shook her head. "It amazes me how young and happy you make me feel."

"Happiness isn't just for young people, you know."

She bit her tongue. She hadn't expressed her thoughts very well. What she wanted to say was, he made her feel young and giddy and loved. But even she, out of practice as she was, was well aware what a faux pas it would be to announce to this man she'd only known a week that he made her feel in love!

So she settled for, "Thank you, Hank. You make me feel wonderful."

He squeezed her shoulders where he held onto them. "Right back atcha, Leslie."

They continued their walk, this time his arm around her waist, holding her close to his side. The chill provided a marvelous excuse for body contact and Leslie threw in a shiver every once in a while to make sure it didn't end.

* * *

The next morning, Leslie showered and dressed earlier than usual, then went and found Marianne. She was in the kitchen, preparing the coffee and muffins for the sun porch. Leslie shared that she was planning a surprise for Marianne's dad and would really love a packed lunch, nothing fancy, just some sandwiches, chips and cans of soda. Marianne's face transformed into a huge smile and she gave Leslie a hug.

"Leave it to me!" she chanted and bustled off.

About 9:45, Marianne carried a family-sized woven picnic basket into the great room where Leslie was reading. The handles dug heavily into her arm.

"What is all this?" Leslie asked.

Marianne grinned, set it on the floor and removed the lid. "Well, you said a picnic lunch, so I gave you a few options to choose from. Fried chicken, bologna sandwiches, potato salad, cole slaw, watermelon." As she named each item, she dug around in the basket and lifted it up, demonstrating it to Leslie. "For dessert, I threw in a few slices of chocolate cake and some grapes."

"Marianne!" Leslie gasped.

She halted her lifting. "What?"

Leslie came over to the basket and peeked in. "There's enough food here for a half dozen people, at least! I said this was just for your dad and I!"

Marianne chuckled. "That's okay. Most of it is leftover anyway. Oh, and I threw in a cooler of my homemade iced tea."

Hank walked into the room. "Hi, ladies." He gave Marianne a peck on the cheek, then did the same for Leslie. "So what are we up to today?"

Leslie eyed the basket. "Eating, apparently. You can thank your daughter for a feast fit for a king."

He chuckled. "Thank you very much." He turned to Leslie. "We eating on the beach?"

"No. Roadtrip. We'll stop in a couple hours for lunch."

Hank gave her a curious expression. "Well now, isn't that interesting? What's our end destination?"

Leslie smiled sweetly. "You won't know until you get there. I said it was a surprise, didn't I?"

He picked up the basket, a relief to Leslie, but he barely huffed under the exertion.

"We can put that on my backseat," she said.

"I can drive."

"Nope. Surprise, remember?"

He threw a look at his daughter like he was going to object. Marianne gave an almost imperceptible shake of her head. "You two have fun now!"

They left the Inn and walked through the sandy front lot. "So glad you could join me today," she said.

"I'm pleased you asked me. Thank you."

They reached her car. She unlocked the back door and stepped aside. He started to hoist the basket in, then hesitated. "I'm sorry." He ducked his head. "I'm really old-fashioned, I guess. I have a hard time with a beautiful lady driving me around. You sure you don't want to go in my truck? Or, I could drive your car for you if you'd rather take it."

She gave his shoulder a playful punch. "If I let you drive, it'd give away the surprise, wouldn't it?"

He shrugged. "You could give me directions, one road at a time."

She gave her head a firm shake.

He sighed and put the basket in the back seat, shut the door firmly. "Okay. I'm in your hands then."

They set off, driving west away from the beach. Because she didn't want to have a set of directions setting beside her that would clue him into their destination, she'd read through her route enough times to memorize it. As they rode through the scenic coastal plain, they shared stories. Leslie told him some of her favorite memories of Jasmine's childhood, those funny stories everyone remembers, sure to bring on laughs. In turn, he shared a couple stories about Marianne, one or two about his other daughter and then a boatload about Stella.

About two hours into the drive, they stopped at a rest area and lugged the laden basket to a wooden picnic table. Leslie chuckled as she dug into the basket. Tucked along the side was a white and red checked tablecloth. She pulled it out, gave it a flip and rested it on the tabletop. They unloaded the contents onto the table and then sat, serving themselves.

The food was delicious; the company was better. Leslie couldn't remember the last time she'd shared a casual outdoor meal with a man and had a better time. Laughter flowed and they'd shared so much about their family members, Leslie felt she was personally acquainted with them all.

Their stomachs were full long before the basket was empty. Marianne had packed enough to feed a family of ten, after all. Leslie gazed down at all the leftovers. She couldn't pack it all back up into the basket and put it back in the car. With the day she had planned, and no refrigeration available, it would all be spoiled before they returned home. She glanced around the rest area. A short distance away, three children of grade school age played on a swing set. A young woman stood to the side, blowing smoke from a cigarette.

She motioned to Hank. "Think they could use some lunch?"

He smiled. They grabbed all the wrapped food they could carry and hiked to the swings.

"Excuse me," Leslie called to the young woman. The woman looked up, then dropped the cigarette to the ground, smooshing it under her foot. "My name's Leslie and this is Hank. We enjoyed a delicious picnic lunch, but we have way too much of it left. It would be a shame to throw it away. I'd feel so much better if I could find someone to eat it instead of letting it go to waste."

The girl didn't speak, but looked curious about what menu choices they had to offer.

"I've got some fried chicken, a couple bologna sandwiches, some potato salad and cole slaw. I assure you it's all fresh, and homemade by a wonderful seaside inn in Pawleys Island. I know it's strange that in this day and age, a stranger is offering you food. But you can rest assured there's nothing wrong with it. I don't have the heart to throw it all away."

The girl's glance swung from Leslie to Hank to the food. Then she smiled. "That's very nice of you. I had planned to take them to lunch soon, but they were driving me crazy with energy and I figured I'd let them run it off a bit first. They're getting so tired of riding in the car."

Leslie gazed at the children, two on swings, what looked like the oldest one standing behind the smaller ones, pushing them higher and higher. "How old are they?"

The woman followed her gaze and her face softened into an affectionate smile. "Seven, five and four. They're a handful."

Leslie nodded. "I'm a teacher. So I work with twenty five eight-year-olds, every day."

The woman laughed. "Enjoying your summer break?"

Leslie automatically responded, "You bet I am." Both women laughed, but Leslie glanced over at Hank.

Yes, she was enjoying her summer break. Given the way it had started, who would've thought it?

"Do you think they'd like this lunch? If so, you're welcome to have it. If not, throw it away after we leave."

The woman laughed and held out a hand to Leslie, then to Hank. "My name's Rona. Thanks so much, this was very kind of you. And you seem trustworthy so I'm going to accept your generous gift. Besides, that chicken smells better than anything I've smelled all week. It's making my mouth water."

"Great! I'm so glad you'll enjoy it, Rona."

She and Hank placed their armloads of food on a nearby picnic table. Rona called to her kids and they readily left the swings and joined them.

"Kids, this is Leslie and Hank. They were very nice to share some of their lunch with us." The kids gave them a busy nod while they settled themselves into the bench. When they saw the spread, they breathed an admiring, "Wow!"

Leslie gave each of them a paper plate and they helped themselves. She smiled at Hank and he returned with a grin of his own.

"Where are your manners?" Rona scolded. "What do you say to Leslie and Hank?"

"Thank you!" they chanted in unison. Rona hovered over them.

"Please, help yourself. We need to leave, so enjoy the meal. So glad you could take it for us."

"Daddy's going to be so happy to see us!" the littlest one said. "Maybe we can save some chicken for him."

Rona glanced at Leslie. "My husband got a new job three months ago, and had to move to Columbia. I didn't want to pull Marge out of second grade this close to the end of the school year, so we've been living separately all this time. We visit on the weekends, but it's not the same. Now, school's done, and we're moving there with him. We'll be together again."

"Oh, that's lovely," Leslie said. "I'm so happy for you all."

They exchanged a few last words, and Hank and Leslie left them to walk back to their own table. They tidied up the area, folded the tablecloth, tucked it back in the basket and returned to the car.

"You are amazing with people, you know that?" he said.

"Me? Why? What'd I do that was so amazing?"

He wrapped his arm around her, resting his hand on her waist and pulling her close as they walked. "You're so kind, and people respond to you. You make friends wherever you go. You're a good woman. A good person."

Leslie blushed. "So many compliments, you're going to spoil me." She giggled and then felt ridiculous for doing it. But she looked over at him and saw nothing but admiration in his eyes.

"You know another thing I noticed?" he asked. "She called us 'Leslie and Hank.' Just like that."

She knew what he meant. She smiled. They reached the car and climbed in. "It has a nice ring to it, doesn't it?"

"I reckon it does."

The journey commenced, along with the chitchat. Leslie turned onto 26 West and began the final leg of the trip. Conversation centered around vacation destinations they'd both enjoyed, and Leslie's favorite students.

Once Leslie exited the highway at Columbia, and pushed the "Go" button on her GPS, pre-programmed with the address she needed, Hank tensed.

"Columbia. What are we doing here?"

She looked over at him with a grin and winked. "It's a surprise."

But in the quick moment she glanced over at him, she was alarmed at his expression. His shoulders were tight, the muscles in his neck tensed and a vein in his forehead pulsed. His complexion reddened to a ruddy color.

"I'm aware it's a surprise," he said, his voice taut with strain. "But now it's becoming clearer to me what this surprise is all about."

She looked over at him, confused at his reaction. It was becoming difficult to follow the city directions being announced by the GPS while also taking her eye off the road to study the befuddling reaction beside her.

"Hank, what's wrong?"

"Where are you taking me? Where are we going?" His voice, normally so calm and kind, had a hard edge to it. Her head swiveled back to stare at him. She'd never heard him with anger in his tone. Heartbreak, yes, but never anger.

"We'll be there soon, and you'll see."

He shifted in his seat, straining to look out the front windshield then back to the limited information on the GPS. "You're not taking me to the prison, are you?"

A dive of panic attacked her esophagus. The nightmare of someone taking on the challenge of executing a surprise was that it would not be well received. Unwanted. Unappreciated. From Hank's reaction, it was clear this surprise was all those things. She just didn't know why.

"Well," she stammered. A car squeaked to a stop in front of her and she barely braked in enough time to avoid hitting it. That's all she'd need, a fender bender on top of everything else. Traffic continued to move forward so she had to move with it. But something was terribly wrong with Hank, and she needed to figure out what was troubling him.

"Leslie, talk to me. I'm not going to the prison. You had no right to bring me here. No right to arrange this at all. Are you listening to me?"

The mechanical voice of the GPS was squawking at her for missing her turn, "Route recalculating" with computer-generated annoyance. Cars passed her on both sides, implying she was going too slow. Unfamiliar roads started causing her blood pressure to rise, when Hank placed his hand on her steering wheel.

They passed a brown sign on the right, "Kirkland Correctional Institution."

"Stop the car." His voice was raised, his anger apparent. But too many things were happening at once. She was completely out of her element. She wanted to scream but managed to hold it in.

"Pull over there." As he said it, he applied pressure to the steering wheel and guided it to the right.

It was the action that broke her.

"Stop it!" she yelled. "You're going to get us in an accident! I can't take this anymore!"

And yet he didn't let up on the steering wheel, so the car followed suit and changed lanes, then continued on into a parking lot. Leslie worked the accelerator, Hank the steering wheel, a team effort, except the team was at odds. Once safely off the street, Leslie pushed on the brake a little too hard, causing the car to jolt to a halt, shaking with the suddenness of the stop. She pushed the gearshift into Park as Hank unfastened his seat belt and slipped quickly out of the car.

She huffed with frustration, watching him leave. What had happened just now? She'd gone to the trouble of planning a meaningful day the two of them could share together — a surprise. Why had it gone so wrong?

She turned the engine off and raced out of the car. He stood a few steps away from the passenger side, his back turned, his head down. She approached him and put a hand on his shoulder, but he jerked it away, unwanted. He took a step further, then turned toward her.

"You had no right to do this."

Leslie was stunned, her eyes widening at the seething emotion beneath his words. "I'm sorry," she started, sure it was a good place to start, but entirely unsure why the apology was necessary. "Hank, let's talk about this. I thought it would be a fun outing to come visit Jeremy together."

If she'd had plans to say more than that one sentence, those plans were thwarted by his raged response. "A fun outing? You thought it would be fun to come visit Jeremy? Together."

Sarcasm dripped from every word and even though he'd done little more than repeat what she'd said, it sounded ridiculous when he did. She cringed.

"After everything I shared with you about my family. After baring my soul, you took it upon yourself to come here without even checking with me?"

He gripped his forehead with his hand, rubbed it absently, then moved his hand into his hair, forming ruffles from his fingers. He turned in her direction and she saw the anger in his eyes. Then he strode back to her until his face was an inch from hers. "This is none of your business. None of your concern. This is wrong. You shouldn't have done this."

Her breath was coming in pants from the intensity of his reaction. She had messed up apparently, but she had to hold on to the fact that whatever colossal mistake she'd made, it wasn't intentional. She'd meant well. He'd understand that if she explained it.

"You're not ready to see him yet. I know it's been a long time. I should have been more sensitive to that. I'm sorry. But I didn't do anything maliciously. I didn't mean to hurt you. I …"

He huffed out a big breath. "Will you be okay driving home?"

She blinked. "What?"

"Why don't you take a break from driving, maybe go to a bookstore and read for a bit. Then will it be safe for you to drive home alone?"

She shook her head. "Are you going to visit Jeremy? I'll wait for you. If you don't want me to go with you, I'll sit in the waiting room. Or the car."

"I'm not going to visit Jeremy."

"Hank, you're not making any sense."

"Six straight hours of driving is too much for you."

She shook her head. "You can help me. You can drive home if you want."

He dropped his head and toed the gravel. "I'm not riding home. I'll get a bus."

"What?" She was astounded. "You're so mad at me you would rather get a bus home than ride three hours with me?"

He quieted. The man was crazy. Juvenile. Completely insane.

"I want you to be safe," he said tentatively.

"Well, how nice of you," she said with a tinge of sarcasm.

She understood. A battle was at odds inside him. He was furious at her for arranging this visit. His first impulse was to storm away and avoid a three-hour drive with her. And yet, the southern gentleman and all around nice guy inside him wouldn't put her in danger. She was so close to being the one to storm off — jump back in her car, leave him standing there. Drive leisurely back to Pawleys Island. She'd driven six hours straight before, it was no big deal.

But fortunately, wiser minds prevailed. She sighed and put some distance between them. And she said a quick silent prayer. She asked God for guidance in this situation, and the ability to put herself in his place. She hadn't foreseen his reaction, but having him storm off and take a bus home, while she turned around and drove three hours by herself, wasn't a godly solution.

So, she marched back to him and held the keys out to him. Doubt was obvious in his eyes. "Here. Take them."

The stubborn man still didn't obey her, so she grabbed his hand and stuffed them in. "You drive, I'll sleep in the back. You won't even have to talk to me."

She flung open the back door.

"Leslie …"

"Don't want to hear it. Just do as I say."

She climbed into the back, and true to her word, it didn't take long after the drive started, the warmth and motion in the back seat lulled her to sleep.

The awkwardness reemerged when they arrived at the inn. Leslie's pride was still nipped at his puzzling reaction and the last thing she wanted was to get into a conversation with him. That was the last thing he wanted as well, judging from his actions. He parked in the lot, left the car, opened the trunk and removed Marianne's picnic supplies. They walked in silence across the lot and up to the inn's front door.

Marianne was leaning down behind the front desk. Leslie glanced over and felt a chomp of pain in her heart at the uncomfortable encounter that was sure to follow. Unless they could sneak by without Marianne noticing them. But it was not to be. Marianne looked up and a huge, happy smile bloomed on her face.

"You're back! Did you have a good day? How was your lunch?"

Hank and Leslie glanced at each other. A question fleeted through Leslie's mind, how's he going to play this? Unfortunately, he dipped his head and said nothing. Men. Figures.

She cleared her throat. "It was a beautiful day, made even better by your delicious meal. Thank you so much for going to all the trouble. Not only did we enjoy it, but we also shared it with a mother and her three children."

Marianne laughed. "Really? I am so bad at judging how much food to make. I guess it's better to prepare for an army, than to have someone go hungry."

Hank turned away. Was he that desperate to leave this day behind? If he was, she'd help him out because she was anxious to end it as well.

"Well, I'm going to take my leave," she said. "Good night, both of you."

Marianne waved and turned back to her work. Hank took two long steps to reach Leslie's side. "Can we have a word?"

She sighed and looked at him. "I don't know. How difficult will the conversation be? Because I don't think I'm up for anything strenuous."

He shook his head. "I'm not either. I wanted to thank you for trying to plan a nice surprise for me. I mean, the beginning of the day was a lot of fun and I enjoyed being with you."

Exhaustion, mental and physical, seeped into her bones. What was she doing? Why had she even gotten involved? Who was she to try to reunite a man and his estranged son when there was so much water beneath the bridge? Maybe he was right to be angry with her. Why did she care? This wasn't her battle to fight and for some reason, she'd grabbed onto it with both hands. And now, it was a big fat mess.

"You're welcome," she replied. "And now, I think I'll call it a night."

She turned quickly so she left him with no choice but to leave as well. She returned to her room and plopped onto her bed. Closing her eyes, she wondered if she could sleep, but it was still early evening and if she slept now, she'd surely regret it when she awoke in the middle of the night. A shower sounded good. She dragged herself out of the bed, gathered her things and went down the hall.

About an hour later, she sat in the comfy chair in her room, attempting to enjoy her novel, but her mind kept coming back to the epic failure of the day. Sure, Hank had confided in her, and in his deepest desire, he wanted to repair his relationship with Jeremy, but did she really think it would be that easy? What was she expecting, that they'd pull into the prison parking lot, and skip hand in hand to the front door, announcing their desire to visit Jeremy?

The more she ran it through her mind, the more she understood his reaction. And was appalled at her own judgment. She tossed the book on her bed and leaned back in her chair. In her mind, she ran through the awe-inspiring experiences of this roadtrip. She'd had so many successes, so many chances to help people and serve the Lord. He'd placed her right where He'd needed her, and she'd made many friends.

She'd gotten smug. She'd come up with the Jeremy idea all on her own. She couldn't say that was God's plan. She couldn't say it wasn't. But prayer was nowhere around.

There was a knock at the door. Marianne stood in the hallway, a look on her face a cross between embarrassment and sheepishness. "Do you have a minute?"

Leslie shrugged and motioned to the room. Marianne swept past her. "I hope you don't mind the intrusion but I spoke to my father." She paused, uncertain. "Dang him! I'm so sorry, Leslie."

Leslie shook her head. "No, don't. Seriously. I had no right."

Marianne's chin dropped. "What? You planned a nice day for him and he blew it. He was so insensitive."

"Well, I can't argue he was insensitive. And yes, he hurt my feelings. But the more I ruminate over it, I realize I was insensitive too. I shouldn't have taken it upon myself to plan a surprise meeting with a son who destroyed his life, who he hadn't spoken to in so long. What was I thinking? How was he supposed to react?"

Marianne stomped a foot. "You were thinking this craziness between the two of them had gone on long enough, and I for one, totally agree with you. I've been talking to my dad for a long time, encouraging him to forgive Jeremy, to give him a chance, to speak to him. It's the right thing to do. But he's so stubborn. He won't do it." She grabbed Leslie's hands in both her own. "My family isn't like that, Leslie. At least, it wasn't until Jeremy pulled this stunt. We were close.

We had each other's backs. That all changed when Jeremy went to jail and my mom died. It destroyed my dad. The anger was killing him. Forgiveness is the answer. But I couldn't get him to open up. And then you came."

Leslie looked up into the younger woman's eyes, basked in the admiration she saw there. The hope.

"Somehow, you opened up my dad's heart. Probably without even trying, without realizing what you were doing. I haven't seen my dad happier than the last few weeks. It reminded me of when he was with my mom. You are so good for him. If there's a possibility my family can reconcile and my dad can forgive my brother, I have the feeling you're our only chance."

A cough escaped from Leslie's lips. The responsibility Marianne had placed on her was too heavy, too important. A burden she, for one, didn't want. She couldn't be the savior of this broken family. Had she learned nothing? This didn't feel like God's will, especially after the disaster today.

She pulled her hands away from Marianne's and took a step toward the far reaches of the room. "I don't know what to say. Let's put this in perspective. Your dad and I have had a few dinners together, a few walks on the beach, a few conversations about our lives. I think your hopes that I can heal your family are unfounded."

Marianne wiped a tear that had formed in her eye. "It must seem that way to you. You didn't know my dad before. But I know him. He has strong feelings for you. If he's going to give Jeremy a chance, it'll be because you convince him of it."

She turned and walked to the door. "I'm sorry. I've laid a huge burden on you, and I'm scaring you away, I can sense it. So please, have a good night's sleep, and things will look different in the morning. But one last request: please don't give up on my father."

And with those words, she closed the door behind her.

Chapter Ten

Leslie awoke after a fitful sleep, and at first glance, things didn't look that much different. She'd prayed. She'd asked God to give her guidance. She was still unsure of her direction with Hank and Jeremy.

But she needed coffee, so she dressed in shorts and a tee shirt and headed down to the back porch. When she was soaking in her hot drink and poking at a homemade muffin, her cell phone rang. She pulled it out of her pocket and glanced at the screen. It was Tim.

Really? Now?

She took a deep breath and answered.

"Hi Les, how's it going?"

She hesitated. Even if she thought he cared how her life was going, she wouldn't tell him. "Fine."

"Are you still out of the state?"

"Yes, I'm still on vacation at the beach."

"Okay," he said, a touch of irritation invading his voice. "We'll have to do this over the phone then. We have an offer on the house and I think it's a pretty good one."

A sound like buzzing bees invaded her ears, and for a moment she couldn't hear or concentrate on anything else. Someone bid on her house. *Her* house, where she'd put her heart and soul for twenty years, raised her daughter, treasured so many memories. Soon, it'd be gone, out from under her. "Tim?"

"Yes, I think we need to give this offer serious consideration and we need to move on it. Our realtor wants to meet as soon as possible. There's usually a short tail on these things."

The buzzing was clearing, slowly, and the total absorption it caused alarmed her. She needed a moment. "Tim?" she said dumbly, and immediately regretted it at his next words in a raised voice.

"Leslie, are you listening to me? Have you heard a word I've said? We need to meet today, this morning if possible, and go over the details of this bid. Our realtor feels it's a viable one."

She recognized the annoyance in his tone. How could she not? Half the conversations they'd had in their marriage involved Tim, the man in charge, being annoyed at her for one reason or another. But with a brief thrill, she realized, things were different now. He wasn't the man in charge anymore. At least, he wasn't in charge of *her.*

She forced the unsteadiness out of her head. That was a brief moment of weakness, and that was over. This was her new life now. "Okay, slow down. This is a big decision and there's no need to rush through it."

"Granted, but there's no reason to dawdle either, Leslie. We need to meet to …"

"I'm out of the state, Tim. Allow me a chance to get home, and then we'll talk."

He cleared his throat and she knew he was trying to control his temper. For a split second, she felt sorry for him. He wasn't accustomed to the Leslie who didn't just roll over and do everything he said. The Leslie who had her own opinions and asserted them, even when they were different than his.

Yeah, time to get over that.

"I can't wait for you to drive home. We can handle this on a conference call, or if you have access to a computer, we could do some sort of video call. We don't want to delay and possibly lose this offer."

Leslie came to her feet, her mind made up. "It's our first offer, Tim, and the house has only been up a few weeks. If this buyer is serious about it, they'll be willing to wait a few days. I'm about done with my vacation. I'll leave today, arrive home tomorrow, and I'll meet with you on Tuesday."

She purposely didn't ask his approval. She was co-owner of the house. Her opinion was just as valid as his, and under the circumstances, she enjoyed being able to control at least one thing in her life.

Besides, she was done here. There was nothing left to stay for.

He emitted a long sigh. "All right, Leslie, if you want it that way. I'll call the realtor and ask for an extension till Tuesday evening. I'll set up the meeting for Tuesday morning and trust that you can make it when it's good for the realtor and I?"

She smiled. "Yes. My schedule is open." Is it ever.

"I'll be back in touch with the arrangements."

"All right, call my cell."

He hesitated before breaking the call and she knew there was more. "I have to ask. You are motivated to sell the house, right? I mean, you're not trying to sabotage this sale?"

A surge of anger flickered at his suggestion, but then it died. It wasn't worth it. And if she were honest with herself, she had to admit he had a point. "I assure you Tim, I want out of the house as much as you do. I want to move on with my life. The best way to do that is to put the past behind me."

It sounded good. Now she just had to work on believing it.

They ended the call and she savored the rest of her breakfast, then went back to her room. Her mind was made up. She was leaving Pawleys. The time was right. She was needed back in her real life, and truth be told, she was no longer needed here. Or, she couldn't commit herself to those that felt she was needed here. Marianne's plan for Leslie was way bigger than she could give. And although she'd thoroughly enjoyed her days with Hank, they were over. Could they get past the faux pas she made? She made a mistake, and now it would be easier to put it in its place. A brief summer romance at a time and place when she'd needed something like that. But nothing more.

She finished packing, a much easier task than unpacking, since all she was doing was returning everything to her suitcase. She took a last look around the room, removed Stella's and Deakon's drawings from the wall and folded them into her bag. She peeked out the window for a last glance at the gorgeous view, and left.

Downstairs, she dragged her heavy luggage to the front desk. No one was behind it so she left her bag and wandered into the dining room. There, she found Marianne sitting with Stella at a table, playing a game of dominos. The little girl laughed as her domino fell against another, resulting in a miniature chain reaction around the tabletop.

"Atta girl!" Marianne praised her.

As Leslie approached, she noticed Marianne's expression change. She didn't want that. This really had nothing to do with Marianne. At least, it shouldn't.

"Good one!" Leslie said to Stella. The girl giggled and started picking up the fallen dominos again. She turned to Marianne. "Sorry to bother you, but do you have a minute?"

Marianne popped up, hope evident on her face. Leslie motioned to the doorway. Marianne followed her out of the dining room, but when she noticed Leslie's packed suitcase, her expression fell.

"What? What's happening? You're leaving?"

Leslie reached out and patted her shoulder. "I am, but not because of yesterday. Well, not exactly."

Marianne sighed. "I'm so sorry I butt my nose in. Please don't leave on account of me."

"No. I got a phone call this morning from my ex-husband. We have a bid on our house. I need to go back and meet with him and the realtor. I'm thinking this will probably be it."

"Oh." Marianne's sad face poked at Leslie. "Will you be coming back?

"Well, no. I mean, I'll need to get the house ready, and find somewhere else to live. I guess I'm done here."

Marianne visibly lifted herself up by the bootstraps. She sniffed. "Of course. I just hoped it'd be different."

An awkward moment of silence filled the room. "Marianne, I don't think I can give you what you want."

She nodded, looked down at the desk. "I'm sorry." She busied herself on the computer, preparing Leslie's final bill. Leslie handed over her credit card and they completed the transaction.

"Are you going to say good-bye to my dad?"

Even if she hadn't asked with such hope and anticipation in her eyes, Leslie knew her answer. "Yes. Of course I will."

"Good. I believe he's over at the Hinthorns' today."

Leslie shook her head. "I don't know … oh! Is that Bob and Martha's house?"

Marianne nodded. "And please come say good-bye to Stella. She's grown quite fond of you, you know."

They returned to the dining room and Leslie gave Stella a warm hug. "Thank you for your drawings for my room. I'm going to treasure them." Stella said her good-byes.

"Do you need help getting your luggage to your car?"

She smiled. "I'll manage. Thank you for opening your beautiful inn to me."

"I thoroughly enjoyed meeting you," Marianne said. "But I can't say I'm not a little disappointed by the way things worked out. And I can't get over the feeling that it's my fault."

Leslie shook her head firmly. "Not at all. Remember, God has a plan for all of us. We can't always write the script. I need to get home. But I'll always remember you. And your family."

She took off before the tears hit.

After she threw the luggage into the back of her vehicle and settled into her seat, Leslie started the engine and headed into the residential part of Pawleys Island. She knew how to get to Hank's house, but she had no more than a vague memory of how to get to the Hinthorns' house from there. But the town was small. Maybe it would come to her if she wandered around enough.

She found Hank's, then focused her memory on what direction they had gone that night. Fortunately, after wandering up and down several streets, she saw Hank's truck parked in front of a house. She pulled in and parked. Sitting there for a moment seemed like a good idea, gathering her thoughts. What would she say to him? She wasn't running away after their first argument. Not really. She had business at home that couldn't be avoided.

Sort of.

A few minutes later, she still didn't have an idea of how to handle it, so she got out and walked to the house. He came to the door when she rang the bell, and she was happy and dismayed, to see the same big smile that always greeted her, do so today.

"Hi!" he said, opening the door wide so she could enter.

"Hi." She stepped into the house, looked up at him and shrugged.

He studied her, then wrapped her into an uncertain embrace. "Good to see you. Thanks for stopping by."

She nodded. "Marianne told me where to find you."

He nodded, then fell silent. After a beat of motionlessness, he held his arm out. "Come on in. I'll show you what I'm doing. Want anything to drink?"

"No, uh, really. I can't stay long."

He led her to the bathroom and gave her the rundown on the retiling project. The floor looked beautiful. He always did amazing work. Soon though, he ran out of work to show her. She ached over the awkwardness hanging between them now, knowing she was the one who had unwittingly introduced it.

"Hank, I've come to say good-bye."

"Good-bye," he laughed. "Where are you going?"

"Home," she said. "It's time to go home."

His chin dropped and a wrinkle of concern marred his forehead. "Seriously? You're leaving Pawleys?"

She nodded.

He turned away, expelled a puff of breath. "Why so sudden?" he asked the floor.

"My ex called. We got an offer on the house. I need to go home and meet with him and the realtor about it."

He turned his head. His gaze turned long.

"This could be it. I might be selling the house."

He blinked and shook his head. "This has nothing to do with what happened yesterday?"

"Nothing," she replied automatically. Maybe it was too fast. Maybe he'd interpreted it that way too.

He brought his hands up to massage his temples. "Look, I've thought a lot about why I reacted the way I did. I panicked. I want to apologize …"

"Don't. You have no reason to apologize."

His eyes met the floor again. "Let me try to finish this." He waited and when she didn't say anything else, he went on. "I want to be able to apologize for reacting the way I did. Hell, I want to be able to talk to Jeremy, to go visit my boy. I want to be happy about your surprise. But I can't. I can't do any of it."

His voice cracked, which was her undoing. He was such a strong, kind, loving man. He didn't deserve any of this. It was ridiculous that life had done this to him.

And yet, we can't control life. It hands us what it hands us, and all we can control is how we handle it.

She walked to him and wrapped her arms around him. She pulled him close and tucked her face into his shoulder. He brought his arms up her back and squeezed her for a moment. When he relaxed his arms, he didn't step back. She breathed in the scent of him — coffee, sunshine and sawdust. How long will she remember his smell? And when will she ever stand in a set of arms that felt as good as his did?

When they separated, he leaned close and kissed her cheek, then her forehead. She grabbed his hand.

"It was so good to meet you," he said. "I can't tell you how much it's meant to me. How much you've meant to me." He squeezed her hand.

"Me too." And because she didn't want to leave any doubt, "You did nothing wrong, Hank. I never should have presumed I knew the right thing to do with Jeremy. I was so naïve to think you'd be happy about it. I didn't think, at all. And I'm sorry."

He shook his head. "Don't blame yourself. You were right. But not right now. I can't."

"I understand." She looked around the house. "So…."

His hand lingered in hers. "Do you have your directions all figured out?"

She smiled. "Yep, I guess I'll go the way I came. Reversed."

"Sounds like a plan." He walked her to the door. "Do you need anything?"

She shook her head. "I'll be fine." Then, because she didn't want to change her mind, she gave him a wave and left. By the time she'd driven off the island, she had to dab her eyes of tears.

* * *

The roadtrip home was different from the first. Just a few weeks ago, she'd set out, escaping an undesirable summer, an undesirable life. God had led her to meet people who'd needed her help, that much was clear. But on the trip home, no such opportunities arose. She drove straight home.

As the miles ticked away, her mind kept returning to her big surprise for Hank. What was different about that one? As she'd planned the meeting between him and Jeremy, it felt like a "God thing." The reunion between father and son, Hank's forgiveness which would not only relieve his own guilt, but Jeremy's too. It had seemed so right.

But it wasn't. It wasn't God's plan; it was all hers. She'd gotten so accustomed to helping others God put in her life, she figured she could do it without Him now. But it wasn't the same when it was *her* in the driver's seat, not Him.

Her plans had backfired so extravagantly and changed the immediate course of her life so drastically. She'd been open to the possibility of some sort of future with Hank. Was that just a pipedream? Now, it was gone in one ill-advised mistake.

Where was God now? Had He turned His back on her? Did He not think she could help Hank get over this family problem? Or had she just gotten so smug in her success in following God's will that He was tearing her down a peg or two?

Did God even operate that way? She didn't think so, but she wasn't even sure about that anymore.

The whole trip home, she ruminated and fretted. She tried to pray but found it hard. Her words, whether spoken aloud or inside her head, seemed wooden and contrived. The contrast between her closeness to her Creator on the trip down, and her return trip was not only vast, but disturbing.

At six on the second day, Leslie pulled into the driveway of her house which in most likelihood, wouldn't be her house for long. She grabbed her suitcase and rolled it through the front door. She stood motionless, looking around. She hadn't been gone that long, and yet it was a lifetime. So much had happened; her whole life had changed since the last time she was here.

She reminisced about the friends God had introduced her to on her roadtrip: she wondered how Norman was getting along with his seizure disorder.

Now that she was home, she really should give Rita a call. They lived relatively close, and she knew they could be friends. She wondered how Nathan was doing with his addiction, and whether or not Rita's husband had returned home from deployment.

She smiled as she reflected on the knitting group at the church in Charlotte, and the preemie babies who received the fruits of their labor, especially little Carson and his mom.

Yes, her whole life had changed on this trip, and definitely for the better. That, at least, she could thank God for. She took her suitcase upstairs and did a hasty unpack. Best to keep busy or else her mind would wander to the three things she didn't want to think about:

Selling her house and finding somewhere else to live,

Hank and her colossal backfire,

Her growing crisis of faith.

She sighed. That was a big list.

Settling into her couch and pulling her feet up underneath her, the man crept into her thoughts first. It was impossible not to think of Hank. She tried to tuck him away in the same category as the people God saw fit to use her for, as their angel on earth, their helping hand. But she couldn't do it. Her feelings toward Hank were worlds different than her feelings toward the others.

She recognized the feelings she had for Hank, because she'd felt them before. Not in a long time, but somewhere in the back recesses of her memory, she remembered. Was she in love with Hank? Probably not, but could she have fallen for him if she spent more time with him?

Absolutely.

But it wasn't meant to be. Their fledgling friendship was too new to bear the weight of what she'd done, and how he'd responded. Not to mention the distance between them.

She'd pray and she'd grieve and she'd move on. What choice did she have?

* * *

The next morning, she opened her house to Tim and a man she guessed to be in his mid-forties, both dressed in lightweight tailored suits. She subconsciously wiped a hand across the wrinkles in her shorts and tugged at the hem of her sleeveless cotton top. Outclassed in her own home.

"Come in. We can sit in the kitchen."

When they arrived at the table, Tim introduced them. "Leslie, this is Randall. Randall, Leslie, my ex-wife."

She fought back a cringe with all her might. Of course he'd introduce her that way. It was factual. So, why did it hurt so much?

"Nice to meet you," Randall said. He pulled a short stack of papers out of a satchel and put them on the table. "Tim's already heard the details of this over the phone, but since you both need to agree on the deal …"

"Yes."

Tim turned at the nastiness in her tone. He studied her with confusion.

She mimicked a smile. "Sure, we both have to be happy with the deal since we'll be splitting the profits on the house."

He nodded, keeping his gaze on her longer than he probably needed to.

Randall pointed to various parts of the document with a ballpoint pen. "As you can see, it's a very reasonable offer. It's under list price, but not by much, what, 7%? That's not too bad in today's market."

Math was never her forte. She glanced over at Tim and he had a happy smile on his face. Why wouldn't he? He would eliminate the house they'd raised their family in, and that would be one less thing to interact with her on. Life was going just the way he wanted.

Randall flipped a page. "Here's where the buyer is requesting some roof repairs, a radon prevention system to be installed in the basement and credit for a new furnace which will probably be needed within two years."

"What?" Rage bubbled in her esophagus. "These are ridiculous terms. How much is all that going to cost us?"

Tim tensed. Randall pulled out a small calculator and tapped the keys. "Between five and seven thousand dollars." He looked at her, eyebrows raised.

Leslie held back the impulse to let out a huff of frustration. Or a scream.

Tim reached over and patted the tabletop in front of her hand, although not her hand itself. "They're asking for a lot, but remember it's a buyer's market right now. Randall told me some bids come back 20% under list, in addition to these other requests. So, it could be worse."

Leslie stared at the offer, the words on the page starting to blur. "It's an insult. This is our first offer, the house has been up less than a month. What's the rush?"

Tim's face took on an expression of controlled irritation.

"I think we should wait and see what else comes in."

Randall looked panicked, and scooted his chair closer to Tim's. "That would probably be a mistake, Leslie. We pass up this offer, and the next one could be worse. Buyers look at how long a house has been on the market, and make a call on how desperate the sellers are. How much dealing they're willing to do."

"I'm not desperate."

Tim piped up, "That's because you're not that motivated to sell. Admit it."

His response was immediate which made her think it was on the tip of his tongue, and he'd been waiting to say it for some time. She opened her mouth, then closed it, saying nothing.

Was there some truth in his words? Was she passing up this decent — not great, but not horrible — offer because she didn't want to sell the house? Would she be happy with any offer or would she find a reason to decline each one?

Oh Lord, guide me, she prayed silently. *Make my intentions pure.*

She stood and took a few steps away from the table. As she struggled to control herself, she said in a shaky, small voice, "Where will I go? What will I do next?"

She heard the scraping of a chair on the floor and Tim's hand rested on her shoulder. When she turned, she saw Randall had left the room.

For a moment, his voice took on the same comforting tone she'd known on many occasions in the twenty years she'd spent with him. Hearing it now, directed at her, tore a hole in her heart. "I know this is hard for you. It kills me that I've caused you pain. But we both have to move forward. You know that, right? And part of moving on with our lives is selling this house and finding the places that will be our futures."

"Out with the old, in with the new?" she said with a sniff.

"Well, yeah, I guess so. I really think it'd be easier for you to adjust if you weren't here where we spent our marriage together."

She was so torn. What he was saying was true. It would be easier to move on if she didn't live here. More painful, like pulling a bandage off a scab. But eventually, easier. But him saying so made her angry. Like she was the weak one, the charity case, and he was in charge. She didn't want to be the weak one. But today, it was exactly how she felt.

"You don't think this offer is taking advantage of us?" she said.

"No, not at all. Plus, we have so much equity in the house we'll be able to pay those expenses, and still keep quite a large amount of cash, each of us. You'll have a nice down payment on a new place."

She rolled her eyes. She didn't want to have to find a new place, large down payment or not. But she had to get used to her new way of life, whether she liked it or not.

They went back to the table and Leslie picked up the pen. Tim called for Randall. The realtor trotted into the room.

"Oh! This is a good sign."

Leslie was paging through the offer. Each time there were two lines with X's by them, she signed the bottom one. She handed the pen to Tim and he signed the top lines.

"All right, thank you very much," Randall said. He stood, then looked at Leslie. "If you'd like my help finding your next place, just let me know. I'm already working with Tim to find his next place."

She glanced at Tim, then back to Randall. "I don't think so, but so nice of you to offer." She hoped the sarcasm didn't drip too awfully much.

She herded them both out, closed the door and flung herself against it before she realized she'd never even offered them a cold drink.

Chapter Eleven

Once the papers were signed, things moved quickly. Randall negotiated a closing date with the buyers and calculated the funds to be disbursed to Tim and to Leslie. He contacted the vendors needed to perform the specially requested jobs and scheduled the work. Such a speedy and expeditious realtor. All Leslie had to do was shop for a new place. She now knew her budget and although it wasn't limitless, there should be a variety of homes to choose from in Pittsburgh in her price range.

The problem was, whenever she thought about the conundrum she was in, she panicked. The "Sold" sign was displayed in front of her house, and she had only a few weeks before she would be out. She really needed to get busy and find her new home.

But she couldn't do it.

Sure, she'd looked in the paper, the Sunday Homes section. She'd circled ads and had even on a few occasions driven around on Open House day to addresses that interested her. But there was no curb appeal. If she couldn't bring herself to get out of the car, wouldn't she hate the inside?

Instead of facing the home problem, she called Jasmine. The six hour time difference meant mid-morning in

Pittsburgh was late afternoon in Paris. She caught her during a rare afternoon in her apartment.

"I'm so tired, Mom. I love Paris, but it goes too fast. A mile a minute. I feel like a slug when I just want to stay home in my shorts and tee shirt and eat popcorn."

Leslie laughed. "That doesn't sound too bad, sweetie. You work hard. You've earned a lazy day or two. Don't feel bad."

Her voice softened. "I'm looking forward to coming home. I miss you so much."

"I miss you too. Big time. But I know this has been the summer of a lifetime for you. And, actually for me too."

"So what's new on the housing front?"

"Nothing. Not a thing."

"Maybe you need a new realtor."

"Or a realtor at all."

Jasmine gasped. "You haven't hired a realtor? Why not?"

Leslie sighed. "I don't know. I really don't. I can't seem to get moving."

"If you don't get moving, you'll be homeless soon."

"Yeah, I know."

"What are you looking for, a single home? Condo? Townhouse?"

"I wish I knew."

They chatted for a while and the doorbell rang. Leslie stood, then thought about it and sat again. Whoever was visiting unannounced could wait or come back later. How often did she catch her world traveler with a free moment to talk?

They talked a little more and the doorbell rang again.

"Mom? Hold on, I have a Call Waiting beep." She came back on after a moment of silence. "Boss Man calling. So much for an afternoon off."

"Oh, dear. Well, don't work too hard. I worry you're not taking care of yourself."

They said their good-byes and ended the call. Leslie headed to the front door and opened it. No one was there, but a work truck was parked on the curb and a man was walking toward it, his back to her. One of the workers the realtor scheduled? But she wasn't told anyone was coming by today.

"Hello? Excuse me!" When he turned around, her heart leapt. Her pulse quickened and she felt dizzy. "Hank?" His face, so familiar, didn't belong in this environment, but strangely he fit right in. She didn't realize how much she missed seeing him till he stood before her.

A smile bloomed on his face and then faded. He jogged toward her and gave her a tentative grin. "Leslie."

"What? What are you doing here?"

He slipped his hands into his back jean pockets with a sheepish shrug. "I have to talk to you."

"Me?" She shook her head to clear it of the cobwebs that had gathered there. Hank was here. On her doorstep. He'd driven 650 miles to see her. "How did you know where I lived?" It was the first question that came into her befuddled mind.

He chuckled and dipped his head, studying his feet. "Well, that's the thing. I hope you won't be mad at Marianne about this, but . . ."

"Marianne?" What did his daughter have to do with this?

"I pretty much twisted her arm. She never would've done it normally."

"What?"

"I got your address from Marianne's record. You know, when you registered at the Inn you provided your home address."

He studied her face earnestly for a reaction. She could imagine Marianne had struggled with the ethics of handing out confidential customer information. However, Marianne had made it clear she thought Leslie and Hank belonged together. So she probably figured providing aid to Cupid was worth a privacy violation.

She gazed at Hank. He looked so good. So Hank, hard-working and capable. She wasn't mad he'd tracked her down, not in the least. In fact, she was elated. She smiled her joy and held her arms out. Within a moment, he had covered the ground separating them and pulled her into his embrace.

Warmth from his hug consumed her. She breathed in deep and knew she was right where she should be. In his arms, it all made sense. All the craziness her life had become since leaving Pawleys Island, now slowed down to the steady, pulsing beat of their two hearts embraced.

He released her and she reached up and caressed his cheek. "It's so good to see you."

A relieved smile covered his face. "Great to see you, too."

"Come in, come in. Are you hungry? Thirsty?"

He followed her into the house. "I wouldn't turn down a cup of coffee."

She led him to the kitchen. "How about an omelet? I could use one myself."

He nodded his agreement. "I have to say when I saw the Sold sign up in your yard, and you didn't answer the door after two rings, I was kicking myself for my spontaneous roadtrip. I thought I'd struck out, I really did."

"So why didn't you call instead? If you could find out my address 650 miles away, wouldn't it have been easier to find out my phone number?"

"I don't know. I got a wild hare and I wasn't sure how it would sound over the phone. I figured in person I stood a better chance of convincing you."

She frowned as she whipped the egg and milk concoction, poured it into the heated pan and went back to her refrigerator and pulled out tomatoes, cheese and mushrooms to chop. "What are you talking about?"

He leaned a hip against the island counter. "I need your help, Leslie."

"Help? With what?"

"I want to go visit Jeremy."

She stopped chopping with her knife mid-air. "You do?"

"Yep."

She shook her head. "You drove the wrong direction, you realize that, don't you?"

His face was serious despite her sarcasm. "I need you to go with me. I can't face him alone."

It made no sense. Why her? And why now, when this same idea had been a colossal fail just weeks ago?

"No, not me. I'm out. God made it clear to me, this was not His will, it was mine. I wasn't listening before but I am now." She shuddered, thinking about the bump in the road she'd had in her faith journey since the "Jeremy mishap." Last thing she wanted to do was misstep again. "How about Marianne?"

He'd been staring at her, now he pulled his gaze away. "Sure, she'd go with me. But, I don't know why, I have this strong feeling I want you there."

"A strong feeling?" It could sound like a crazy vagueness to someone else, but she knew exactly what that strong feeling was. She'd been following strong feelings all summer and look what new adventures had opened to her. Opening your heart and following the will of God required a person to recognize strong feelings for what they were.

But was this strong feeling from God, or merely from Hank? There was a difference.

"So you came here to pick me up?"

"Yeah. I drove all day yesterday to get here, but it was too late to stop by. I got a hotel room and was hoping I could convince you to get in the car with me. It'd be a long drive, but we could probably get to Columbia late tonight, and be there for visitors' hours tomorrow."

She finished her chopping and tossed the ingredients into the eggs on the stove. Then he stepped in front of her and captured her hands in his.

"I wasn't sure I'd be welcome here. I didn't know how much making up I'd have to do."

She grinned. She let herself settle down and sink into the comfort of his hands in hers, the knowledge that he was standing here in her kitchen. That he had come after her. That he needed her. She looked into his eyes and saw there what she needed to see.

"You're welcome here, Hank."

He leaned closer and his lips brushed against hers, his strong hands moving to her back, pulling her in against his chest. She closed her eyes and soaked in the sensation of his lips on hers, the rush of her heartbeat, her senses filling up with everything Hank. She loved the solid feel of him in her arms, the taste of him on her lips, the security she felt in her heart when she was with him. She remembered this feeling from long ago, but this time it was different. It was experienced and mature. She wasn't a young college student losing her heart to the good-looking football player destined for med school. Back then, she'd felt so lucky he'd chosen her because he had his pick of so many beautiful girls and instead of them, he'd chosen her. Who was she to say no? Her future was secure and he was such a good catch.

Or so she thought then. Her feelings for Hank were so different, not based on his credentials or his potential for a strong match. She liked him because of the person he was today. Who cared what the future held? They were only guaranteed today. And he was a strong man with a good heart who made her feel loved.

She pulled back so she could look in his eyes. "I've struggled since I left Pawleys Island, with several things. But at the heart of it was this situation between us. I had no business setting up that surprise visit …"

"It's okay, darlin'. You were right, I was just too stubborn to see it at the time. You setting that up was exactly what I needed to jolt me out of my status quo. To get me starting to think about making a change, a positive change. It took me a little while of thought and prayer before God revealed it to me. But you were right."

She stared into his eyes, wanting to believe him. Maybe the disturbing distance she'd felt from God since she left Pawleys was more her own doing, and not His. Suddenly, she knew what she needed to do.

"Will you pray with me, Hank? I need to know if it's God's will for you and Jeremy to reunite, or was that my own will?"

His forehead creased as he looked at her. "Well, of course it's God's will. God always wants us to forgive and love each other."

She stammered and shook her head. How could she possibly explain to him the crisis of faith she'd been struggling with since her return? God's idea, God's timing, God's direction. That's what she strived to follow, not her own.

Still standing with him, hands clasped, she closed her eyes and bowed her head. "God, I open my heart to you and ask you to put a blessing on our intentions. We want Hank and Jeremy to forgive each other, to love each other, to open their hearts to each other. We want to follow Your will, and not plow ahead on our own without You. Please guide us and keep us on the right track."

There, that should do it. And that's what had been missing last time. Life was too short to beat herself up, and she doubted that's what God wanted for her anyway. She loved being with Hank, and she knew God now had a hand in this roadtrip ahead of them. She would go and enjoy the moment. And worry about her own problems later.

"Yes, I'll go with you," she said with a smile.

In response, Hank lowered his lips to hers, enveloping them with warmth, caring and passion. It was a delicious, heart-racing kiss. He gripped her upper arms and squeezed them and when her knees were starting to go weak, he pulled away, leaving her breathless.

But reality intruded. The smell of burning food on the stove turned her toward it. "Oh!" She grabbed a spatula and scraped at the mixture. "I think I can salvage it."

As she worked, he smiled. "I wouldn't care if you couldn't. That kiss was worth a burnt breakfast, and much more."

She turned to him and beamed her appreciation at him.

In the end, it wasn't too bad. They ate the well-done omelets with toast and coffee. Afterward, Leslie washed dishes and Hank dried. She ran upstairs and packed a few days' clothing. By 9:30, they headed to the car.

"So, you sold your house. What's next?"

She shook her head. "I have no idea. I have a block against looking for someplace new. I can't explain it. I know I should be looking and narrowing my choices. But I can't motivate myself to do it. Tim thinks I'm in denial."

"Have you prayed about it?"

"Sort of, I guess."

He shrugged. "Do it again. He'll lead you."

That comment stuck with her for the first hour of the trip.

They spent the next eleven hours driving, stopping occasionally for gas, food, drink or bio breaks. They talked easily, their previous argument forgotten. They chatted about Marianne and Seaside Inn. He told stories about Stella that made her laugh. He talked about his work, having finished the Hinthorns' home and moved on to the next set of old vacation homes down near the Old Gray Barn.

She told him about the bid from the buyers, her thoughts that Tim had rushed into accepting, and how Jasmine's internship was progressing. And how desperately she missed the beach. She loved the beach and felt most herself there.

Late that night, they pulled into Columbia, SC. Darkness covered the small city, but just off the interstate they pulled into a hotel. Hank grabbed their suitcases from the backseat and they walked into the lobby. He stepped up to the desk, asked for two hotel rooms and pulled out a credit card. She started to object.

He put a hand on hers on the counter. "No, let me."

She studied his face a moment and saw he had already planned this — the separate rooms, the fact that he'd pay the bill. It was important to him things go according to plan. She nodded and stepped back.

The rooms happened to be adjoining. They went to the second floor and found them. Hank walked comfortably into hers, tossed her bag beside the bed and gave the room a quick once-over. He strode into the bathroom, pulled the shower curtain back, looked in. Back in the main room, he glanced into the closet. Over to the window, he pulled the drape back and looked outside. His actions warmed her heart.

"Looks like everything's in order." He was back at her side and she couldn't help her happy smile at him being there, right where he should be.

"Thanks."

He shook off her thanks like it was unnecessary but she appreciated his actions. She had no one else to watch out for her and help her stay safe. Sure, she'd made it this far on her roadtrip independently. After 20 years of being part of a couple, she was adjusting to being solo.

But it never hurt to need someone. Isn't that what the song was about? *People who need people are the luckiest people in the world?*

He lingered now. "So how about we meet about 8:30 to go down to the breakfast buffet? Then we'll head over. Visiting hours start at 9."

She nodded, her heart feeling full and happy. He reached for both her hands again, squeezed them and pulled her in to him. His kiss was gentle and soft, but it still made her heart increase its rate.

"Good night."

Lying in bed, she said a fervent silent prayer, thanking God for helping her find her way back to Him. She asked God to guide her, to lead her, to allow her to release her heart to follow Him. Hank could be a second chance at love and she wanted to include God in their fledgling romance.

The next morning they ate their breakfast, then headed to the car. The prison was a short drive away and Hank knew where it was. His talking decreased during the drive and came to a halt when they pulled into the parking lot. He stopped in a spot close to the building and turned the engine off, then sank back in his seat, his chin resting on his chest.

Leslie turned to him. The tension in the car was palpable. "It's going to be okay," she started.

"Will you pray with me?" he asked, looking into her eyes.

"Of course."

They joined hands and Hank spoke quietly. "Lord, this is it. This is a big day and I want Your help in getting through it. I thank You for sending Leslie into my life to, among other things, make me see that not talking to my boy for this long, despite what he did in the past, is wrong. I need to forgive him, but I'll need Your help with that one. Thank You for putting Leslie at my side today."

He stopped and sighed. She waited. He didn't continue speaking, but didn't end the prayer. She eventually spoke, "Lord, put a spirit of acceptance and love in both Hank's heart, and Jeremy's. Watch over us today during this visit."

Hank squeezed her hand and after a moment, he murmured, "Amen." He looked at her, his eyes moist. "Thank you. You don't know how much …"

She patted his hand. "Don't mention it."

He managed a smile and they got out of the car. They walked to the nondescript building, a gray cement block construction surrounded by a chain link fence. They followed the signs to the visitors' section. Inside, they stood in a short line in a colorless room with dull linoleum and painted cement block walls. Leslie had never been inside a prison before, but this was exactly what she would've pictured in her mind — hopeless, lifeless rooms that were part of the punishment for the people who lived there. If this was what the visitors' section looked like, she could only imagine what the prisoners' quarters were like.

Leslie stood with Hank, but when they got up to the window, she let him do all the speaking.

"Names?"

"Hank Harrison and Leslie Malone."

"Have you been here before?"

"No." His answer was quick, accompanied by a slight reddening of his face Leslie was sure she was the only one to notice.

"Fill these out." The man in uniform behind the window handed out some forms and two pens. Hank started to take them when the man said, "Prisoner you're here to see?"

"Jeremy Harrison."

The man tapped on the keyboard of his computer. "Okay. Bring these back up when you're done filling them out, along with a source of ID."

They sat in metal folding chairs, again, no source of comfort or luxury. Leslie could almost convince herself she was filling out a form like at the doctor's office, but they weren't asking about her medical history. They were asking about her history of trouble with the law: arrests, misdemeanors, felonies. Fortunately, she had none and breezed through the paperwork. Hank did too, then they walked back up to the window and handed the forms through, along with their drivers' licenses.

The officer took them, studied them a moment, tapped into the computer again, then handed them back. "Everything's in order. We'll call you when the prisoner's brought forward."

Hank nodded. Leslie returned to her chair but Hank stood near the door. A small window allowed a view into the visitors' room and he stared through it. Leslie knew the minute he saw Jeremy. A tensing in Hank's back and neck, and a widening of his eyes told the tale. Unsure of her place here, she stayed in her chair.

Soon, the officer called their names and the lock on the door into the visitors' room automatically released. Hank was there to grip and pull it open. Leslie got up and followed him into another listless room, same colorless tile and walls, this one filled with tables and chairs. The bland room reminded her of a high school cafeteria, but the purposes of those two rooms were completely different.

Leslie hung back. What was her role? Moral support for Hank, sure, but she didn't know Jeremy, and after so long without a visit from his father, she was sure the presence of a strange woman with his dad would be awkward at the least.

Hank came face to face with his son in the same room after a decade of no communication. His chest heaved as his breathing came heavily. Jeremy stood at one of the tables, positioned as if ready to sit. He studied his father and watched him take a step away from the door, keeping a conservative distance between the two of them. His face was void of expression. Two men standing a distance apart, weighing each other before committing to words.

Jeremy broke the silence first. "Dad. Good to see you."

That was enough for Hank. He covered the distance between them in a few long steps and pulled his son into a rough embrace. Arms wrapped around torsos, sobs catching in throats, the two men held onto each other. Quiet words were exchanged, pats on backs. A decade worth of bitter silence evaporated in a few moments of forgiveness. Leslie found herself repeating silently, "Thank you. Thank you, God."

"Let me see you," Hank murmured and pulled back from his son. Placing his hands on the younger man's cheeks, he took him in, his eyes darting from eyes to hair, to haggard cheeks to frame. Ten years of prison life had passed, leaving its toll on Jeremy's appearance. Ten years that Hank had not taken part in.

"You've lost weight," he observed.

Jeremy laughed. "You try eating this food three squares a day."

They chuckled together and Hank pulled him in for another, quicker hug before releasing him and gesturing to the table. The two sat. Leslie lingered by the door, not wanting to interrupt this miraculous reunion she was observing.

The silence broken, now both of them had words to say. They started, stopped at the interruption, looked at each other and laughed. Hank said, "You go first."

Jeremy nodded. He wore a uniform of sorts, a prisoners' uniform of blue dungarees and denim shirt, tucked in, hair cut as short as a military buzz cut. "I'm sorry, Dad."

Hank gave his head a firm shake. "No. We're not starting out like that."

"I have to. It's the start of everything. I screwed up, I know that, and I've never had the chance to apologize."

Hank huffed out a lungful of breath. "I have apologies, too."

Jeremy scoffed. "No. You have nothing to be sorry for. I messed up. Listen." He tapped his dad's hand until he knew he had Hank's attention. "You were the best father I could ask for. You gave me everything, loved me, trusted me. You set me up in business. But I screwed it up. I lied to you, betrayed you, and ultimately, ruined your life. And Mom's."

Hank pulled his hands back, leaned far back in his chair. A swipe across his eyes, and Leslie knew he was struggling to fight tears. "I can't handle this today. Let's not do this, okay? Can it be enough that I'm here?"

Jeremy studied him a moment, then shook his head. "Okay. Let me say this: I'm sorry. I really am. I'm getting out soon and I'm going to spend my life, Dad, making it up to you. I'm not sure how. But it means the world to me that you're here."

They spent the next ten minutes talking softly and Leslie gave them their privacy. She hung close to the door, looked through the small window, anything but stare at Hank and Jeremy and make them feel uncomfortable in their reunion. Then Hank said, "Leslie."

He had turned in her direction and motioned her over. "I want you to meet Jeremy."

Jeremy stood and held his hand out. "Nice to meet you."

Hank got to his feet too and said, "Leslie is a big reason why I'm here. She convinced me, in her own gentle way, I was being an idiot not visiting all these years."

"I never said that!"

He chuckled. "Not in so many words, but you got me thinking and I came up with that one myself." He put an arm on her shoulder as they faced Jeremy across the table.

"Well, however you got him here, I am very grateful. And I hope we can spend some time together when I get sprung."

"I'd like that," she said, not having any idea how or when it would happen.

They sat and relaxed at the table. "So, when is that, Jeremy?" Hank asked.

"Should be around the first week of August."

"That soon! That's great. What are your plans?"

Jeremy sighed. "I'm not exactly sure, long term, but Marianne offered me a room at the inn for as long as I need it, and free meals in the dining room."

Hank nodded his approval. "Can't beat that."

"I'll probably try to find a job with a contractor if I can find one that'll take a chance on me." He rushed on, "I've been working on my portfolio while I've been in here. They have a woodshop here and I've been building furniture."

"Really?"

"Yeah, something I've picked up during the empty hours. I made a few pieces, tables and dressers mostly, of my own design. They allowed me to sell them online. They keep enough of the funds to cover expenses but they let me put the rest in my account. So I'll have a little money when I get out."

"That's real good, Jeremy. You were always a good worker."

The visitors' hour passed quickly and when it was time to leave, Jeremy pulled his dad into a farewell hug. Hank rubbed his son's crew cut head playfully. "See you in a little while, son. You keep your nose clean, now."

"Oh yeah, no problem there." He turned to Leslie. "So nice to meet you. Thank you for coming."

Leslie smiled. "My pleasure." She hesitated, then reached for a hug, which Jeremy immediately gave her. He murmured for only her to hear, "And for bringing him here."

They left first, before Hank had to watch his son being taken back to his cell by the prison guard. Back in the car, Hank turned to her and released a deep breath.

"That went well," she said.

He nodded. "It's a start, long overdue." He turned the key and the engine revved. "Now a decision for you. Where to?"

She stared.

"Pittsburgh or Pawleys? Your choice."

She chose Pawleys. Funny how Pawleys and the Seaside Inn was feeling more home to her these days than "home."

A few hours' drive deposited them in the sandy parking lot of the Inn. When they reached the great room, Marianne looked up from her place at the reception desk. And shrieked.

"Oh my gosh! Leslie! Dad! You're here! What's going on?" She trotted around the desk and hugged them both at the same time. Leslie couldn't help chuckling at the animated greeting.

"You didn't tell her?" she asked Hank while still in her grasp.

"Not yet." He raised his voice. "All right, all right! Let us go. We have something to tell you."

Marianne gasped, a gallon of assumption resting in that breath.

"Tell her quick, before she jumps to the wrong conclusion," Leslie muttered.

They sat in the great room and Hank jumped right in. "We saw Jeremy today."

Marianne's eyes popped wider. "Oh! I didn't think you were going there but okay, that's good news too." She exchanged glances with both of them. "Great news, actually, fantastic news! So tell me."

Hank gave a succinct description of recent events, leaving out a million details, but Marianne visibly held her tongue. Both ladies knew Leslie would fill in the blanks later. "Now, a question for you, daughter dear. Do you have a vacant room for our friend Leslie here?"

Marianne smiled. "In fact, I do."

"Then, get the lady set up for a stay of undetermined length."

"Will do."

He stood and reached out to Leslie. "Could I have a private word with you?"

"Of course."

They walked to the back porch and then outside to the boardwalk. He turned and gave her a serious expression. "I can't thank you enough. For helping me see that visiting Jeremy was the thing to do. For going with me, even though I showed up unannounced and you have plenty else to do. And for being here with me now. I don't know how long you can stay, but I would love to shower you with attention while you're here. Like tonight, dinner?"

Leslie smiled. "I'd love to."

"And whenever you need to go back to Pittsburgh, let me know and I'll drive you. Meanwhile, I think I can sweet talk the boss into giving you a free room."

"Oh, no! I can't do that. This is Marianne's livelihood. She can't make money giving rooms away for free."

He took her hands in his. "Whatever she can't discount, I'll pay for myself."

"No." Leslie shook her head.

"I won't take an argument. You've done so much for my family. It's the least I can do." He leaned in for one of those soft, gentle, soul-shattering kisses of his that left her absolutely breathless. "Tonight at 6? Jambalaya is on the menu here."

She nodded, watched him leave, then settled down and checked into her room.

They enjoyed the jambalaya dinner, as well as more delicious homemade seafood dinners on consecutive nights. During the day while Hank worked, Leslie relaxed on the lounge chair on the beach, reading, or ventured into the ocean and rode the waves. She shopped in the quaint artisan stores in town, and even bought a hammock, Pawleys Island's trademark. Of course, she had no idea where she would put it since she'd be homeless soon. But she had to trust in God her housing arrangement would become clear to her.

One noon-time, she got in her car and wandered over to where Hank was working, two sandwiches and a bag of chips packed in an iced cooler on her front seat. It was early for a lunch break, so on her way to the big beach house where he was working, she parked her car across from The Old Gray Barn. She gazed up at it, the old wooden house on stilts with its gorgeous back view of the beach, a dinosaur by today's architectural standards. It couldn't hold a candle to the new beach homes, so full of luxury and beauty. And yet, none of those new homes down the beach held any appeal to her.

She had no idea how long the old house had been sitting there, but it had survived at least one hurricane she was aware of. Deceivingly sturdy. Took a beating and stayed standing. Sort of like her, and this summer adventure.

So little about the house had changed since she had spent summer after summer here as a girl. Good things were meant to last.

The longer she stared at it, the more a feeling instilled itself in her heart. Other than her house back in Pittsburgh where she'd raised her family, this was the only place in the world that gave her a sense of home. Of belonging. Of nostalgic love of place. And her home in Pittsburgh had been sold to the highest bidder. So, by process of elimination, this was the only place for her in the world.

The moment the thought hit her brain, her pulse increased, her breathing became labored in her chest. What was this? Was this God speaking to her, or just her crazy mind wandering to places it had no right going? The Old Gray Barn could be her new home? How crazy was that?

She quickly bowed her head and said a quick prayer, asking for clarification. "Please guide me, please lead me. Help me understand what I need to do regarding my next home. Should I go buy a condo in Pittsburgh? Why? What's left for me there? Should I buy an old beach home in Pawleys Island? Why? What's in store for me here?"

She ended her prayer, feeling slightly better that she'd prayed, but still with no answers. That was okay, that was the way of prayers. By placing her open heart in God's hands, she'd do her best to understand His answer. But answers don't usually come immediately.

She started her car and continued on to find Hank. She spotted his truck parked two blocks down in front of an old beachfront house, also on stilts. She carried the lunch box up the stairs and finding the door unlocked, let herself in.

"Hello?"

"Hello!" His voice floated from the back porch. She found her way.

She stepped down onto the porch floor, now converted to a 4-seasons room. The wall facing the ocean was one window after another, providing a non-stop view of the magnificent private beach. He stood and covered the distance to her in a couple steps. He took the cooler.

"What a pleasant surprise."

She couldn't stop staring out the windows. "Is it hard to get anything done with this view? Look, the ocean is sparkling today."

He chuckled and turned to face it. "It sure is. And yes, it's hard but I have to keep my nose to the grindstone. I have another three days' work here, then I have another job lined up after that. "

She shook her head. "You rarely have a day off, do you?"

He considered it. "No, but until recently I haven't had much of a reason to." He came close and put his arms around her, pulling her against him. They both breathed in the other, enjoying the feeling of body against body. He locked eyes with her, then moved in for a gentle kiss.

Once her heart rate recovered, she pulled herself together. "I brought you lunch. Are you hungry?"

"Sure."

She pulled the sandwiches and chips out and they settled on the wooden floor. Halfway through the sandwich, Leslie's phone rang. Glancing at it, she groaned. "Tim."

Hank ducked his head and smirked.

"I have half a mind to let it go to voicemail." Leslie stared at the phone as if it held answers. "Then again, he rarely calls unless he has news." She pushed the button. "Hello?"

"Hi Leslie. Is the work complete that we scheduled?"

Leslie was speechless.

"The roofers should've come Monday and Randall said the radon installers called him on Wednesday asking for a key to get in."

"Oh, uh huh." She'd forgotten to tell Tim she'd left town again. Ooops.

"So are you satisfied with the work? I mean, I'm sure you haven't climbed up on the roof, but is everything to your satisfaction?"

She sighed. "Tim, actually, I'm out of town. I haven't inspected the work done. "

"Oh." His sudden silence made her almost smile. She knew him well enough to predict the internal workings of his brain. He was dying to ask where she was, why she hadn't told him, reprimand her for not being around to inspect the work done to the house. But he knew it wasn't his right anymore, it wasn't his business. She supposed you could teach an old dog new tricks.

"I should've informed you of my plans since they impacted the work done on the house, but they came up rather suddenly. "

"Oh."

She had stunned him, caught him surprised, made him unable to come up with a word other than "oh." Under the circumstances, she couldn't help but consider that a victory.

"If you'd like to inspect the work, feel free, or since Randall still has a key, he could do it. "

"Right." She heard some papers shuffle on the other end of the line. "Leslie, there's one other thing. The buyers have an additional request." He hurried on. "During their walkthrough, they noticed several of our custom-made furniture pieces and wondered if they could purchase them from us. Pieces made specifically for the house. For example, the bookshelves on either side of the fireplace. The leather circular couch in the sunken family room. And the armoire in the bedroom. "

Leslie could picture the pieces in her mind as he listed them, and she also replayed the scenes in her mind of their creation. She had worked with a furniture store in town to design the circular leather couch. And the armoire was custom-made by an artisan in central Pennsylvania. The bookshelves had been built specifically for their family room by a local wood worker. All of them were her creations, her design, her ideas. She waited for a pang of pain to hit her at the thought of letting them go, like had happened with the carpet, the countertop and the blinds.

But nothing hit. No pain. She glanced over at Hank. He was making a concerted effort not to eavesdrop.

Tim continued, "These items are negotiable Les, as they weren't included in the purchase contract. But I really think we ought to consider their request. Since they were custom fit, it's unlikely they'd go in any future place …"

"Yes, let's go ahead and sell them," Leslie said. "Whatever price you think is fair." She listened to a few seconds of silence before she went on, "In fact, do you want any of the furniture? You can pick what you want, and we can offer the rest of it up to the buyers. I won't have a spot for them in my new place, I don't know about you. I'll probably start fresh.

New furniture, new color scheme." New life, new hopes, new dreams.

"Uhhh," Tim stammered, which caused Leslie's lip to curl up. "I hadn't really considered selling *all* the furniture. I figured we'd try to split it up equitably."

"Well, you can have all of it then. I'm sure you'll be fair in compensation."

Tim wasn't a stammerer. He was too sure of himself and in control. So Leslie didn't really know the right word to describe what he was doing. But if she didn't know better, she'd think "stammer" was close.

"Thanks for the call, Tim. I need to get going."

"Uh, Les? Where are you and when are you coming back?"

She glanced over with a smile at Hank. "I'm right where I want to be, where I need to be, where I've always loved to be. And I have no idea when I'm coming back. Call if you need me!"

Chapter Twelve

Two months of Leslie's summer break had slipped by. August was right around the corner, and along with it, the feeling of anxiety that accompanies every teacher's heart at the turn of the month. Leslie had always loved teaching, but even so, the thought of turning the calendar page to August meant her carefree summer days were coming to an end and the school year, and all its work and early mornings and late nights, was imminent.

This year, the anxiety was more prevalent than usual because of how up in the air her living arrangement was. What was she doing here, 650 miles away from home, when she should be in Pittsburgh, finding her next place? But every time she thought and prayed about leaving Pawleys, she ended feeling uncertain. This new lifestyle of letting God lead her actions was unsettling, but exciting for its possibilities.

She was sitting on her favorite lounge chair on the wooden deck behind the Inn. The day was a hot one, in the upper nineties, the sun direct by mid-day. She had lathered up with sunscreen, and she wore a big floppy hat for good measure to shade her face. Marianne and Stella walked by on their way to the beach, then when Marianne noticed Leslie sitting there, she waved Stella on.

"You go on, sweetie. I'll be right there."

Marianne lowered into the lounge chair next to Leslie. "How's it going today?"

"Fantastic," Leslie answered.

Marianne rested her head back onto the cushioned back and closed her eyes. "I can't believe my baby's going to kindergarten in a month. "

"Oh! What an exciting time. She'll be fine, Mom." Leslie reached over and patted Marianne's arm. She had grown so fond of Marianne over the weeks they'd spent together. They had a bond and could talk openly about any number of topics. She was a fine mom and a great businesswoman and she loved her dad, wanting the best for him. Maybe that's why they got along so well. Marianne was convinced Leslie was the best for him.

"I wish the school wasn't in such disarray. It would be easier to deliver my firstborn to them if they had their act together."

Leslie glanced over at her. "What do you mean? What's going wrong at the school?"

"The kindergarten teacher had her baby, but the administration hasn't named a replacement yet. It's only weeks till school starts and we have no idea who her teacher will be."

Leslie nodded. "I can see how that would be disconcerting to you, but unfortunately this is very common. Because public schools rely on state budgets, we're often in the position where non-tenured teachers are laid off every spring, then wait with baited breath to see if they get rehired in the fall. Often, the rehires happen just a few days before the school year starts."

"How awful!"

"It is, not only for the children, but especially for the teacher. Can you imagine being given a class of twenty five or twenty eight students, with two days' notice?" Leslie turned back to the ocean. "I'm sure they've got a long list of applicants. They need to go through the process of selecting the right one."

Marianne sat quietly, then said softly, "Maybe you should go throw your name in the hat."

Her voice was so low, Leslie wasn't sure she'd heard right. She turned to her. "What did you say?"

Marianne smiled. "Go apply! I'd love for you to be Stella's teacher."

Leslie chuckled nervously. "But I have a teaching job. In Pittsburgh. And it's starting soon."

Marianne waited a beat or two. "You sounded so sad as you said that."

"Did I?"

Marianne nodded. "Are you going back?"

"I suppose. What else would I do?"

"Stay here."

Leslie sighed. "That sounds like one of those dreams that can't possibly turn into reality."

"Why not?"

But the more Leslie pondered the idea, she couldn't come up with a concrete reason. She no longer had a house, a husband, or a daughter in Pittsburgh, nobody who needed her day in and day out. She did have a job, and a classroom full of kids who would need her soon. But there were classrooms of kids needing teachers all over the country. What was so special about Pittsburgh?

She turned to Marianne. "This may be crazy talk but I think I will apply at the school. What's the principal's name?"

Marianne squealed like a teenage girl and clapped. "Mrs. Robinson."

* * *

The meeting with Mrs. Robinson went well. She seemed interested in Leslie's long tenure and experience teaching a variety of grades. They discussed Leslie's ideas for improving the kindergarten curriculum, and Leslie discovered there were actually several openings this year due to a retirement and a sudden resignation. Walking out of the school though, her sense of well-being was replaced with anxiety. Her breathing was ragged as she got in the car and her head filled with dread. What on earth was she doing? She couldn't leave a long-term stable teaching job. They were hard to come by these days. She'd worked up her salary to higher than average. She'd need it now as a single income person. She'd better put this crazy pipedream behind her and head back to Pittsburgh … today.

So she bowed her head and prayed a fervent prayer, "Lord, guide me. Help me know what is right. What is Your will for me? Help me follow Your will. I need help here. Make it clear to me which way You want me to go." She repeated various versions of the same prayer for a good ten minutes. When she raised her head, her anxiety had lifted and she no longer felt the need to race "home." She drove back to the Inn.

When she got to the great room, Marianne was on the phone behind the desk. Leslie couldn't help but overhear her side of the excited conversation since her voice was louder than usual. "Yes, Dad. Today. I don't know why. Evidently they don't give them tons of notice. But he just called me.

No, he doesn't need a ride. He's taking a bus. He's coming straight here. I know. I can't wait. It's unbelievable. After all this time. Okay, come on over. Yeah. "

She hung up and noticed Leslie lingering. "Jeremy's being released this morning!"

Leslie danced over to her and pulled Marianne into a happy hug. "That's wonderful!" Then she asked the first thing that popped into her head, "Do you need my room?"

Marianne laughed. "Not this time of year. I have room for him and you, too."

The next few hours were spent cleaning the already spotless inn and creating and hanging a huge Welcome Home Jeremy banner in the great room. Leslie drew big block letters on a flowing roll of blank newsprint and Stella decided on the color scheme and colored in the letters with her markers. Marianne bustled around with the duster and the vacuum. When Hank arrived, he helped attach the banner behind the couch so it would be the first thing Jeremy saw when he came in the room. When they were done decorating, they estimated another hour to fill before Jeremy arrived so Hank swooped Stella up in his arms, took her to the car and they went shopping for colored balloons to place around the room as well.

The Prodigal Son was returning, Leslie mused. Warmth filled her heart over the excitement the family felt over his return. She had a bit to do with that, she realized. How would Hank be feeling about Jeremy's release if she hadn't arranged the prison visit? If they hadn't spoke recently? She said a quick word of thanks to God for the joy in their hearts today.

While they were waiting for Hank and Stella to return with the balloons, Leslie went to where Marianne stood, idly dusting the bookshelves she just dusted moments before. "Anything I can do?" she asked with a smile.

Marianne turned to her and wrapped her in a hug. "Not a thing. You've done so much. I'm so glad you're here."

Leslie smiled and shook her head.

"You've made such a difference in our lives, you know."

"No."

Marianne gave her shoulder a playful pat. "Don't deny it. It's true. We've all become so fond of you, not the least of which, my father. I haven't seen him so happy since, well, since before my mom died. He was surviving. Moving forward, one day at a time. But you brought him back to life."

Leslie knew she was blushing from the warmth that plunged into her cheeks.

"For that, I will always thank you. And for the miracle of getting my dad to go talk to Jeremy, face to face. I'd tried and tried to convince him till I was blue in the face. He'd never do it. I tried for years, I honestly did. But you managed to get through to him. Not right away! But you were effective where I failed. Now, what does that tell you about what you mean to him?" She gave Leslie another squeeze. "I'm so glad he's got you."

She didn't know what to say to that, so she said nothing. Hank and Stella came bursting into the great room with big fistfuls of colorful helium-filled balloons, and Leslie ran to help organize and hang them.

Ninety minutes later, Marianne, Tom and Stella sat together on the couch, having run out of preparation activities to perform, their work ground to a halt in the empty minutes waiting for Jeremy. Hank and Leslie shared a chair, Leslie sitting on the arm, half-on, half-off Hank's lap with his arm around her. Empty iced tea glasses sat around the room, Marianne's attempt to keep herself busy over an hour before. Conversation had ended at least a half hour prior. Jeremy had not been in touch since the initial contact with Marianne earlier this morning. He didn't have a cell phone so there was no way to speak to him in transit. They were simply in wait mode, unable to concentrate on anything other than Jeremy's pending arrival.

The silence ended abruptly when the front door opened and Jeremy stepped into the doorway. He wore khaki pants and a plain white button up dress shirt over a white tee shirt. He carried a small backpack, which he hiked off his shoulder and onto the floor.

"Jeremy!" It was Marianne, shrieking with joy. She ran to him and grabbed his hands, pulling him into the center of the room where she wrapped her arms around him, squeezing his slight frame and pounding his back. Leslie peeked a glance at his face. He was laughing and rolling his eyes. She hoped he'd survive Marianne's enthusiastic greeting.

"Hey sis, good to see you," he managed.

She pulled back, held his face in both hands and gave him a long kiss on the cheek. Her husband, Tom stood and rescued Jeremy with an outstretched palm. The two men shook hands, Jeremy dipping his head and looking up at his brother-in-law through his eyelashes.

"Welcome home, man," Tom said.

"Thanks. I can't tell you how much it means …" Jeremy's voice broke and he shook his head.

"No need," his brother-in-law said and patted him on the back.

Marianne gestured for Stella to come over. "Baby, we want you to meet your Uncle Jeremy. Jeremy is my big brother. He's been away for a long time and now he's come home. I've told you about him, remember?"

Stella walked up easily and stopped in front of Jeremy. He kneeled so he was closer to her height. Stella held a hand out, which Jeremy took gently. "Nice to meet you, Uncle Jeremy. Are you going to live here with us?

Jeremy swiped a thumb over first one eye, then the other, then looked over her shoulder at Marianne who was watching the exchange, beaming at them. "She looks just like you, sis. In fact, she's a carbon copy of when you were a little girl."

Marianne nodded and curved her lips into a closed-mouth smile.

Jeremy turned back to his niece. "Nice to meet you too, Stella. It's so cool to finally talk to you. And yes, I'm going to stay with you for a while. Is that going to be okay with you?"

Stella gave her head a vigorous nod. "Do you like the beach?"

Jeremy smiled. "I love the beach."

"Great. We can go swimming and digging together. And I can show you how to crab and fish, too."

"Oh sweetie, Uncle Jeremy knows how to do all that stuff," her mom said. "He grew up on the beach, just like you."

Jeremy swung his head from his sister down to his niece. "But you're right, I've been away from it for a while. I need your help, Stella. How about we do that together later?"

Stella nodded and wandered away, and Jeremy got to his feet, his stance tentative now after all the hugging and greeting. He glanced around the room, grinned at the balloons and the banner, and then his eyes lighted on his dad. Hank had stood when Jeremy first came, but stayed in the corner, his hand joined with Leslie's, more for moral support than romance.

"Hey, Dad." Jeremy stayed where he was in the center of the room, facing Hank. His eyebrows rose, cutting a crease in his forehead and his arms hung at his sides. He seemed uncomfortable in the position the family had placed him in: in the center of everything, both literally and figuratively.

Leslie turned to Hank. The older man gazed calmly at Jeremy, not saying a word, but memories probably running a highlight reel through his mind. Jeremy being born, Jeremy as a little boy, Jeremy as a teen learning his dad's craft. An expression of pain flickered across his face before clearing and Leslie could pinpoint exactly when, in the memory slideshow, Jeremy's life and therefore the family's, had taken an awful turn. But today wasn't a day to dwell on the destruction of their lives. Today was a day for redemption.

Jeremy had paid the price for his crimes, his family had forgiven him, and he was home.

Hank freed his fingers from Leslie's and covered the few steps to his son quickly, holding out his arms. The two men embraced and held on, their closeness giving comfort to them both.

"Great to see you, son. Welcome home."

"Thanks, Dad."

"Marianne, you got a room planned for our boy?"

And with that, Marianne grabbed Jeremy's shoulder and directed him toward the stairs, Jeremy dodged to grab his small bag of belongings before following her to his room. Marianne yelled over her shoulder, "Family dinner in the dining room at 6:15. Be there, everyone!"

* * *

The summer days continued on, one after another. Leslie savored each beautiful, sunny beach day, painfully aware her deadline was approaching. It wouldn't be long before school would start in Pittsburgh, which meant she had to spend at least a week in preparation for her class. Getting her class list, making nametags, posters for the walls. A variety of personalized wall hangings designed to make twenty-five potentially anxious third graders feel at home in their new classroom. Every year she simultaneously dreaded and looked forward to the return of normal after a heavenly three months of carefree.

But not this year. The dread was there alone, no trace of giddy anticipation. Probably because everything was so up in the air. Her house was sold, waiting for its new owners. She needed to get back home, clean out her closets, pack and move. To where? She didn't have a place to stay. She hadn't gone through the work of house hunting, of deciding on a new permanent place, of buying a new property.

Why? What was wrong with her? This was so unlike her. Some moments she was sure she should leave immediately and return home, and others, that feeling of panic would pass and she'd thank God for the cozy room at the Inn and the happiness she found there.

That night, she walked with Hank on the beach. The sunset painted a gorgeous pallet of orange, pinks and purples across the sky. They held hands and pushed their speed past the comfort zone, agreeing the walk was for exercise and help digesting, not a leisurely stroll. Later, when they stopped to catch their breath, Leslie told him, "I think it's time I get back to Pittsburgh. I've got to finalize the house before closing, and I've got to figure out where I'm going to live once the school year starts."

He looked at her and she could make out the sadness in the set of his mouth. “I suppose you do. Or, you could stay here.” He said it with a smile.

“As much as I’d love to, I can’t just stay on vacation mode the rest of my life.”

“Why not?”

She considered it a moment. “I don’t know. I guess I have to get back to reality. Much as I dread it.”

“Why can’t this be your new reality?” He reached for her hand and rubbed the back of it with his thumb.

She choked out a half laugh, half scoff. “Some days I think it is. I love it here, always have. But a couple problems. My job is in Pittsburgh. I have to go back to it. And I’m homeless, basically. I need to wrap up my housing plans, preferably before school starts. Because once the school year is off and running, I won’t have any time or energy for anything else for a while.”

Her mind raced ahead to those first weeks, months of a new school year, and how it would be her first one without Tim or Jasmine at home. Her routine as a teacher was so familiar to her. But not the home part. She’d be all alone, in a different house, probably a different part of town. Everything would change.

Could she do it? Would she be happy? Could she thrive?

She’d learned so much this summer about opening herself up to God’s will in her life. It was amazing what experiences God could place you in if you were willing to be where He placed you. Would a tiny one-bedroom apartment in Pittsburgh, all by herself, be the place God wanted her?

She gripped Hank’s hand. “Would you pray with me, please?”

He nodded.

"God, where do You want me when this summer ends? Is it Your will that I go back to Pittsburgh and teach children there? If so, where will I live? How will I bear being totally alone? Is it Your will that I stay here? If so, where will I work? Where will I live?"

She squeezed her closed eyes and sighed. "Please help me listen to Your answer. Make it clear to me, Father, just what it is You want me to do. I want to follow Your plan. I need to know what it is." She waited for a few moments. "Amen."

Hank put an arm around her, rubbing her shoulder with his palm. "That's pretty clear. Now you wait."

"Now I wait," she said nervously.

As it turned out, she didn't need to wait very long. A few days later, she was at the grocery store with Hank, shopping for a dinner she planned to make at his house.

"How about spaghetti and meatballs tonight?"

He agreed. "I'll go get the pasta. How about you get the meatballs?" He pointed at the freezer a few feet away. She pulled open the heavy door, but soon he tapped her on the shoulder. She pulled her head out of the icy freezer and looked at him.

"Your cell phone is ringing." He handed it to her. The number was unfamiliar but local. She answered. It was Mrs. Robinson from the local elementary school.

"Well, Leslie, I've finalized my decisions about the job openings, and I'd like to offer you one. We were impressed with your interview, and your teaching experience made you one of our top candidates. I know you were interested in the kindergarten opening, but we didn't slot you there. We see you in the sixth grade opening. Would you be interested?"

A wave of dizziness struck her and she gripped the grocery cart, locking eyes with Hank and begging him wordlessly to stop its movement so she could lean heavily on it, regaining her balance.

"Um, wow. You've given me a huge surprise and a lot to think about. "

Mrs. Robinson let out some sort of emission of air, most likely an amused one. "Are you still looking for a job for the fall?"

Was she? She had no idea.

"Could I think about your generous offer and get back to you in a day or two?"

There was a slight pause. "Tomorrow, please. Then I'll have to move on to the next candidate."

"Absolutely. Thank you very much." She barely remembered pushing the End button on her phone and slipping it into her purse but she must have. "I got the job."

Hank emerged from expectant silence with a whoop. "You got the job!" He fist pumped the air and lifted her up, off her feet, swinging her easily in a circle right there in the produce section. His mouth curled into a sly grin. "Do you believe in answered prayer?"

Anxiety started in her chest and was growing into full-blown panic. "Do you think? Is this God answering my prayer? Or am I pretending it is?"

Hank made an unbelieving scoff. "Are you serious? Of course it's an answer to prayer. God is putting this new job right in your lap. I believe that means, He wants you … here."

He returned her feet to the floor. "Sure seems that way," she muttered.

"Let's celebrate."

"Not yet."

He let his head drop backward and rolled his eyes good-naturedly.

"Hey, God knows I'm cautious. It's all part of the deal." She glanced around. "Can you finish up this shopping without me? You have the list. I'm going to make a few phone calls in private."

"Sure. You wouldn't be you, otherwise. Love you, darling." He rolled the cart away as she dug in her purse absentmindedly, found her phone and pulled it out. She'd flipped it open and pushed a few digits when she jerked her head up. "Wha—?" What did he say?

He'd already pushed the cart half an aisle length away. She shook her head. She'd have to worry about that one later.

She went outside, punched Jasmine's number and waited till her daughter's treasured voice answered. "Jasmine."

"Mom. What's up?"

"I've got some awesome news to share and I need help interpreting it."

"Sounds intriguing."

"You know how Hank and I prayed for a clear sign whether God wants me to go back to Pittsburgh or stay in Pawleys? Well, I just got off the phone with the school principal here in Pawleys. They offered me the sixth grade teaching position."

A second of silence, then an explosion of joyful laughter. "Congratulations, Mom! Sounds like things are falling into place, doesn't it? You sold your house, you found the man of your dreams, you got a job near him."

"Wait, whoa, whoa, whoa." Leslie gasped. "I never said a word about Hank being the man of my dreams. Why would you say that? We are friends. Acquaintances, really. He's easy to talk to, at a time when I needed a friend."

"Mom, come on. Seriously?"

"What?"

"Righteous indignation? It's me, Mom. And friends? Acquaintances? Get real."

Leslie's head was spinning again, like when she'd gotten the job offer.

"When you talk about this guy, your voice changes tone. You go softer and happier, thinking about him. And he sounds so sweet. He does so many nice things for you. I've actually thanked God for sending him to you. He's exactly what you need, and he's more than just someone to talk to."

"I'm barely divorced."

"Yeah, from my dad. But life moves on. People aren't meant to be alone and I think it's cool you found a man friend you enjoy spending time with. I get the impression he's hot too."

"Jasmine!" Leslie darted her head around, looking to see if she spied Hank anywhere. Of course, she didn't. He was inside shopping. "Have I ever said anything about his physical appearance?"

Jasmine considered. "No, but I guess I'm picturing him in my mind as a Richard Gere type."

Leslie let loose an unbidden chuckle. "No, Richard Gere's the stuffy suit type. That's not Hank." She bit her tongue because she nearly said, "That's not my Hank," before she refrained. "I always considered him more of a Harrison Ford type."

"Oh! Nice work, Mom!"

Leslie shook her hands out, then put her phone back to her ear. "Stop this. He's simply a good friend who I enjoy spending time with. I was married more than twenty years, you know. The last thing I need to do is jump into another relationship."

"Okay, Mom. That's fine. Just have fun and enjoy your new life. I'm jealous you get to be that close to the beach all the time."

"So your advice is to take the new job?"

"In a heartbeat."

"And not move back to Pittsburgh?"

"To what? Not trying to be funny, but you obviously don't need to go back for the house or Dad. I still have a year left of college, so I won't be there. You have a new job, so that battle's done. Grab this, Mom. Grab hold and savor it. A lot of people dream to be in your position. In fact, I'm proud of you."

They wrapped up their conversation. Leslie felt better, more at ease, knowing Jasmine's reaction. She had one more call to make. She called the cell number of her boss back in Pittsburgh. Mrs. Peterson, but because they'd known each other so long, Bev.

Bev answered on the second ring and they chitchatted about Bev's summer as educators do. Then Leslie dove into the condensed story of her summer — the divorce papers being final, the sale of her home, her roadtrip and finally, the offer of a job down here at the beach.

"You're quitting?" Bev's voice took on a tinge of alarm.

"Well," Leslie faltered.

"You have a job here, and now a job there. You can't do them both."

Leslie sighed. "For some reason, this is so stressful for me."

"Can I ask you a question? Is there a man down there?"

"My gosh! Why is everyone asking me that? Jasmine just said something similar. It doesn't have anything to do with a man."

Bev smirked. "That doesn't really answer my question."

"I have met someone …"

"Say no more."

"No, but it's not like you think."

"Do you like him?"

"Well, yes, but …"

"Leslie, after what I saw you go through with Tim, I couldn't be happier for you. Life's too short, honey. You have to go where you're happiest."

Leslie sat silent.

Bev's voice was quiet and gentle. "You did the best you could with your marriage, Les. It wasn't salvageable."

Although she had rummaged through the same line of thought hundreds of times in the last year, now was not the time to re-rummage. "It's a big, big change and I don't want to do anything I'll regret later."

"So, your options are come back to Pittsburgh, find someplace to live, and go back to your old job, or move to South Carolina …"

"Right on the beach …"

"Yes, take the new job, and get to know this new guy better, see if it's something more permanent."

Bev had a way of getting right to the heart of the matter. "I guess so."

Bev sighed. "I know which one I'd take. Door number two!"

"Really?" Leslie's heart soared. Even her boss thought she should do it. "I want to make sure it's God's will for me."

Then, she asked tentatively, "Do you believe in God, by the way?"

Bev laughed. "I sure do. Have you prayed about this decision?"

"Endlessly. In fact, both Jaz and Hank think God's answer is clear. Why am I so wishy washy?"

"Because change is hard. And you've had more than your share of it lately. But it sounds like you've got a good thing going on down there. And if you've prayed about it, then I think … as crazy as it is for me to say this, since I'm negatively impacted … I think you've got your answer, Leslie."

Tears popped into her eyes. People were so good to her. She looked skyward. His message was clear to her now. "I can't thank you enough."

When she ended the call, she took a moment to control her emotions and thank her God for doing exactly what she asked Him — making it clear to her what His will was. And being patient with her while she came to accept it. She was staying.

One last call. She selected Tim's number from her contact list. He answered on the third ring. "Hello Tim, it's Leslie."

"Hi."

"I have big news. Well, for me, at least. This shouldn't impact you much."

"Okay."

"I'm not coming back to Pittsburgh."

"Ever?"

"I mean, I'm not going to live there. I'm staying in Pawleys Island."

She listened to him trying to form words, to catch up. "Where?"

She realized she'd never told him where she'd been all summer. "Pawleys Island, South Carolina. It's where I've been all summer. I've decided I'm staying here."

"Leslie, that's crazy. Think about it. Your whole life is in Pittsburgh. Your job, your friends, your family. Why on earth would you leave all that behind?"

"Tim, my whole life *was* in Pittsburgh. My family, you, Jasmine, our home. None of that is there for me anymore."

He sighed in exasperation. "Jasmine will need a place to stay when she comes home from college."

"Yes, and she can stay with me here, or you there."

"You want to make her travel to different cities to see us both?"

She shook her head. "You were the one that separated us, not me, Tim."

There was a pause on the line as he considered that. "What about your job? You've been there a long time. You're going to abandon your students and what about Bev?"

"Bev has a long list of applicants she can choose from to replace me. And she wished me well in my new life."

"Leslie, I advise you against this. You're not thinking straight. The child support and alimony I'm paying you will not last. You're going to need to find a job to provide income."

"I have a job."

At that announcement, she succeeded in striking him speechless. "Where?"

"Here, at the beach. I have skills, Tim, and experience. I got a new teaching job pretty easily. They said I was a top candidate. Jasmine is happy for me. And I've made new friends. I can always visit my old ones in Pittsburgh whenever I want. Or better yet, they can visit me here. It's a wonderful place to vacation."

Silence on the line made her wonder what he was thinking. "So…"

"So," she replied.

"I guess you're moving on."

"I had to, Tim. You pretty much forced me into that, didn't you?"

They discussed the house closing. No, she wouldn't be coming back for it, he will need to take care of it. Yes, she'd come back one more time to pack up her clothes and decide what to keep and what to donate. Of course, he didn't know it, but her car was still sitting there in the garage. She held firm with her decision that he'd be in charge of disbursing the furniture.

She was done with all of it.

Her new life stretched gloriously in front of her like the endless waves of the ocean surf.

Chapter Thirteen

The third week of August, following the quick trip to Pittsburgh that she'd promised Tim to finalize house business and retrieve her car, Leslie finally experienced the familiar sense of excitement over the pending school year. That little nip of "oh! It's coming!" all good teachers feel, if only for a moment or two. Now that her school year plans were set in stone, she was ready to prepare for her new class.

She drove to the school, a short distance from the Inn. She pulled a bag of supplies out of the back seat and carried them into the school. A secretary worked at a desk inside the office door, so she stepped in and introduced herself.

"Nice to meet you. Want to see which room is yours?"

"Sure, thanks."

The woman led her down a long hallway of doors to the very end. "They're in order. Kindergarten and first are closest to the office, older grades are further away. Sixth is the oldest we have at this school. I'm Pam, by the way."

"Leslie Malone. So glad to be here."

"We're glad to have you. It's unusual for us to have openings. Mrs. Robinson was glad to have experienced teachers to choose from."

Leslie nodded, but it wasn't until later when she'd been working in the classroom for a half hour or so, the comment came back to her. It was unusual for them, such a small school, to have teacher openings, several the same year. She smiled. God had a hand in that. She imagined Him up there, working desperately to answer her prayer, making every piece fall into place so she wouldn't miss it. He must really want her here.

And she was happy to obey.

Three hours later, the room had a respectable start to welcome her sixth graders. The walls were covered with interesting posters and thought-starters. The desks were arranged in clusters of four, conducive for group projects, and their nametags were laminated and taped to the backs of their assigned seats. She'd arranged the classroom into several breakout areas, so the students could leave their desks and take advantage of independent learning projects in other parts of the room. She gathered up an armful of additional laminates to cut out, along with her empty lesson plan book.

The late day sun was making its trek west when she got in her SUV. She headed to Hank's house to share what she'd accomplished in her classroom and see if she could convince him to celebrate with her, dinner outside the Inn, her treat for a change. She pulled up outside his house and knocked on the screen door before letting herself in. Jeremy stood in the living room, a ball cap on his head, the visor backwards, wearing a pair of khaki cargo shorts and a dirty tank shirt dripping in sweat. A leather belt, slung low on his hips, served as a home for a number of tools, and he wore a pair of worn work boots.

He looked up, surprised at her arrival. "Oh hi, Leslie."

"Hey there. You look like you're working hard."

Jeremy nodded. The living room was a mess of productivity and Jeremy was surrounded by evidence of home improvement projects. Furniture was shoved into the far corner the living room shared with the eating area, to allow room for what looked like two projects going on simultaneously. Four sawhorses were set up, a closet door resting on each pair. The pungent smell of wood stain permeated the tiny house. Resting against the front wall were two brand new vinyl replacement windows. At closer look, Leslie saw the two window frames in the living room were empty, the original contents had been removed.

"So, doors and windows, huh?"

"Yep. I bought two new doors to replace some nasty old ones, the coat closet and the powder room. I stained them, and I'm letting them dry some while I replace the two front windows. See here?" He stepped over a wrinkled tarp covering the floor and hoisted up one of the window units. "Whole set. The frame, the pane, the screen, all together. Just have to install it and nail it in, reinforce with glue. Only trick is making sure you double and triple checked the measurements." He smiled and his whole face lit up with the happiness of a kid on Christmas morning.

She nodded, not knowing a thing about window or door installation, but feeling warmth in her heart that he was using his talents and being productive. "Can I get you a glass of water or soda while you work?"

"That'd be great. Thank you."

She made her way carefully to the kitchen, poured a large glass of water with ice, grabbed a can of Pepsi from the fridge, and carried them both back. "There you go. I figured you could gulp the water first, then use the ice for the Pepsi."

"That's kind of you." He did exactly that with the water, drained it, and popped open the Pepsi can. "I'm sorry I can't really offer you anywhere to sit."

She looked around. There was literally nowhere to sit. "No, that's okay. Is your dad around?"

"Not yet, but he should be home in the next twenty or so. Want to stick around?"

"As long as I don't bother you."

"Not at all. I welcome the company."

Jeremy worked on the windows, and it amazed Leslie how quickly and easily he popped in the replacement window, following it up with nails and caulk. He expertly drew a line with the gun, swift and straight. When he was done, no cleanup was necessary. As he worked, Leslie told him about her afternoon in the classroom.

"Sounds like your class will have the luckiest kids in that whole school. I used to love having teachers like you. Even as a kid, I could tell which teachers were there because they loved kids, and which ones just wanted the end of the day to come."

"Really?"

"Absolutely. It seems to me a teacher who loves teaching would get a lot of satisfaction, every darn day."

She chuckled. She had to agree.

"So, you're doing work here for your dad?"

"Yep. Oh, I'm also putting out job applications, believe me. I really need to secure a paying job. Dad's got a big heart, letting me work on projects to get my skills back. It's been ages since I've done some of this stuff, but of course, I can't live off charity from my family forever."

The windows done, he moved to the doors. He tested the stain with his fingertips, rubbing them together to judge the wetness. Satisfied with one side, he picked the big door up in the air and flipped it over, resting it on the sawhorses so he could test the other side.

"I think this baby's dry. At least dry enough to put back in place." He made fast work of retrieving the hinges, screws and doorknobs. Leslie watched him secure the door on the coat closet, helping him by holding the door in place while he tightened the screws, then she followed him to the powder room while they repeated the task there.

Their chitchat continued while Jeremy cleaned up his work area, folding up the tarp covering the wood floor, moving the sawhorses back into the garage, mopping up the floor and moving the furniture back in place. His muscles strained with the fast effort and his skin glistened under a sheen of perspiration. Before long, the entire house was put back together, not even a trace of its former mess. Leslie sank into the brown leather couch and admired the new windows and door.

"Thanks for keeping me company. I better get going."

Leslie sat forward. "Don't you want to wait till your dad gets home?"

"Uh, no. That's all right. I've got something to do tonight and I think I'll want to shower up before I get started." He shook his arms out and Leslie laughed.

Her words popped out before she thought of how they might make him feel. "Got a date tonight?"

He smiled, but it was a sad one, and he didn't answer right away, as if he were actually considering how different his life would be if he were rushing home to take a shower after a long day of hard, honest work and freshen himself up for a lady he was fond of. "No, not a date. Not by a long shot."

"I'm sorry, Jeremy."

He squeezed her arm. "Don't be. Listen, if you leave before my dad gets home, could you lock up?"

"Sure. I plan to stay and see if he'd be interested in going out to dinner."

Jeremy paused and studied her face, his smile this time close-mouthed but sincere. "He's one lucky guy." He made for the door.

Leslie stood. "Jeremy, you don't have a vehicle out there."

He shook his head.

"How are you getting back to the inn?"

He shrugged. "I'll walk. It's not that far."

She grabbed her purse. "Don't be silly. I'll drive you."

"No, that's all right."

"It'll take me ten minutes to drive you over there and get back."

He waved his hand, palm facing her. "No, no. You sit down and relax. Believe me, I've been walking the streets of this island my whole life. It's relaxing to me. Bye now."

Ten minutes later, Hank's truck pulled into his driveway. Leslie still sat quietly in the living room, pondering the fast departure, almost like he knew exactly when to exit to avoid running into his father. When Hank entered through the open door, his expression turned from confusion to joy. "Hey, beautiful. What a nice surprise."

She rose as he approached and wrapped her in his arms. She inhaled and reveled in the sensation of being enveloped in him, his scent, his strength and his love. "I came by to tell you about my day of setting up my classroom."

"Ah, gotten started, have you? When's school start again?" He scratched the back of his ear and squinted at the ceiling.

"Two Wednesdays from now, starting with a half day."

"Wow, that's soon. You ready?"

"I will be." She squeezed him and stepped back. "I got to talk to Jeremy while he was here working."

He shook his head, then looked around with a suspicious glare. He pointed at the closet door. "This is new."

"And a matching one in the bathroom."

He left the room and returned moments later, looking angry.

"What's this about?" Leslie asked, confused.

"I don't want him spending what money he has on improvements for my house." He walked into the kitchen and she followed him. He reached into the refrigerator and pulled out a Pepsi. "His guilt is eating him up. It's not healthy."

"So, you're not assigning him this work?"

"No! He sneaks in like a Secret Santa, does jobs for me and sneaks out before I can say a word."

"And you're not paying for anything?"

"Nope. Although most of the jobs have been low cost." He pointed to the miniscule amount of wall not covered with cabinet or tile. "New paint." He pulled her into the great room and pointed to the walls, which, now that she was looking, Leslie could see were freshly painted. "Every inch of wall space in this entire house has fresh paint." He gave his head a brisk shake. "That, I don't mind. Buying a couple cans of paint is no big expense." He led her out the front door and turned, pointing at the house. "He's done the entire exterior, scraped, repainted."

Leslie ran a few fingers over the gray exterior and saw, indeed, it wasn't flaky like it had been. The paintjob made it look much more maintained and cared for.

Hank pointed at the wooden porch attached to the front of the house. "He's completely repaired and stained the lattice work on the porch, given it some reinforcements to the boards. Porch is much safer and more attractive now.

Those kinds of jobs, I don't mind. Minimal cost, just elbow grease and labor. But lately he's been buying expensive pieces. Like those doors."

They headed back inside. Leslie said hesitantly, "Then, continue the treasure hunt, because he replaced something else besides doors that probably cost him."

Hank squinted at her, then swung around in a semi-circle. "Holy mackerel! Windows?"

Leslie laughed and took a closer look around her. "You know, he's made quite a difference in here. This place is looking great. You haven't had time to do it. He's enjoying the work and getting good experience till he can get a job of his own. What's the harm in letting him?"

Hank shrugged. "I don't want him to feel guilted into it."

She laid a hand on his arm and said softly, "Maybe you need to give him this. Maybe he needs to pay you back some. Make him feel better."

He studied her for a minute, then nodded.

"How do you suppose he gets the money to buy some of these more expensive supplies?" Leslie asked.

"He told me he started building furniture in prison. They let him sell a few pieces and keep the money. I assume it's either out of his savings, or who knows, maybe he's made more."

"He's very hard working."

"Always was. That wasn't his problem."

She said no more.

"But I know he's having trouble finding work. There's one question on the application that, when answered honestly, stops them all in their tracks."

She rubbed his arm. He was aching for his boy, but there was nothing he could do about it. "I've come to take you out to dinner." Changing the subject seemed to be a good thing. "To celebrate the start of my class preparation."

He smiled and kissed her. "You're sweet. Give me fifteen minutes and I'll be out here, showered, shaved and fresh clothes."

Leslie chuckled and waved him off, amazed at how simple a man's preparations were. She had a seat and turned on his television for amusement until, as he promised, fifteen minutes later he emerged, hair damp, skin smelling of soap, dressed in a fresh pair of shorts and a button down cotton shirt. A smile jumped to her lips and he returned it. A few minutes later, they were in his truck.

They went to a rustic seafood place called the Crab Trap. It was a tourist favorite so they waited forty minutes for their table, but they passed the time easily with conversation.

"I've got some exciting news," Leslie said over her salad.

Hank nodded.

"Jasmine is coming back to the States next week."

He smiled. "Will you get to see her?"

"Yes. She's coming here next weekend. She'll have over a week before she has to head back to school. Tim will pick her up from the airport and she'll stay at his place for about three days, then she'll drive down here for a little beach time. And Mom time." Just saying it made her heart jump with excitement. She put her fork down. She was so excited, even eating lost its appeal.

"And that's before your school starts, eh?"

"Yes! I'll have uninterrupted time to spend with her. Guess I better work hard over the next few days to finish up my room and my lesson plans."

"So happy for you, darlin'. I can't wait to meet her."

Leslie ducked her head. "I've told her all about you."

"Oh boy. The good, the bad and the ugly, huh?" The topic didn't seem to affect his appetite. He finished his salad and pushed the plate away.

The joy of the evening took over and she let out a happy giggle. "I have a feeling she'll like you. She's a good judge of character."

"I'll have to be on my best behavior."

"Don't you dare. Just be yourself."

They ate their dinner, sharing three pounds of crab legs. Leslie liked crabmeat but had never done all the cracking herself. Hank reached over the table to show her the technique and after some practice, she was doing pretty well. However, when all the legs were devoid of meat, she had to wonder if it was worth all the effort.

After dinner, they walked the beach outside the restaurant. They talked about how good life was, how much had changed for both of them since they'd met that day at the Old Gray Barn. Jeremy and Hank had reconciled a decade-long riff, resulting in healing and forgiveness for both of them. Jeremy was out of prison and getting his feet on the ground, preparing for the next stage of his life. Leslie started out taking a roadtrip with no destination and ended up making a life-changing move. Amazing what can happen when you put your faith in God and follow where He leads.

They did not discuss, however, the two of them. It was the one topic they didn't want to touch, for fear of it falling apart like leaves holding fragilely onto their branches in the last gasp of fall. He wasn't just a person her age to chat with, to share similar life experiences with. She'd always known, from the moment she saw him, that he was a handsome man. Now, she'd started thinking of him in terms of being *her* handsome man. She enjoyed the sight of him, no matter if he was working, sweaty and dusty, or cleaned up and sitting across from her at a dinner table. It mattered not. She found him attractive either way.

And what about that off-handed "love you, darlin'" comment he'd made a few weeks ago? There had never been a repeat, and she'd been too apprehensive about broaching the subject again. How would she, without feeling like a total idiot, or putting him on the spot?

She loved the feel of her hand in his as they walked the beach, loved when he reached out to capture her hand. It was such a simple, yet romantic gesture. He wanted to touch her, to be connected with her. When was the last time Tim …?

She gave her head a brisk shake at that line of thought. It didn't matter what her relationship with Tim had been like, because her relationship with Hank was completely different. Tim had his faults, but he had been a good husband and father for a long while. She wasn't going to completely trash all memories of her two decades with him. Because Tim was in her past. Did that mean Hank was her future?

A sigh escaped her lips, and Hank turned his head toward her as they walked. "I get the impression you're thinking something up there in that beautiful head. Care to share?"

She smiled. "Not a thing. Enjoying the sand under my feet, my hand in yours, and the warm breeze in my face. How about you?"

* * *

Later that night after Hank left, Leslie arrived back at the Inn. The great room was a hustle bustle of activity. It appeared a new family, who had arrived today, were meeting there, lengthening their evening after a delicious dinner in

Marianne's dining room, not quite wanting to say good night yet.

Leslie knew the feeling. She didn't want tonight to end yet either. Her heart was bursting with excitement about how life was evolving: her new classroom, her new relationship, Jasmine coming to visit soon. Life couldn't be any better. The only thing left on her list was to remedy the housing situation — find a more permanent place to live. But if that was the worst thing to worry about, then life was definitely good. Living full-time in an ocean front inn where most people go for vacation, was not a hardship.

She skirted the edges of the great room, leaving the family to their celebration, went through to the back porch, then out onto the outdoor patio. Leaning over the railing, she let the sound of the massive ocean waves overtake her. She closed her eyes and thought about how much she loved the ocean, and how lucky she was to live here now.

Mingled amidst the sounds of the waves, came another sound. A hammer pounding nails. A motorized machine, possibly a sander or screw driver. Someone was busy working on something. Creating something, possibly. Curious, Leslie pushed off from the railing and headed down the boardwalk toward the beach. When she reached the sand, she turned and walked back toward the inn. Led by the sounds of construction, she walked to the side of the Inn, then out to the front of it. There, bathed in a surprising amount of light by a makeshift set of lanterns, Jeremy worked. Pairs of wooden sawhorses held cut pieces of wood in various stages of staining. A huge piece of stained, finished wood lay on a tarp on the grass. He wore earbuds connected to thin wire cords. He concentrated on his task, rubbing sandpaper over a circular tube of wood, occasionally running his fingers over it, then back to the sandpaper. The electric sander provided rare help with a particularly rough patch.

She stood nearby, but he hadn't noticed her, so entranced was he in his work. She didn't intend to spy on him, but she paused before announcing her presence, and studied him at work. Patient and diligent, working with the sandpaper, then rubbing lovingly with his fingers, transforming the wood from a rough natural resource to a useful thing of beauty.

She waited until he laid down his tools. "Jeremy, hello again."

He looked up and saw her, gave her a wave and a grin. "Hi, yourself." He took off a dusty ball cap and drew his arm over his forehead. Moisture glistened on his scalp, visible through his short-cropped hair.

She gestured to the work he was doing. "Whatcha got going on here?"

He glanced around at his makeshift workshop, pulling the buds from his ears. "I'm making wooden furniture. It sort of started as a time burner, a chance to practice a new skill. I found out I liked it, then I found out I'm pretty good at it. I made a few pieces for customers, and sold them." He looked back her way and puffed out some air. "While I'm between jobs I figured I'd build up an inventory. Maybe sell them at craft fairs or make a deal with some stores in town. You know. See if anyone would want to partner with me."

She only saw the sadness in his eyes because she was staring into them, listening to him. Her mother's heart broke at the position this young man was in, had put himself in. And he wasn't complaining, no, not at all. He was taking responsibility and doing the best he could, with help from his family. But she couldn't help but imagine where he'd be in life if he'd gone down the path intended for him, instead of the detour he'd thrown in his own way. Successful family business, take over the management from his dad, probably a big house, maybe a start of a family of his own. Instead, he was an ex-con tiptoeing back into life, trying to figure out where he fit and dodging one roadblock after another.

She didn't know him well, and she wasn't his mother, but she followed her maternal instinct. She took a few steps to him and pulled him into a hug. "Jeremy, you're such a hard worker. You're going to get back on your feet. Your dad will be proud of you again. And your mom would be proud, too."

His shoulders tensed at her last statement and she feared she'd gone too far. He stayed motionless while she patted him on the back, then stepped away. "Oh believe me Leslie, I've given neither of them any reason to be proud of me yet. But I intend to. Don't you doubt that. I've got a ways to go to pay for my mistakes. And I won't take a dime more from my family than I have to." He turned and waved at the Inn. "My sister is so generous to let me stay here, but I hate taking up one of her rooms. I'll help out by doing any home repair jobs she needs. I've asked her for a list."

"And you're doing a lot over at your dad's house."

He ducked his head. "It's my fault Dad lost his big, beautiful house. He's done paying the price for my mistakes. That's my job now. So, although I can't buy him his house back, I can sure spend time fixing up the one he's got."

"You've made a lot of improvements. It's made a big difference."

"Well, thank you, but no. It's made a miniscule difference. But when I get done with it, it'll be a nice place he can be proud of. I've got a lot of landscaping and yard work to do, some plumbing and general modernization. It's fun. Heck, all I've got right now is time."

"So, you're working on your dad's house by day and building furniture by night?" She motioned to his work area.

He turned back. "Yeah. This here's gonna be a dining room table, a big jobber. It'll seat twelve easily." He took a few steps to the large piece of finished wood leaning against a pair of sawhorses. "This here's the tabletop. I finished it tonight." He drew the fingers of one hand over it.

"It's beautiful. Look at this grain." Leslie came closer and took in the full beauty of the piece. "What kind of wood is it? I love the lighter blonde color."

"Maple. Dining room tables generally get knocked around, setting dishes on top of it and what not. Maple's a durable hard wood that should work well." He picked up one of the tube-shaped pieces. "I'm working on the legs now. Pretty simple design. The top, the legs, and a pedestal underneath to strengthen it. I picture it in a big beach house dining room or casual kitchen."

"I love it."

"Thanks. Marianne's got a shed over here she's offered to let me store things, but I need to start selling pretty quick here. To bring in cash for more projects, and to alleviate crowding." He let his hands drop to his sides. "So, that's what I'm doing."

"I'll be happy to spread the word however I can."

His face softened. "I sure appreciate that. And Leslie, thanks for asking and being interested."

She gave him a squeeze, right at the elbow and decided to call it a night. "See you."

* * *

The next few days were taken up with putting the finishing touches on her classroom, writing the first week's lesson plans and talking to Jasmine on the phone. It killed her that she wasn't in Pittsburgh to pick Jasmine up from the airport after such a monumental trip in her daughter's life. But she had to remind herself, life was different now. Jasmine was practically an independent woman, she and Tim had split up their parenting duties, and Leslie had a life to live at the beach. That didn't mean she couldn't keep in close touch with Jaz as she made her way across the ocean, landed in the US, and finally got picked up safe and sound by her dad.

Now, her daughter would have a few days to acclimate to the US, her dad's new digs, and then … it was all about mom and daughter time.

On Thursday, Leslie's jitters were so intense she couldn't concentrate on anything. Fortunately, her lesson plans for week one were done. The few tasks remaining in her classroom didn't require a brain, just some hands, so she headed over there to finish up. Mrs. Robinson chided her for being ready almost a full week early, but when Leslie told her Jasmine was coming, the principal understood. Mothers have a way of knowing how children can turn plans around.

Jasmine had said to expect her around five, but Leslie knew from periodic phone calls throughout the day, she was making excellent time. Leslie returned to the Inn by 3:30. At 3:40 her cell rang and it was Jasmine.

"I'm here!" she sang. "I think. It's rustic, isn't it?"

Leslie let out a whoop. "Well, it's not your Marriott or Hilton."

"That's okay. So I park in the sand lot, then up the stairs?"

"Yep. I'm leaving now. I'll meet you in the front."

Chapter Fourteen

The girl looked more beautiful than Leslie could imagine possible. Long, silky hair, waves of brunette bouncing over her shoulders as she walked, then broke into a run to meet her. Her smile was salve for a sore heart after months of being apart, and Leslie bathed in it before grabbing her and pulling her close. She sank her face into Jasmine's hair, breathing in the scent of her, familiar yet different, a new perfume picked up in Paris, but still her little girl, now grown, back in her arms again.

Leslie couldn't help the tears sprouting in her eyes, and she didn't even try to tamp them down. Jasmine wouldn't mind the waterworks; in fact, she'd probably be crying herself when they parted.

"I love you so much, Jaz. I'm so glad to see you," she murmured and Jasmine squeezed her arms tighter around Leslie.

Finally they parted and Leslie captured Jasmine's face in her hands so she could study her closely, see how much this summer abroad had changed her, transformed her from the Jasmine she'd always known. She'd picked up a heavier makeup style this summer, but her skin was glowing and healthy and there was absolutely nothing that looked better to Leslie.

"I'm so glad I'm here! You have to show me around. I can't believe all the changes you've made this summer." They strolled to the car and retrieved Jasmine's suitcase. She grinned at her mom. "You sold the house, sold your furniture, quit your job, moved to the beach! Look at you, woman! Awesomeness!"

Leslie chuckled. Not to mention the divorce. "One other big change this summer. I'm letting God lead the way. I'm listening constantly for His guidance, and I'm following His plan, not mine. I can honestly say, this is exactly where God wants me to be." She chuckled. "How lucky am I?"

Jasmine shook her head in amazement. "Wow. Lucky, indeed. I'm proud of you, Mom."

They headed across the street and climbed the front steps to the Inn. In the great room, Marianne bustled as usual behind the front desk. But she was aware of Jasmine's planned arrival time, and the minute she saw them, she broke into a huge smile and came out from behind.

"Marianne, I'd like to introduce you to …"

"You don't have to!" Marianne interrupted. "This child is your carbon copy. Jasmine, so nice to meet you."

"And this is Marianne, the innkeeper."

Jasmine grinned and they shook hands.

"I've had so much fun getting to know your mother. So glad she's sticking around now."

Leslie could feel her face blushing. "That's so sweet of you."

Marianne continued, "You make yourself at home and enjoy the beach, you hear?"

Jasmine nodded.

"How long can you stay?"

"My semester starts next week so I'm glad I have a few days to spend with her, see her new place, her new job, her new m…"

Leslie nudged her. She knew Jasmine was going to say "man." Her lips had formed around the m, and she could hear it popping out. And that would be a definite mistake, considering Marianne was the "m's" daughter. Of course, Jasmine didn't know that.

Jasmine turned to her mom with a confused expression. "M … m … map!"

Marianne frowned. "Her new map?"

Jasmine stared at her mom. Leslie shrugged. Jasmine turned back to Marianne. "Yes. Mom has trouble with directions. Can you imagine how she'd get along down here on her own, driving all over creation without a good map? I want to check it out, you know, make sure she's safe."

Marianne laughed and Leslie joined her. "Oh, she's safe. And she's rarely on her own. Usually, wherever your mom is, my dad isn't too far away."

Jasmine stared. "Your dad is …?"

"Hank. Surely she's mentioned …"

"Oh! You're Hank's daughter! Of course. I can't wait to meet him."

"You'll probably have a chance soon." She turned to Leslie. "Is he coming over for dinner?"

Leslie shook her head. "No, he wanted to give Jaz and me a chance to re-acclimate. He said he'd catch up with us tomorrow."

"That makes sense. Well, have a good stay." She dipped her head to Jasmine, then went back to work.

Their evening was spent walking the beach, Jasmine sharing endless stories about her summer in Paris, her excitement over interning in the most important city in the fashion world, her experiences that would launch a resume. They talked about Leslie's summer in Pawleys Island, how she was looking forward to teaching a new class at a new school, her sense of security that God was looking out for her and all would work out the way it should.

In the middle of the talk marathon, they attended dinner in the dining room and enjoyed a delicious meal of grilled shrimp primavera, salad and pecan pie ala mode for dessert. They ended up on the patio with a cup of decaf coffee before turning in to their shared room.

As Leslie drifted off to a happy and satisfied sleep, she whispered, "Thank you God, for sending Jasmine here."

The next morning, they slipped into their suits and set up shop on the white sands of the beach, their reclining chairs tucked under a big umbrella, sunscreen, magazines and books, along with a cooler of cold drinks.

"It's been so long since I've done this," Jasmine said. "I haven't gotten any beach time all summer. I never had a moment for it. Ahhhh…" She rested her head back on the padded chair and closed her eyes. "This is the life." She rolled her head in Leslie's direction. "I can't believe you can do this every day if you want."

Leslie smiled. "Not for much longer. School starts in less than a week."

Jasmine let her eyes drift closed again, soaking in the sun. "I wonder if island kids are any different than Pittsburgh kids."

"Maybe in some ways. But probably not by much."

A drowsy ten minutes quieted them. Then Jasmine said quietly, "I'm so sorry for what Daddy did to you."

Leslie popped her eyes open, glanced over at her daughter, who still had hers closed. "It's not your fault, you know Jaz. I mean, it had absolutely nothing to do with you."

Jasmine nodded. "Oh, I know. But I can still be sorry. I hate that he cheated on you and broke your vows and destroyed your marriage. I'm sorry for how he made you feel. And I'm so proud of you for living your own life, even though it means a bunch of changes."

"Our family has changed forever. And it'll never be the way it was before."

"You guys gave me a great childhood. You are both super parents."

Leslie's heart warmed hearing that.

The afternoon passed with breaks for dips in the ocean, walks along the shoreline and lunch in the Inn. By late afternoon, they packed up and headed back for showers and cool clothes. They rubbed lotion on each other's shoulders to moisturize their sunburns.

"Hank's coming over to join us for dinner here."

Jasmine flipped around, causing Leslie to squirt a dab of lotion on her blouse. "Goodie! I can't wait to meet the new man."

Leslie rolled her eyes. "Jasmine, remember all those times you told me not to embarrass you in front of your boyfriend?"

Jasmine giggled.

"Well, I beg of you. Don't say or do anything embarrassing. I'm serious. I'm so new to the dating scene, I don't even know what I don't know. Besides, I don't know where we're headed. And I certainly don't want a serious relationship, just months after I signed my divorce papers. I should probably go solo for a while and figure out who I am as a single person." Leslie shook her head, then grinned at her daughter. "Be cool, okay, and go with the flow."

Jasmine bounded across the room and took her mother by the shoulders. "That's me, floating along. Up for anything. And I'm not about to embarrass you, don't worry. I can't wait to meet the hunk." Leslie started to protest. "I mean, the Hank!"

They went down to the great room. She spotted Hank before he realized he was being watched. He stood by the fireplace, his hands in his pockets, then he pulled them out and rested them at his sides. He ran fingers through his hair, then back into his pockets.

She walked up to him and placed a kiss on his cheek. He jolted, then gave her an eyebrows-up greeting with a smile. "Hi, beautiful." And he leaned in for another kiss, this time right on her lips. When she pulled away, she wasn't the only one blushing. Jasmine was too, watching the show.

"Hank," she took his elbow and reached out to Jasmine with the other hand. "I want you to meet Jasmine. Jasmine, this is Hank." She pulled the two most important people in her life right now, together to meet. As they shook hands, nodded and made friendly introductory comments together, Leslie pulled her mind away from the action for a moment to wonder, two most important people in her life?

Jasmine, of course. But when had she started thinking of Hank that way? And what did it tell her that she'd come to the conclusion without analyzing, without ranking, without any thought whatsoever? It was a natural conclusion.

Marianne rescued her from her runaway thoughts by calling them to their table. They followed her in, then sat, Hank pulling out first Jasmine's chair, then hers. Southern gentleman to a tee. She almost forgot how unusually nice it was, except that Jasmine flashed her a "get a load of this" look. And then she remembered how impressed she'd been with Hank's manners at first. She must be so used to them now she didn't give them another thought.

After salad and before the entree, Jasmine asked if Leslie would show her where the rest room was. Leslie nodded and herded her out of the dining room, through the great room and into the hallway to the rest room door. Jasmine leaned in close with a huge grin and whispered, "Hank is a hunk, Mom! You were right. He definitely reminds me of Harrison Ford!" She giggled and stepped into the restroom.

Leslie's heart rate picked up its pace and she felt her cheeks blushing again. Never in her life had she introduced her "boyfriend" to her daughter. It was unnerving and her body was reacting to the experience.

"What's up?" Hank asked as she sat down.

She picked up his hand and rubbed it with her thumb. "My daughter thinks you're a hunk."

"Oh, Lordy." He shook his head but she hoped he was pleased with the assessment.

"I think she really likes you. Well," she patted his hand and put her own back in her lap, "who wouldn't?"

Jasmine returned and the three of them talked easily about a number of topics, enjoying their dinner. They ordered coffee when the plates had been cleared away. While they were waiting Hank said, "Jasmine, do you mind if I have a few minutes of private time with you? Leslie, if I may?"

Leslie glanced over at Jasmine who looked delighted. "Be my guest." The two of them stood and Hank led her daughter into the great room, then out the front door.

Curiosity gripped her, which quickly turned into worry, dread and was working on a full-blown panic, when they returned. Maybe ten minutes had passed, and they slid into their seats, followed closely by the arrival of the coffee. Her heart returning to a more manageable rate, she couldn't help but ask, "What was that all about? What are you two up to?"

Jasmine let out a soft screech of excitement and her eyes sparkled. "Nothing, Mom. Not a thing. Nada."

Hank watched her, amused. "Nothing for you to worry about, sweetheart."

The rest of the evening passed, three people enjoying each other; stories shared, laughter spilled and affection flowed freely. When it was time for Hank to leave, he took Leslie's chin in his fingers, brought her close and took his time with a long, slow kiss. Leslie momentarily forgot about Jasmine, lost herself in his kiss. When she said good night and watched him leave, Jasmine pinched her arm.

"Oh, you've got it bad, Mom. I'd say … you're in love!"

"No," Leslie started, instinctually denying the allegation, but not sure why. "I don't know. It's too soon …"

It was the same argument she always came up with when she let her mind wander to the exact nature of her feelings for Hank. She'd spent twenty years married to Tim. It only ended three months ago. Wasn't it too soon?

"Ridiculous. If you love him, and he loves you, and you have nothing holding the two of you apart, then why not go for it?"

Leslie started to sputter. "What? First of all, go for what? What exactly would I be going for? And I don't know if I'm in love with him, and who on earth said he was in love with me?"

Jasmine tsked and gave her hand a patronizing pat. "Oh Mom, it's so obvious he's in love with you, I'm surprised you can't see it."

Leslie's breath hitched. "Did he tell you that when he pulled you aside? What was that all about, by the way?"

They headed back to the room. "No, he didn't have to tell me. It's written all over his face. When he looks at you. When he looks *for* you. When you talk, he listens. He cares about what you think and what you say. Let's face it, how long has it been since D …, I mean, since a man did that?"

Leslie shrugged.

"Mom, it's totally up to you of course, but Hank's the real deal. The only advice I can give you is, listen to your heart, and don't say no just because you think that's the responsible thing to do."

She shook her head. "Say no … to what? What am I saying yes or no to?"

Jasmine grinned. "Nothing. In case a question pops up." They reached the door and Leslie used her key to open the door. The rest of the evening, they were like girls at a slumber party, painting their nails and chatting endlessly until they could no longer keep their eyes open.

The next few days with Jasmine passed so quickly, it pained Leslie's heart to watch them slip by. She kept reminding herself, she was home. She was back in the US. It'd be easier to see her now.

But it wasn't long before she and Hank walked her to her car, Hank carrying her suitcase, sliding it into the trunk for her, shutting it firmly. A million admonishments circled through Leslie's mind … drive safely, good luck at school, study hard, watch your grades, etc. But she said none of them. Her little girl was a grown up now, and the last thing she needed was a bunch of words from her mom they both knew wouldn't make any difference.

So she said the words that always made a difference. "I love you, Jasmine." She pulled her daughter into a long embrace and worked to memorize the feel of her in her arms, the smell of her in her nostrils.

When they parted, she stepped away and into Hank's arm, wrapped around her shoulder, and it felt good. Great not to be alone, and great to be with this man her daughter had deemed "the real deal."

Chapter Fifteen

School started. As it turned out, kids on Pawleys Island weren't too drastically different than children in Pittsburgh during their first week back to school after a long summer of fun, leisure and sleeping in. Of course, her kids were sixth graders this year, not the third graders she'd grown accustomed to. And sixth graders were close enough to being teenagers that they checked at the door anything resembling enthusiasm or optimism about a new school year, or for that matter, a new teacher. It wasn't cool to appear excited. But she knew their game, and she could tell which students were in fact, excited and which ones absolutely weren't.

The first week flew by, and the evenings were accompanied by the familiar exhaustion she'd known for sixteen Septembers now. The desire to plop into a recliner immediately upon hitting the front door, feet up, eyes closed, voice resting. Maybe a glass of wine to calm her nerves. Stay there until the grumbling of her stomach required her to go find some food, which currently, while staying at the Inn, was blessedly easy to find. Then, it was back to schoolwork — grading papers, preparing lessons for tomorrow, arranging displays to hang on the walls. It would get easier as the year progressed, as she got to know the kids better, to understand the dynamic of this particular class. But for now, her days were dedicated to school, school, and more school.

The end of September, her life started to be hers again. Her class was under control. She could spend a few weekend hours on lesson plans and be pretty well set for the week. Sure, she graded papers every evening, but generally she could do that type of work while watching TV, listening to music or the sound of the ocean waves.

Hank had developed an evening routine of coming to the inn and sitting with her while she graded papers. Tonight, she was rubbing the kink in her neck and stretching her back before proceeding on to the next stack. He looked up and noticed, then patted the seat on the recliner he sat in. "Come here."

She looked over at him. "Hmm?"

He motioned to his lap, and she came over to sit on his recliner with him, tandem style, him straddling the chair and her nestled into his outstretched legs. She rested her stack of paper on the seat in front of her, and massaged her neck and shoulders.

"Oohhhh," she groaned, unable to stop it.

He chuckled behind her, rubbing the kinks out of her neck and shoulders, up onto her scalp under her hair, and back again. And he never got tired. The massage lasted upwards of an hour. It felt so good. He knew just where to touch her, and how hard or soft to rub. What had she ever done without him? And how would she have ever gotten through this first month at a new school, a new class, a new grade, without him?

As she wrapped up the papers for this evening and soaked in the pleasure of his hands, she let her mind wander for a moment. She wouldn't even be here if it weren't for him.

Sure, she loved Pawleys Island and always had, but she would not have made such a life-changing move from Pittsburgh if it hadn't been for him.

Over the last month, their relationship had grown closer, stronger. Together, they were like pulling on your best pair of jeans that fit you to a tee. It was so comfortable, talking, laughing, sharing each other's days. Their personalities melded, a custom fit. She never had to bite her tongue to avoid a subject that would make him explode, like she at times had to with Tim. The man didn't seem to have any explosion points. No ticking time bombs. He was a simple man, and he was easy to be around.

But that didn't mean there wasn't a burning attraction between them. So far, they had remained positively chaste in their physical interactions. They'd kiss, and Leslie would feel her heart rate soar, feelings long dormant coming to the surface. They'd seek each other's hands to hold, and they'd caress shoulders and necks and faces.

It was nice. But it wasn't enough.

Lately, Leslie surprised herself with her level of desire. Sometimes she ached with her need to explore him more, to open herself to him. She wanted to know if he felt the same way, and she thought he did. At times they'd be kissing and he'd stop, stand up, take a few steps away, shaking his hands out. Then suddenly, there'd be a reason for him to leave. "Early morning tomorrow," was his favorite line, or "Gotta go pick up Jeremy."

She never pushed him, but she wondered. Did he want her as well?

One Saturday afternoon at the end of the month, they were shopping for groceries. Leslie picked up a bag of potatoes and put it in the cart. No need to ask him if he needed them. The last time she'd made dinner for him, she'd used the last one. And Hank was a man who loved his potatoes.

"The Old Gray Barn is going up on the market," he said out of the blue.

"What? You're kidding."

He shook his head as he pushed the cart. "Owners want to retire out west and they need the capital to buy their own place out in Arizona or wherever."

Leslie nodded, pondering the timing of her absolute favorite house in the world going up on the market, around the time she had equity money she needed to reinvest. As much as she loved the Seaside Inn, she'd tired of living in a hotel. Sure, it was convenient and quaint. But unconventional. She was starting to yearn for a real home. (Would she be considered homeless?) "I wonder how much they want for it," she mused, then looked up at him.

"Let's find out." He grinned broadly.

"Probably way over my price range. That place is huge. And oceanfront."

They headed for the checkout line. "You may be surprised. For one thing, it's old, and although it's in great shape, it does take a lot of effort and TLC to keep it that way. Many buyers looking for beachfront property want something more modern."

He paid for the groceries and loaded them into his truck. Then they drove to the realtor's office. In a display rack right inside the front door, he scanned the full-page informational sheets, spotted the one he wanted, and whipped it out. He took a look, then handed it to her.

She gasped when she saw the price. It was high. But what did she expect? It was a beachfront single home at a vacation destination. She sighed and handed it back. "So much for that."

He didn't take it. He squinted at it. "Over your price range?"

She nodded, disappointed. She had really wanted it to work out. She was searching for a home, and what house had felt more like home for her entire life? She wanted answers about where she should settle for good, here or Pittsburgh. What would've been a clearer answer than if she could move into The Old Gray Barn?

"By how much?"

She stilled and looked at him. "What do you mean?"

"How much did you want to spend?"

She thought about it, then shrugged. "I really don't know. I haven't thought about it."

A realtor strolled over. "Hi Hank. You here on the job?"

"Nah. Just looking." He motioned to the brochures.

The realtor's ears visibly perked up. "You interested in something in particular?"

He poked a thumb in her direction. "This little lady's stayed in The Old Gray Barn every summer since she was a young'un. She can't believe it's up for sale. But she's got a bit of sticker shock."

Leslie glanced at him, wide-eyed. The way he was talking made it sound like she was really interested. Which she wasn't. Definitely not, at that price. She couldn't afford it. No way.

Could she?

"That's a new listing, and we probably won't be lowering the list price until it's been on the market a few weeks. But I do know the owners have plans to leave the area. I think they'd consider any reasonable offer." The man shuffled in his breast shirt pocket for business cards, handing one to Hank and one to Leslie. "My name's Doug Martin. I'd be happy to work with you, answer any questions you may have."

Hank took charge. "Why don't Leslie and I figure out her financials, and we'll give you a call?"

They shook hands, then Leslie and Hank headed back to his truck. The whole drive back to Hank's house, she studied the paper, mainly focused in on the big six-digit number with a dollar sign in front. Hank carried the groceries inside and quickly put them away. When she noticed the absence of activity, she looked over at him. He stood in the kitchen, studying her.

"Do you want me to help you figure out your price range?" he ventured.

"Yes. Yes, I do." Who was she kidding? She'd never bought a place on her own before. And even when she'd bought their last house, her income didn't qualify for the loan, it was Tim's. She'd never been a numbers gal.

He strolled over to the table, a pad of paper in his hand. "You don't mind sharing numbers with me? It's mighty personal stuff."

"No, I don't mind." She smiled. It hadn't even occurred to her to hesitate sharing her information with him.

So, the next forty minutes they bowed over the paper, Hank asking questions about assets and debt, bills and income, inheritance and equity. Finally, they came up with a six-digit number of her own on the bottom of the page. Hank circled it in red.

"It's not as big as the number on the sheet." She shuffled underneath their papers and pulled out the realtor's sheet. "I'm short."

"Mmmm hmmmm." He tapped on the number with his pen. "But not by much. Would you want to rent it out? Get some income from it?"

She shrugged. "Why would I buy a beautiful house on the beach and then not even live in it myself? Especially when I don't have anywhere else to live, other than a hotel?"

"That's what I figured."

She shoved the papers away. "It's a pipedream, Hank. It doesn't even make sense. It's a huge vacation home. It can accommodate dozens of people. Why would I live out there all by myself?" She sighed. "I think I'm just feeling nostalgic. I've always loved that place, all my summers there, and I have so many wonderful memories there. I need a place to live, so I think I'm trying to force-fit it. If I want to live on the beach I should probably find a condo or something. Don't you think?"

She turned to him but he didn't look convinced.

"What if you weren't alone out there?" he asked. "Would that change your mind?"

"A roommate? I don't know. I'm not crazy about living with someone I don't know. Not at my age."

He looked like he was going to say something, but he shook his head instead. "Give me a week, will you? Don't make a decision for an entire week, and let me work on something. If it works out, I'll tell you. If it doesn't, you can look for something else."

She took in the determination etched into the lines on his face, the optimistic look in his eyes. "What are you up to?"

"One week."

"Okay."

"Now, what about those steaks?"

* * *

The week passed quickly with Leslie's new school year routine: waking to the sounds of ocean waves crashing on the beach, taking a brisk two-mile walk on the sand, enjoying a continental or hot breakfast with coffee at the Inn, heading out to school. Her class had settled in. She was enjoying teaching the older kids, while still adjusting to their inflated attitudes. In the evenings, she'd see Hank and they'd spend simple time together, eating, shopping, occasionally taking in a movie, but always talking and sharing their day, their stories. At the Inn, Marianne had become a friend and Leslie looked forward to seeing her as well as Stella, who always brought a smile to her face.

The next Saturday, Hank came over to the Inn for lunch. Guests had diminished due to the end of summer, so they had the corner of the dining room to themselves. Once Marianne had served them their tuna salad on croissants and fruit plate, Hank said, "I have some news about the Old Gray Barn."

Leslie nodded. She looked up from her lunch plate to see his intense look of concentration.

"Do you remember that number in red I circled last week? The amount you're short for buying the Barn?" She nodded. "Well, I've come up with a way to cover that amount."

She stilled. "Hank, I don't want to be in debt up to my ears. This stuff is all new to me and …"

He placed his hand on top of hers. "No additional debt for you."

She frowned. "Tell me."

He cleared his throat and put his fork down. "Darlin', I can't give you many details at this time. But I can tell you I've researched it and I know it'll work. This is the answer to your fund shortage. You put a bid in on the house. If it is accepted, I'll put this plan into play and I promise you, you'll eventually know everything about it. But I gotta do things in the right order, in the right time. It's not the time to reveal everything right now."

She stared. A flicker of nerves penetrated. "I don't understand. This is something really important. I know you're helping me, but I don't get it. What, is this some phantom investor or something?"

He smiled. "No, not at all. You don't need to know the whole story right now, trust me. All I need to know is, if you were able to buy the house for the amount we wrote on the paper last week — the amount you could come up with, before the shortage, would you want to? Would you buy the house?"

All went silent. It felt like her life was on the line. So much rode on the answer. If she bought the Barn, she'd be committing to staying here on Pawleys Island long-term, paying off a long mortgage loan, something she'd never done on her own before. Was she jumping into this? Was she making an impetuous decision because of her childhood sentimentality?

Or was God leading her here? It was always so difficult to tell.

So she grabbed both Hank's hands and held them in her own. "Let's pray about it, Hank. Right now. I want to know what God wants me to do."

He smiled, bowed his head and closed his eyes. She admired his profile for a short moment before she did the same.

"Dear Lord, first I want to thank You. Thank You for all the blessings in my life, and there are so many, I can't even count them all. They're all due to You. Thank You for putting me in the position that this decision is even possible. I can't imagine my good fortune in being able to buy the house of my dreams, the house I've spent so many wonderful months in. But here it is, God. Hank tells me I can afford it. I have no idea what that means, or how much money I'd be spending every month, but I trust him, God. He wouldn't lead me astray. What I want to know now, and You know You have to make it clear to me, is, what is Your will? What do You want me to do about this? Did You lead me down this path? Is it a blessed path or will it lead to disaster? Please tell me." She looked up at Hank. He was concentrating on her words. "And quick. Please."

He chuckled. Together, "Amen."

"Take your time. An answer will come. You'll feel it."

"I know. But it's sure feeling right." She stood and shook out her hands. "I don't know if it feels right because I want it so bad — selfishly — or if God is giving me the green light."

Hank picked up his fork. "How about we finish lunch, then go for a swim?"

She couldn't think of anything better.

* * *

Monday evening, Leslie headed over to Hank's house. He wasn't home from work yet, but she let herself in with the key he'd given her. She walked through the living room, straight to the kitchen. On her way to the refrigerator to see what she could start for dinner, she gasped. The kitchen cabinets. They'd all been re-stained and they were practically glowing with a fresh, new pecan color. Jeremy'd been at it again.

Delighted, she inspected the cabinets more closely. They were gorgeous. Jeremy had worked very hard on them and done a professional-caliber job. Fitting them in between paid odd jobs, and his new furniture building venture. Why did he take the time to re-do his dad's cabinets when she was sure Dad hadn't requested it?

She ran her fingers over the smooth, glossy surface. Did Hank know? Oh, he'd grumble about Jeremy spending his time doing this free job when he should be working for pay. But Jeremy's heart was in the right place.

Leslie pulled two chicken breasts out of the freezer and stuck them in the microwave. She thawed them, and dug into the small pantry. She found a can of cream of chicken soup. Making a simple concoction, she combined the chicken, light seasoning, sliced potatoes and soup, covered it with a lid and slid it all into the oven. It'd be ready in less than an hour.

She'd brought a bottle of wine to share over dinner and had left it in the car. She headed out the front door, to find Hank pulling his truck in behind her car in the driveway.

"It sure does my heart good to see you here after a long day of work." He pushed his truck door closed and leaned in to kiss her, careful not to wipe dust or sweat on her.

"I've got dinner in the oven."

"Magnificent."

She grabbed the wine from her front seat and they walked into the house.

"I'll go take a quick shower and be right back down."

"Before you go, were you aware of some changes in your kitchen?"

He gave her an odd look, then walked there. He sighed, shook his head. "They look nice, don't they?"

"They sure do. He does good work," she said. "And with good intention."

"I knew he was working on them. He took the doors down on Saturday. He worked fast."

She couldn't help recognize the pride in his voice.

He turned to her and placed a quick kiss on her lips. "Something for you to mull over while I'm up there. I talked to Doug today, you know, the realtor. The sellers would consider a reduced bid."

He jogged up the stairs. She opened the bottle and poured herself a glass. When he returned, smelling heavenly and looking even better, she'd drank one and had poured a second. She fixed her eyes on his and he stopped before reaching her.

"Yes. Yes, Hank. I want the house."

He pulled her to her feet, lifted her up and swung her around.

* * *

The bid process went much smoother than the worst case scenario Leslie had dreamed up in her head. With Hank at her side and Doug guiding them, her lack of experience didn't matter. Because Hank had done such a great job laying everything out for her on paper, she knew exactly what financial commitment she was comfortable with. Because Doug advised them on what was a reasonable bid, they chose an amount to offer, and came up with a Plan B if it came back rejected. Doug drew up all the papers and headed off to talk with the sellers. All Leslie had to do was wait.

On the way back to the Inn in Hank's truck, she said, "So when are you going to tell me about this phantom investor? Why are you keeping that a secret?"

He glanced over and his lips twisted into an affectionate smile. "Ahh, darlin'. Don't worry about that. It's not as mysterious as it sounds, you'll see. Once the bid is accepted, I'll tell you."

They walked on the beach, trying to forget Doug was speaking at that moment to the sellers, but Leslie kept her cell phone in her hand, not wanting to miss the ring if it were buried in her pocket. She tried not to dwell on it, but every time she pushed it out of her mind, the magnitude of her action overwhelmed her.

She could be buying a house! On her own. Not just any house. Her favorite house in the world, a very expensive house, a house hundreds of miles away from home. But … that wasn't home anymore. Nothing there was home for her. This … this was her new home. If they accepted her bid.

Ahhhh.

Fortunately, the swirling in her mind only went on for a few hours because Doug called. When his number appeared on her phone, she gasped and showed it to Hank. His eyes went wide and he pointed at it, nodding.

She pushed Speaker and answered.

"Leslie, the meeting with the sellers went very well."

"Really? How well?" Her voice was breathless, but let him think it was the wind from the beach blowing past the speaker.

"They are willing to come down from their asking price, however not quite as low as you offered. They're willing to meet you in the middle. So you need to decide if that's acceptable to you."

She had no idea. No, wait. She did. She needed to think. No need to rush. She looked at Hank, he was motioning.

"Tell him we'll discuss it and call him right back."

She relayed the message into the phone and hung up. Her heartbeat raced and she felt like a boxer in the ring. She had the strange desire to bounce on her toes.

Hank was the voice of calm. "What do you think about the counter offer?"

She shook her head. She had no idea. Well, wait. Yes, she did. "It was our Plan B, right? If they didn't accept our original bid, we already decided what we would do. As long as we stay within Plan B, we're comfortable with it. Right?"

He smiled and wrapped an arm around her waist. "You got it, gorgeous." He leaned in and gave her a kiss. "And don't worry about financing the extra amount. That won't be on you. That'll be on my side."

"Your secret financier?"

He smiled and nodded.

"Don't you need to check with them?"

"No, I'm well aware of what he can do. This is within his guidelines."

She inhaled deeply and puffed it out. "So we call Doug back and give him the counter offer?"

"Sounds like it."

And she did. Doug took the information and told her to stand by because he didn't think it'd be long. The buyers' acceptance was a matter of course now.

Leslie and Hank spent the few moments sharing a long, excited kiss on the beach. In fact, when the phone rang, they almost neglected to answer it.

"Hello?" Her voice this time was deep and unfocused.

"The house is yours. The sellers accepted your counter offer."

Hank gave a whoop and a holler and Leslie refrained from her impulse to throw her phone up in the air. He wrapped her in a warm, close hug and they ended with a kiss.

* * *

The next night, Leslie took inordinate care in her room to make sure her hair and makeup were perfect. After the excitement last night, Hank had invited her out to a dressy restaurant for a celebration dinner. Not only did she want to thank him for all his help with the house purchase process, she was craving a little romance.

Because of the additional effort on her face, she ran late so she had the pleasure of answering the knock on her door, swinging it open to find him standing there, dressed in a full suit. Charcoal gray, cut to fit him to a tee, mauve shirt and burgundy tie. She'd never seen him this dressed up. The man dazzled in his masculinity. Suntanned face, all sign of stubble shaved away from his chin, his hair not only clean and combed, but the attempt to tame it was evident with some sort of product he'd undoubtedly rubbed through it with his fingertips. Little did he know she'd always liked his casual, loose hair.

She'd always loved a man in a sharp suit, as well, and with a pang she remembered Tim dressed this way routinely every day. However, there was only one reason Hank was dressed this way tonight.

For her.

The fact that he'd pulled a suit out of his closet, or wait, bought a new one? "Where did you get the suit?" she blurted.

He chuckled. "Believe it or not, an old low country boy does own a suit. Don't wear it that often. But I pull it out, brush it off every now and again."

Now she felt bad because that was certainly not the first thing on her mind and by starting with it, it seemed to demean him somehow. To make up for it, she grabbed his hands and pulled him into the room.

"Stand right there." She pointed to the middle of her rug, then took measured steps around him, 360 degrees. He turned his head to watch her as far as he could, his cheeks coloring.

"Mr. Harrison, you look mighty fine." She drawled the "mighty fine" into a southern accent, drawing laughter from him. "No, now," she admonished when he started to move. "I get another round to fully admire my dinner date this evening. I do believe I'll be the luckiest lady in the restaurant tonight. Maybe even the whole island."

She'd made her way around him again, scanning him up and down and was face to face when he grabbed her and pulled her in for a long kiss. Heat seethed down her body and she went breathless under his lips. When they broke, he pulled her close for a long embrace. "I love you."

Just as his whispered words registered, he pulled apart enough to see her face. "I love you, Leslie. You've become such a big part of my life and I don't want to think of a future without you in it." He ducked his head, then focused in on her again. "I know the time is bad for you. I know you're newly divorced and you're not as sure as I am. And that's okay. I'm not asking for you to say it back to me. I want you to know it."

His words flowed over her. She closed her eyes and waited for a natural reaction. Would they make her scared?

Nervous? Want to run? No. They were welcome. Because she felt the same way.

"I love you too, Hank."

His face did a transformation. She knew his expressions because she'd spent so much time watching them. But anyone could read this one.

"Ah, sweetheart, I can't tell you how much it means to me. But I don't want you to feel obligated to say it, now."

"I don't." She gave her head a fierce shake. "But I do. I love you, I mean. Why else would I take a job here? Buy a house here? I want to stay here. And the only reason I can think of, besides the gorgeous beach, of course, is you."

He laughed and came in for a kiss. She loved the feel of his lips on hers, loved how his kisses made her body react. "I haven't been as sure of anything lately as I am about this. You've helped me become whole again." He shook his head, frustrated. "I'm not that good with words, but darlin', you've made me happy. You've made me want to rise above the failures of the past. You make me want to see the future."

She shook her head, speechless. Tears stung the corners of her eyes. How had she gotten so lucky to have met this man? When her life was in pieces, and her self-esteem was as low as it could go, she walked into the house where so many wonderful childhood memories had taken place, and there he was. Simple, gorgeous, hardworking Hank. The Old Gray Barn had brought them together, and now they were going out to celebrate the indisputable fact that she would become its new owner.

Life was absolutely amazing.

They headed out to a restaurant called Perrone's. Hank had seen it ranked as the best restaurant on the island in a recent newspaper article, so he had chosen there to celebrate the new house. And, as it turned out, their newly declared love.

"Get whatever you want," Hank assured her. When she spotted the prices on the menu, she started to object. "No," he insisted. "Whatever strikes your fancy. I know the food is fantastic here."

She sighed and tried to push the expenses out of her mind. He wanted to be sweet and create a memorable evening for her. Who was she to rob him of that? This was his choice and she wouldn't worry about his spending for him.

After scanning the menu and throwing possible choices to each other, she settled on the fresh catch selection, and he chose duck. A knowledgeable waiter made suggestions on accompanying wines, and they each chose a glass, savoring the memory they were forming, holding hands over the tabletop.

"In all the fuss about my suit and all, I don't think I told you how beautiful you look tonight."

She blushed, a smile coaxed. She hadn't gone for the typical sundress she favored. She'd dug deep into the back of her closet and chose a dress that had arrived with her other clothes from the house in Pittsburgh shortly after it sold. She'd worn it to a wedding years ago. It was a navy blue satin, two piece dress. The sheath hugged her form, skimmed her knee and was sleeveless with a crew neck, topped off with a lacey jacket of the same color. It complimented her light brown hair and with all the beach walking she'd been doing, she was pleased to see it fit her even better than the first time she wore it. Living on the beach must agree with her.

"Thank you. I'm glad I didn't send this one to storage. I needed a fancy dress, and there it was. Must be fate."

"Speaking of storage, it won't be long now till you can pull everything you've got out of storage. You'll have so much space in the Barn, you won't possibly fill it all."

She nodded, a bubble of giddiness rising in her throat. "Can you imagine how much furniture it'll take to fill that place?"

"I'm sure Jeremy will help out with that."

"Yes! I bet he will."

They were halfway through their entrees when she remembered. "Oh! Tell me about this secret donor."

"Uhh." He looked down at his plate, then put his fork down. "See now …" He cleared his throat and looked back at her. "There is no secret donor, darlin'. I mean, the extra investor is … me."

"You." She blinked.

"Yep." He gave one firm nod.

"I don't understand." She put her fork down too. "Why didn't you just tell me? Why the big mystery?" She shook her head.

"Because." He reached across the table. Now that neither of them were eating, he could put both her hands in his and squeeze them. "Think about that. How would that look?"

"What do you mean?"

"I tell you I want to buy the house with you. I want to share the mortgage. And move in."

"Okay."

"It sends the wrong message. Sure, I want the house too. And I can help you with your dream of qualifying for the loan. But that's not all I want."

This moment seemed important. Significant. Monumental.

"I want to live with you, Leslie, sure I do. But I want to do this right. I want us to live together, as man and wife. I want this to go in the right order. The last thing I'd want you to think is I'm interested in the house, and in order to get to live with you, then I'd propose. No. Wrong order, see what I mean?"

"I think …" But she couldn't think. She couldn't form a sentence.

"It's you I want, Leslie. I know it's sudden. So I can wait. Meanwhile, I want you to buy this house of your dreams, because it's what you want. And I can help you with the piece of the funding you couldn't do on your own. And someday, when we're both ready to be married, we'll live there together."

She brought her hands up to her face, covered her eyes, ran her fingers through her hair.

"Too fast. Darn it all. I'm sorry, Leslie. I'm movin' way too fast," he said.

"No," she assured him. "No, it's just … sudden. I mean, five months ago I was married to …" But she didn't want to say it. She didn't want Tim's name to mar the excitement and joy of finding love a second time. He was irrelevant. "My head's spinning," she admitted.

"How about we finish our dinner, then take a walk on the beach?"

She nodded, shot him a beaming smile and concentrated on her fish. They talked during the remainder of dinner, but kept the topics as mundane as possible. She was glad. She needed to give her heart a chance to recover from the bombshell.

They finished dinner, had coffee, and while Hank was paying the bill, Leslie stood by the picture window facing the ocean. The restaurant stood on stilts and a door opened from the dining room to a back porch, which led down to the beach via a set of wooden stairs. He joined her and taking her hand, they walked down to the sand. Walking on the beach with Hank had become one of her favorite activities in the world.

"So," she began. She wanted to talk about it again, needed to. But she had no idea how.

"So," he echoed. Then he chuckled.

"You definitely had a surprise for me tonight. More than one," she amended. "You want to invest in the Barn so I can afford it. And you're in love with me. And you want to marry me."

He ducked his head but she caught his white smile in the growing darkness. "That about sums it up, don't it? Thanks for the recap."

"I have to say for a man of few words, you sure poured them on tonight." They took a few more steps and she stopped to slip off her shoes, then picked them up so she could walk barefoot in the cool sand. "You been thinking about this long?"

"Honest?"

She nodded. *No, lie to me*, she mused.

"I realized I was in love with you when it dawned on me what you were trying to do at the prison and that ill-fated first visit with Jeremy. I would've never tracked you down to Pittsburgh if I weren't in deep. You're such a sweet, loving woman. I was a total jackass to react the way I did."

She began shaking her head. She didn't want to go back there. What's past is past and no need to trample over bad ground.

"That's when I knew I loved you. I was waiting for the right moment to tell you."

Sunshine dawned in her heart. Her resulting smile couldn't have been stopped.

"As for the house, when I heard you wanted to buy the Barn but was short on funding, I was determined to help. It took a meeting with my banker to find out I could fill in the hole you were in. So of course I wanted to. I didn't want you to think I was doing anything underhanded, that's why I couldn't be up front with you until now."

She reached an arm around his waist and squeezed him while they walked. He brought an arm around her shoulders and she recognized the instant warmth. They walked in silence and she wondered if he'd forgotten about the third revelation tonight: he wants to marry her!

"When did you start thinking about marriage?" Saying it into the dark night made it so much easier than saying it in daylight.

He took a deep breath through his nose, held it a moment, then puffed it out. "You know, Leslie, the kind of man I am, I guess you'd say, traditional. Yeah, I'm a traditional man with old-fashioned values. When I fall in love with a woman, I look to the future. Love isn't just for the here and now, it's for a lifetime. I was in love with my Ruthie. Every day was a treasure. But she was robbed from me and I spent a lot of years being bitter and angry.

"You are a new gift from God. Can't say I deserve that gift or not, but by God, I'm takin' it. Or at least, doing my best to try to take it. I've been lonely for years now. I'm the kind of man who loves being in love. Loves having a companion, loves being married. It's the way I'm made."

They stopped walking and he turned to face her in the sand. "I've known for a while now I want to marry you, but I don't want to make mistakes. Don't want to scare you, don't want to move too fast. Don't want to get so wrapped up in what I want, I don't think about what you want. I know you love me, you told me that tonight, and I believe you. But I'm not in a rush, darlin'. I can wait because you're worth waiting for. You're the best thing that's happened to me in a good long time."

He seemed to have more to say but she couldn't stop herself from grabbing his cheeks and kissing his lips, any more than she could stop her blood pulsing and her heart beating. She pulled him in and poured as much love and affection and passion into the kiss as she possibly could, hoping he got it. She ripped her lips from his, kept hold of his face and looked deep into his eyes. He huffed slightly, his breathing ragged. His eyes locked in with hers, his pupils darkening and heat emanating from his skin.

Then, he pulled her close for a kiss of his own. Her heart raced with the sensations his kiss let loose in her, feelings she hadn't experienced in a long time, if ever. He slid a hand under the lace jacket and cupped her shoulder, caressing her bare skin. While his lips kept hers engaged in a hot tangle, his fingers grazed over her bodice. He rested his hand over her breast, squeezing gently and tentatively testing its weight, its shape, familiarizing himself with her body's curves, even while clothed in blue satin.

It didn't seem foreign, somehow. Even though the only man who had ever explored her in that particular spot over the last twenty years was not this man. It felt good, it felt welcome.

With his other arm still wrapped around her, he pulled her lower body closer to his, and his warmth enveloped her. Their bodies were studies in opposites, hers small and chilly and soft, his large and warm and hard. His body was tight from a lifetime of physical labor, his muscles well-toned. She ran her hands up under his jacket and across his back. Lost in the dance of their lips and tongues, she pressed herself closer to him and discovered another part of his body that was hard and tight.

A gasp escaped her lips and he broke away. "I'm sorry," he murmured, and he turned and took a step away.

"No, Hank, don't go," she said, following him, hand out. She was a grown woman, a mother, familiar with the functions of the human body. There was nothing here to be sorry about. She reached him and grabbed his arm, spun him around till he faced her. He was adjusting his belt, his pants.

"I didn't mean to …" he fumbled.

"You didn't mean to what? To kiss me? To touch me? To make us both want to explore each other further? Why not? We're in love, Hank. We're nearing our fifties." She laughed. "If we're not entitled to go beyond a kiss, who the heck is?"

His head was dipped, listening, not looking. Now he turned enough to catch a glimpse at her. His lips curled and he laughed too.

"Don't apologize for that. I'm very attracted to you."

He let out a breath. "Glad to hear it. And, uh, I guess it goes without saying I'm attracted to you."

She smiled. "I got that."

"Did you now?" His reddened cheeks revealed his embarrassment but he was loosening up. "Leslie, I want you. I really do. But in my day, you only did that if you were committed. It's served me well my whole life. I'm not about to change it now."

He really was a man of honor and integrity. And somehow, she was lucky enough to have fallen in love with him.

They started back to the car. As the night wore on, the temperature had dropped and Leslie shivered in her thin dress. He noticed, he always did, he was so attentive to her. He pulled off his jacket and rested it over her shoulders. She reached her arms through the sleeves and dug her hands in the pockets for the walk back. Something was in the right pocket. A small square box, velvet covered.

Without thinking, she whipped it out of the pocket and held it up, looking at him. His mouth dropped, eyebrows up. He tried to take it but she moved it out of his grasp. "What's this?"

His cheeks colored again. Poor guy had had a rough night. "Well, I, now, you don't need to …"

She knew exactly what it was, at least she knew what she hoped it was, what she wanted it to be. She brought her other hand over to lift the lid and before she did, it hit her. She wanted it to be an engagement ring, she wanted it to be for her, and she wanted to say yes. In fact, she wanted the whole nine yards. She wanted her handsome Hank, down on one knee, taking her hand and asking her the question. She wanted to say yes, and she wanted him to slide it on her finger. And she wanted a big celebration kiss while he swung her around.

She saw the whole thing in her mind. Along with the next several decades being this man's wife.

He put a hand over the box, her hand trapped underneath his. "The last thing I want to do is rush you. I don't want to ask you before you're ready to say yes. I can wait. I want you to be comfortable."

"But you had it in your pocket. You must've planned to ask me tonight."

"No."

"No?" Her eyebrows scrunched. "You planning on asking someone else tonight?"

He shook his head. "Dang, you're rough, woman. Give a guy a break." He took the ring box from her hand. "I've carried this along with me every time I've seen you since I bought it. Waiting for the right moment when I think you're ready."

She stared at it. "When did you buy it?"

"When I was positive I wanted to ask you."

Her eyes widened. "Which was when?"

"Do you remember when Jeremy first came home? And Marianne had the big welcome sign up at the Inn and everyone greeted him and welcomed him home?"

"Sure I do."

"That's when I knew. You see, if it weren't for you, Leslie, I wouldn't have even taken part in Jeremy's homecoming. My heart was so hardened over that boy and what he did, I didn't think I'd ever speak to him again. It took you to get me to see the error in my ways. It was because of you I got my son back and could form a new relationship with him." He rubbed his palm over the velvet on the box. "That's when I knew I wanted to make you my wife and be together forever. And it's just one of many reasons why I love you."

"That's when you bought the ring?"

"Yep." He looked at her, a new idea forming in his eyes. "And I can prove it. Jasmine could tell you."

"Jasmine!"

"I took her aside while she was visiting, told her my intentions and showed her the ring. I guess I wanted to get her blessing. Not that it would've stopped me if she'd said no. But I was relieved when she gave me the green light."

She felt like laughing as loud as she could at the sky. "She did? She never told me!" It'd been way too long since she'd spanked that girl.

"Don't be mad at her. I made her promise to keep it a secret until the time was right. It's probably killed her the last month not saying anything to you."

Hmmm, she had no idea Jasmine was that good at keeping secrets. She wondered what else Jasmine hadn't told her.

He quieted and took her by the shoulders, forcing her to look into his eyes. "So, what do you say, Leslie? Is the time right?"

Chapter Sixteen

She got everything she wanted. The proposal on the beach, Hank on one knee, even the celebration twirl and kiss. The ring was a diamond solitaire on a gold band. It was small and simple but exquisite. And it came with the love of the finest man in the world behind it. The best part of it was, she had not one regret.

Later that night, Hank returned her to the Inn. Marianne was in the dining room, setting new cloths on each of the tables before calling it a night. They joined her, hand in hand.

"How was your celebration dinner? Have a good meal?"

Leslie frowned, looking at the ceiling. "I think it was." She turned to Hank. "Do you remember your meal, Hank?"

He played along, rubbed his chin. "Barely."

Marianne looked perplexed. "You guys all right? Not having a senior moment, are you?"

Leslie couldn't wait anymore. She held out her left hand.

Marianne took a second, then gasped. "Oh my gosh! You did it!" She banged her dad on the arm. "And you! You said yes!" She rushed forward and wrapped an arm around each of them, dipping her head between them. "I'm so happy for you!" She popped a kiss on her dad's cheek, then Leslie's. "Congratulations."

They basked in her enthusiasm, but then she dashed off. "Just a minute!"

Hank shook his head. "That girl … what's she got up her sleeve?"

"She's so full of love for everyone."

"You're right about that."

Marianne came back, now winded from her running. She had a hold of Jeremy, pulling him by the arm while he objected.

"What is it, sis? What's going on?"

"Hey, son."

He focused on his dad. "She pulled me away from sanding a dresser I was making for the Petersons. It better be good."

Leslie and Hank shared a smile, then Leslie presented her finger again. The little diamond glistened.

Jeremy's mouth dropped and he stared at it for a while, his emotions playing out across his face. When he tore his eyes away from the ring to look at first his dad, then at Leslie, his voice was choked with sentiment. "Ah, Dad. I can't tell you how much this makes me happy. You found love. A man like you should have a woman to love him, and you couldn't have found a better partner than Leslie." His face colored as he took Leslie's hand and brought it to his lips. "Thank you," he whispered.

He didn't need to thank her. Hank was the finest man she'd ever met. He was kind, hard-working, thoughtful, and she loved every moment she spent with him. She couldn't believe her good fortune in finding him.

Later, after Hank had walked her up to her room and they had shared a long, warm kiss full of promise for the future, he left and she immediately picked up the phone to call Jasmine, that rascal. When she revealed her big news, Jasmine let out a whoop.

"I wondered when it would happen! It was hard keeping a secret for so long! Congratulations, Mom. I'm so happy for you."

Leslie fingered the light quilt on her bed. "You sure you're okay with me getting married again, so quickly after divorcing your father?" She never had any intention of it happening this way. But you couldn't always plan what life threw at you, especially when she'd been praying every step of the way, and felt convinced it was God's will for her.

"Mom, I want you to be happy. Hank makes you happy. If you're sure, I'm sure."

* * *

The closing date for the Old Gray Barn was set, about a month away. Leslie settled back into life on the beach, teaching her sixth graders, enjoying the family around her, Marianne, Tom and Stella, Jeremy, working hard to put his life back together and realize his dreams of building a business, her frequent phone calls with Jasmine, and of course, her moments with Hank. She savored her routine of teaching all day, going back to the Inn, grabbing some relaxation time on the deck with a book and a cool drink while letting the powerful sound of the ocean waves come over her. Then, when Hank was done with work for the day, they'd spend time together. It was never elaborate. Simple time spent talking, walking, sharing, laughing and kissing. Getting to know each other better. Growing their love stronger. She couldn't remember ever being this happy in her life.

She felt remarkably calm about the purchase of The Old Gray Barn. She wasn't plagued with restless nights or upset stomach, as often hit her when she was faced with a difficult decision. She was at peace.

Hank, however, as the day got closer, seemed nervous. Several times, while they were at dinner, he'd take a phone call, glance up at her and excuse himself to take it away from the table.

"Who was that?" she'd ask.

"Oh, some questions about the closing."

"From who? Why aren't they calling me?" He may be an investor, but she had the primary investment.

"Oh, you know how it is around here, sweetheart. They know me and know I can answer quick enough."

"Are there any problems?" Worry gripped her.

"No, no, not at all. Smooth as silk." He patted her hand, shot her a reassuring smile and went back to his plate. If there was anything to worry about, she felt sure he'd fill her in. Meanwhile, it was sort of nice to have someone take care of the endless details.

The morning of the closing finally dawned. It was a Friday in October and she'd taken the whole day off of school. She'd accidently left her curtains open an inch-crack last night, so the sun blazing through woke her before her alarm could ring. Turns out, it was beautiful way to wake up.

She showered and dressed casually in slacks and a sleeveless top, then set to work on her hair and face. Halfway through, her cell rang. It was Hank.

"Good morning, darlin'. How are you feeling today?"

She stretched luxuriously at the beloved sound of his voice. "Couldn't be better. I'm buying the house of my dreams and will move in later today. I'll have the man of my dreams by my side, helping me every step of the way. And guess what, once we get this out of the way, we can start planning our wedding date."

"First things first, huh?"

"Yes, I'm a big proponent of that."

"Everything in its proper order."

She laughed. "I guess."

"I think this is going to be a fantastic day. What are you wearing, by the way?"

A surprised laugh escaped her. "Why Hank, is this one of *those* phone calls?"

He chuckled heartily. "No, no, no. I want to suggest we dress up. Make the event more memorable. Maybe be camera ready when we're signing the papers and opening the front door."

She shook her head. He was so sentimental. One of the many things she loved about him. She never would've predicted at their first meeting he had this romantic side. But it had sure come out.

"I like that. How dressy?"

He took a moment to think about it, then told her which dress he preferred. She went to her closet and found it. It was a sundress, gauzy and breezy, a beautiful off-white with lace. She'd worn it once when they'd gone out to dinner and he'd complimented her on it. How sweet he'd remember it.

When they hung up, she changed her clothes and finished her preparations. By the time he came to pick her up, she was waiting for him in the great room. He spotted her the minute he stepped into the room, and stopped in his tracks. He was dressed in the suit again, from their engagement night. The charcoal suit fit him perfectly and made her breath catch in her throat.

"My, oh my. You are the picture of loveliness." He took a few steps toward her, his arms outstretched. She stood, laced her fingers in his and smiled into his eyes.

"You look very handsome," she said shyly. He looked so much more than handsome. He looked rugged and strong and sexy. Very sexy. But she stopped with handsome.

His lips came down on hers and her breathlessness was complete. The man literally took her breath away, the sight of him, the touch of him and the taste of him.

"Ready to go?" he asked.

The closing meeting went smoothly. Doug was there, helping them through the steps. Everything was in order with Leslie's down payment money and Hank's mortgage. No surprises. When they left thirty minutes later, they held a stack full of papers and the keys to the house.

"I can't wait to see it," Leslie said. She hadn't been to the house since their official walkthrough a few days ago. Would it look different somehow now that it was actually theirs? Her heart pounded.

"Let's go." He drove across the island slowly, which only added to her suspense. He kept glancing down at the clock in his truck.

"What's the matter?"

"Not a thing."

"You're acting strange," she noted. "Like you're hesitant to get to the house."

He shook his head, ducked with a smile. "No. It's not every day you open up your newly acquired house where you plan to spend the rest of your life with your new bride. Let a guy savor the moment, huh?"

She squeezed his arm. Her romantic.

They parked the car in the sand driveway, got out and slammed the truck doors, gazing up at the house on stilts that held such special meaning for both of them. She glanced first to one neighboring house, then the other, then turned her head to peek in between to catch a glimpse of the gorgeous ocean view out back. Soon she'd be waking up to that view every morning.

They climbed the stairs and Hank fumbled with the key in the lock.

"Your hands are shaking," she realized and put hers over his, helping guide the key into the hole. Soon, they had the door unlocked, pushed it open and found …

"Hi Mom! Surprise!"

"Jaz! What are you …? Oh my gosh!" She rushed forward and pulled her daughter into a hug. "Did you arrange this?" She stared at Hank in amazement over Jasmine's shoulder.

He was interestingly silent and she was unable to read his face.

"Oh, if you only knew, Mom. Come on in."

"What? What are you …?"

Jasmine took her hand, and Hank slid in beside her and grabbed her other one. Stepping aside, Jasmine waved her arm to the huge rustic great room of the Old Gray Barn. Her view unobstructed, she didn't know where to look first. Because it was filled to the gills.

With people.

The entire room was filled with people she knew, all dressed up. "What …?"

"Surprise!" came a unison shout, then lots and lots of noise. Her heart pounding in her ears, she looked out and saw several of her teacher friends from Pittsburgh, who must have traveled here to help her celebrate her new house. She picked out at least four, before she then noticed her new principal here in Pawleys, and a few of her new teacher friends. She saw her old next door neighbor in Pittsburgh, who she'd known for twenty years. She waved to Leslie, a bright smile on her face.

"What did you do?" She looked at Jasmine, then swiveled her head to Hank. "What is all this?" Why would all these people travel six hours or more on the day she moved into her new house? But they weren't all.

Moving to the front of the small army was the trio she had met at the beginning of this transformational summer: Deakon and Norman Foster, and Joan Lundeen. Little Deakon had grown at least an inch since the summer began, and Norman looked healthy. They came forward and stood in front of her, Norman resting a hand on his son's shoulder.

"Hi, Leslie," Norman said, and his mother-in-law Joan came around and hugged her.

Leslie was tongue-tied but she managed, "So good to see you again! How are things going?"

Norman nodded. "They're going well. I've been on an anti-convulsive medication for five months, with no seizures. If I get through the next month, they're going to let me have my driver's license back."

"That's wonderful!" Leslie kneeled down to Deakon's height. "And how is your new school year going? Do you like your teacher?"

"Yep!" He nodded vigorously. "They let me do a lot of coloring. And I learned how to read!"

Joan winked at her. "We do a lot of reading at home, don't we, Deakon?" She turned to Leslie. "I'm so lucky to have them close by. They help me as much as I help them."

Leslie knew how important in life it was to feel needed.

"Well, you've got a lot of other guests to greet, so we'll talk to you after."

They started to move away, but Leslie said, "After? After what?" She darted her head around, looking at Hank and Jasmine, but they were both amazingly closed-mouthed.

"Leslie," she heard, and turned back to the crowd in front of her.

"Rita!" It was her impromptu girlfriend Rita, the owner of the Front Porch restaurant. They embraced. "So great to see you! I've been meaning to call, and I've been awful at staying in touch, but I really want to become friends."

Rita laughed. "I think you've been pretty busy since I last saw you." She shook her hand at someone. "Hey, I have someone I want to introduce you to." A tall and ruddy man stepped up, dark-complected with curly hair. "This is Gary, my husband. He's home from Afghanistan. Just arrived last month!"

"So nice to meet you, Gary. And I'm so happy you're home." The look exchanged between Gary and Rita was so full of love and passion, it was immediately clear to Leslie what kind of relationship they shared. She turned to Hank, "This is Hank, my … fiancé." It rolled off her tongue, but she realized it was the first time she'd introduced him that way. Which reminded her, when she'd met Rita, she hadn't even met him yet.

Life was strange.

Rita turned and grabbed her son's arm. "You remember Nathan."

The teenager looked weirded out but was polite, held his hand out to her and shook it. "Nice to see you again."

Rita excused him to go look at the beach, then said in a conspiratorial whisper, "He's getting straightened out. Gary and I set the house rules, and made him understand if he breaks them again, he's out. And no paying for college until he's drug-free."

"That's wonderful! How's it going?"

Rita shrugged. "Better than when he was walking all over me. I realized tough love was the best way to straighten him out, and he needs it to be a self-sufficient adult."

"That's right. Best of luck."

Rita and Gary strolled after their son to the beach view in the back of the house, arms around each other's waists. Leslie turned to Hank, "How did you find them? And why?"

But they were interrupted by a "Leslie, dear." She turned to see Evelyn Fletcher, the white-haired lady in charge of delivering warm blankets and caps to the premature babies at the hospital. "Evelyn! Oh my gosh!"

They hugged and Leslie listened as Evelyn filled her in on all the good work her group continued to do for Levine Children's Hospital, and the camaraderie shared by the ladies each and every week.

Wrapping up their conversation, Hank approached Leslie with a young man in his thirties in tow, dressed in a black suit. The loud swarm of conversation noise died down suddenly, leaving the room quiet enough for her to hear Hank's next words. Quiet enough for everyone to hear, in fact.

"Leslie, I'd like you to meet Brad Cummings."

Leslie automatically held her hand out to shake with him. "Nice to meet you, Brad."

"So nice of you to have us all in your new home."

Leslie rolled her eyes toward Hank and Jasmine, who lingered nearby. "Well now, it wasn't me who planned all this, and although I have an inkling of who did, what I don't know is why." She took in all the people in the room. "Everyone in this room has played an important part of my life. Some of you I've known a short while, some of you a long time, but all of you have had an impact. It took someone," she laid a meaningful glare on Hank, "a lot of work to track you all down, and get you all here in this room at this moment."

"I think it'll make sense in a minute, darlin'."

With that, Hank took her shoulders and positioned her to stand beside him, facing Brad in the front of the room. All the guests maneuvered to stand in rows behind them. Jasmine slid into place beside her, and Jeremy appeared out of nowhere to stand beside his father. Jasmine was handing her something, and she looked down to see it was a bouquet. Glancing closer, Jasmine held one already.

Her head was spinning but yes, it was all starting to make sense.

Then Brad opened a Bible and said, "Dearly beloved, we are gathered here today …"

She gasped and darted a startled look at Hank. He shushed her and leaned in close to whisper in her ear while the minister continued the ceremony. "Are you ready? When we move into this house together tonight, we're going to be man and wife."

"Oh, my gosh," she breathed, her head clearing. He'd planned a surprise wedding for her. He was serious about making a life with her, and once he knew she wanted it too, he saw no need to wait.

"You're not backing out on me, are you?" His eyes were amused, but held the slightest trace of dismay.

She didn't want him to have one second of doubt she wasn't as committed as he was. "No!"

His surprised expression told her she'd said it louder than she'd intended. In fact, the minister stopped talking and paused, staring between the two of them. The gathering of friends in the room was quiet.

She leaned in close to him so only he could hear. "I meant no, I'm not backing out on you." She turned to Brad, "Minister, please continue. We're getting married!"

Laughter rippled through the crowd and the rest of the short service was uneventful. When they got to the part where Hank could kiss his bride, he left no doubt in her mind theirs would be a marriage of love, laughter, passion and togetherness.

And his kiss gave her enough of a rush to highly anticipate their wedding night.

"I now pronounce you man and wife."

The crowd cheered, no polite, subdued clapping here. Whistles and loud applause. She looked out to the people who meant the most to her in the world, who'd shared this substantial moment with her. Then she turned to the man who made it all possible, the man she'd gladly spend the rest of her life with. She grabbed his cheeks and looked deep into his eyes. "I love you, Hank."

Marianne and several waitresses from the Inn swept by, distributing flutes of champagne to the guests. Hank grabbed two, handed her one.

"To the best woman in the world. The one who saved me from myself and gave me a reason to keep on going."

"Cheers!" shouted the guests.

The rest of the day was spent catching up with friends, new and old, sharing in the love in the room, but never roaming far from her new husband who had secretly planned this whole day for her. Later, when they had all departed, and

Leslie and Hank plopped onto the couch (that Hank had sometime moved over from his house), she said, "You know, it really wasn't a bad summer after all."

THE END

A Word About the Author

Laurie Larsen is a multi-published author of romance and women's fiction. She became an award-winning author when her inspirational romance, *Preacher Man* won the EPIC award for Best Spiritual Romance of 2010. Laurie spends her days working in the high-paced world of Information Technology, and her nights writing love stories that touch the heart. Laurie has been married for 25 years, and is the proud mother of two remarkable sons. She and her husband are empty-nesters now, which makes spending her evenings writing a little easier than it was when she had a house-full. Next year (2015) will be Laurie's 15th year as a published author.

Tide to Atonement
Book 2 of Pawleys Island Paradise
by Laurie Larsen

Chapter One

Jeremy Harrison was in the zone. He laid one last swipe of his brush across the top surface, then took a step back to study his latest creation. A homey shade of blonde maple, the dresser reached slightly over waist-high — at least, to a six-foot-two body like himself. It was his latest design, the "his and her" model, a column of five drawers on each side, separated by an open armoire-style cabinet. The stain was complete. Now, to soak in for a day or possibly two, to allow the high sheen to be brushed with fingertips without danger of leaving prints. After that, he'd check the drawers and make sure they rolled in and out smoothly with no sticks. Then he'd choose handles — brass? No, something more burnished.

He absentmindedly rubbed a hand over his lips, then spit out the taste of polyurethane. Searching for a clean cloth, he lifted his feet high, careful not to knock over any cans of thick liquid, the finishing tools of his trade.

A distant sound wormed into his consciousness. Buzzing, sort of like a mosquito or an angry pack of them. Infuriating in its persistence. Sounded like an alarm. Had he set …?

"Well, dang it!" He ran off the canvas tarp laid in his backyard that he called his work space and into the house through the backdoor. The timer on the microwave was buzzing away and after a quick study, Jeremy realized it had been sounding for at least four, five minutes. He turned it off. He'd set it this morning because he knew he'd get wrapped up in furniture-making and lose track of time — he always did. And normally, that was good. But not today.

Today he had an important appointment in town he couldn't miss. Miss? Heck, no, he couldn't even be late. He hustled to the bathroom at the back of the tiny house and shucked off his sweatshirt, boots and jeans. Jumping into the shower, he emerged two minutes later, dried with a towel, and raced into his bedroom. A quick study of his closet had him pulling out a pair of khaki pants and a button-down light blue shirt. Didn't take much study. There weren't that many choices in there anyway.

Who needed a Wall Street wardrobe when you lived in a beach town in rural South Carolina?

Dressed now, he swung back to the bathroom and made a quick swipe of his hand over his jaw. Shave? His eyes lighted on the digital alarm clock on the counter. Nah, no time. He'd shaved sometime in the last, what, three days? Neil wouldn't mind.

Passing through the kitchen, he peered out the window for a glance at the dresser in the backyard. He shifted his gaze to the sky. No rain in the forecast, nothing but sun expected today. The dresser would be fine.

He raced out the front door and jumped into his truck. These monthly meetings were part of his life now, and he best learn to accept them. At least he'd moved to monthly from weekly. That was one thing to be thankful for.

And one meeting a month with Neil was a heck of lot better than where he came from.

* * *

He didn't mean for his truck tires to squeal as he maneuvered into a parking space. But tardiness was frowned upon and he was cutting it close. He jumped out of the old pickup and took a cleansing breath, lowered his shoulders and walked intentionally.

The County Courthouse in Georgetown was a mere eleven miles from his home on Pawleys Island, but tourist traffic being so erratic, he'd settled into the habit of allowing at least forty minutes for the drive. Now that tourist season was over and autumn had made residence, he didn't need the full timeframe, but as Neil had taught him, it was better to be prepared. Early was always better than late.

Screvens Street sparkled today with the sun glittering off the scrubbed sidewalks and immaculate brick buildings. At the center of them all stood the courthouse, a Pawleys Island historic landmark. It was a pastel yellow and white wooden building with six impressive pillars adorning the second floor balcony. In order to reach that level, Jeremy had the choice of identical closed stairways on the right or left of the building that circled up and met at the front door.

His visits to this landmark had become so routine that he barely noticed the grandeur today. He trotted up the stairs, entered the building, walked to the Probation Office at the back of the third floor, gave his name to the receptionist and sat down in a folding chair in the waiting room, amidst about a dozen other offenders. He was twelve minutes early.

He lowered his head to examine his shoes. No eye contact with those seated around him, that was something he learned during his decade in prison. Mind your own business. Keep to yourself. There was no telling when you might see something or hear something you would be asked about, just because you had your head up, curiously looking around. Not worth it.

"Hey, man." The voice came from the chair beside him. He swiveled his head and recognized a guy who'd spent a few of his last months with him in Columbia at the pre-release center. He scanned his brain for a name but couldn't come up with one.

"Hey." He nodded at the man, dressed in a similar outfit as his — neat-looking khakis and a button-down shirt. This man had sneakers and white athletic socks on though, instead of dress shoes like Jeremy's. Heck, it didn't matter. The ex-con was making an effort. Scraping up extra money for luxuries like leather shoes when the only time you wore them was to your probation appointments, took time. "How you doin'?"

"Good, good." He was nervous, Jeremy could tell. He sat hunched, his shoulders rounded, and rubbed his palms briskly together, creating an uncomfortable slipping sound. "Trying to find a job. Ain't easy."

"No. No, it's not." One of the court's requirements, hold gainful employment. You had to report on your job-hunt attempts at every appointment. Among other things. Drug testing, community service.

The man sighed, his manic tension cutting through Jeremy's calm façade, making him feel nervous, too. Jeremy turned his head and tried to create an invisible wall between them. He didn't mind helping, but he needed to stay calm, serene. That was the name of the game with this process.

"I'll do anything, man. I've tried the most menial jobs. Fry cook, bus boy, bag boy at the grocery store. They just don't want me. I'm dying here."

Jeremy squeezed his eyes to the desperation in the guy's voice. There were consequences to not meeting the court's probation requirements. He himself hadn't had to serve them, thank God. But you had to keep your nose clean. Don't stand out. Follow the rules, as best you can.

"Sorry, man. Keep looking. Ask your officer for a hand. Maybe he could make some calls for you."

The man wiggled in his chair. "What about you? You working? What're you doin'?"

Jeremy exhaled. "I'm trying to start up my own business."

"Oh yeah?" The man looked over at him with interest and in Jeremy's opinion, leaned a little too close. "Doin' what? You wanna hire me?"

Jeremy let out an uncomfortable chuckle. "Nobody on the payroll. I'm barely making ends meet. But doin' what I love. Wood working. I make furniture."

"Oh." The man shrugged and turned away, to Jeremy's relief. "I don't do nothing like that. I wonder if I could start my own business. Might be the only choice I have left."

"Harrison."

Jeremy looked up, glad to be called. "Good luck, man." The man nodded as Jeremy checked in with the receptionist. Jeremy said a quick silent prayer, not even fully formed thoughts and words – just a sincere sentiment to God: *help this man, help get him on his feet.*

"You can go on back to Neil's office."

Jeremy nodded and headed back.

The word "office" was a stretch, but hey, who was he to judge? He edged into Neil's closet-sized room stuffed full with a desk, Neil's chair, two facing chairs and a filing cabinet. A few framed certificates scattered across the walls, but Neil didn't seem to be much into decorating. Stacks of files littered his desktop and the man himself was so big, he dwarfed everything around him.

Neil had been Jeremy's parole officer since he'd been released towards the end of the summer. He'd quickly recognized Neil as an advocate to help him adjust to life in the free world. Neil had high expectations and held him accountable for his behavior, but he made the rules clear and praised Jeremy when he saw results. That was fine with Jeremy. He never should've made the mistakes that had landed him in prison anyway and after serving his sentence, all he wanted now was to get his life back on track. He understood the odds stacked against him — he'd earned every single one. But by following the rules, he'd get there.

One step at a time.

Neil was bent at the waist, his powerful lineman's body folded in half in his chair as he tried to get a closer look at something under his desk. They had talked once or twice about his college career at Clemson. Football had never been Jeremy's sport, but he could certainly see how Neil would intimidate the defenders lined up across from him before the whistle blew. But inside that monstrous body and competitive scowl was the heart of a saint.

Jeremy waited in the doorway. Neil mumbled, sounding frustrated. "Can I help you find something?" Jeremy ventured.

Neil straightened at the sound and banged his head on the partially-opened desk drawer. "Dang!" the big African-American man eked out in pain.

Jeremy scooted around a chair and over a box of papers sitting on the floor, trying to get closer. "I'm sorry. Did I surprise you?" He reached out a hand toward the big man.

Neil was rubbed his aching head, distracted, a smile playing on his face. "When do I move out of this cubicle into a space befitting my size and accomplishments? That's what I want to know."

Jeremy smiled, thankful that he was cracking jokes.

"Can you reach that business card on the floor there?" Neil asked, pointing.

Jeremy leaned, reached, picked it up, handed it to Neil.

"No, it's for you. Keep it."

Jeremy frowned at the card. "Seminal Magazine?"

"Yeah. Have a seat."

Jeremy made his way back to his chair and did as he was told. He waited for explanation, knowing it was coming.

"Do you know what the word seminal means, Jeremy?" Neil slid into his own chair, folded his hands on top of his desk and focused on Jeremy.

Jeremy took a breath. He was never good at English, had a horrible vocabulary. Books were never really his thing, he was always good with his hands. "Ummm …"

Neil shook his head. "No matter." He reached under a stack of files and pulled out a thick book — a dictionary. He handed it to Jeremy.

Jeremy flipped pages till he located the word. "Influential, formative, pivotal, inspiring."

"Good." Neil held a palm up and Jeremy handed the dictionary back. "Nice name for a magazine, huh?"

Jeremy nodded cautiously, wondering what this had to do with him.

Neil continued, "I got a call from them last week. They like to do stories about people who display some of those words you read. Pivotal, inspiring. Ground-breaking. Me and the editor talked over some story ideas. Turns out they want to do a feature on some of our success stories."

Jeremy fidgeted, not liking where this was going.

"I told the lady some of our Values Statements. You know all those. You memorized them a few months ago."

Jeremy nodded, hoping to God Neil wasn't going to call on him to recite them.

"Promoting and maintaining a safe community. Treating people with dignity and respect." Neil leaned back in his chair, let his eyes roll thoughtfully to the ceiling. "What are some others?"

Jeremy sighed, the small card now digging into his palm. "Uh, the ability of offenders to change."

"Yes! That's a good one." Neil's smile formed, white teeth amidst dark complexion. "What else?"

Jeremy could come up with one more, so he hoped that was the last one Neil was after. "The relationship between staff and client can have a profound impact on successful outcomes."

"You got it. I knew you would."

That was one of the things Jeremy liked about Neil. He was genuinely happy when one of his caseload succeeded. The man could scare the crap out of him, and had on several occasions, but he was not without his virtues.

"So, I shared those values with her, and all the rest …," he pointed to the framed paper hanging on the wall behind him. Jeremy swore to himself. They were right there, behind Neil's head! "…and she asked me if I had any success stories she could interview and feature in an article about Georgetown County."

Jeremy went motionless and felt his eyes widening as he stared at Neil.

"I had a few. And you're one of them. Jeremy, you're one of my best success stories."

Jeremy shook his head. "No, no. Thanks for recommending me, Neil, but no, I'm not interested."

Neil's forehead creased, his lower lip protruded a little bit. "You don't want to be seminal? You don't want to help influence others to overcome challenges and be successful? I have to tell you, I'm surprised at that, Jeremy."

His palms were starting to sweat and his breathing was a little labored. "I'll help however I can. But not to be featured. I don't want to tell my story and I don't want to be made public. You understand. But I'll help organize the other offenders and drive the reporter around? Uh, what else …?" He was grasping at straws now.

Neil's mammoth face twisted into a pained expression and it about killed Jeremy to know that he'd caused it with his refusal. Everything about the man was big. He had big emotions, big disappointments, big pride and big hope. So far, Jeremy had worked hard to fulfill all the goals Neil had set out for him. But this … he really didn't want to do it.

"I have to say that's very disappointing, Jeremy. You are a role-model, whether you know it or not. You have a story to tell, and I want you to have the chance to tell it. I can't force you, of course, but part of my job is to rehab you. To get you out of your comfort zone, to try new things. I know you can help others. And isn't that one of our values? To help the community and make things better? I really thought you bought into all those values. You said you did, back when you first got released."

A sinking feeling hit Jeremy's stomach. Neil was using the ole guilt trip on him. Of course he believed in the county's probation values. Of course he'd memorized them and recited them when Neil ordered him to. He was trying his very best every day of his life and he'd never allow himself to fail again. He looked up at the big man before him and realized that he couldn't tell him no. He admired him too much and Neil had been too good to Jeremy to disappoint him.

"I don't want to talk about my crime. I've tried hard to work through that and …"

"No, no. The focus is on your transformation, your new story, how you're making yourself a success. Very little about why you were in jail."

"I'm not what I'd call a success …"

"Not yet, but you're working hard, aren't you? And look at it this way, it might generate some interest in your work. You might get some orders out of this. That would be nice, wouldn't it? Call it free advertising."

Jeremy took a deep breath and let it out.

"Well, if you're gonna be stubborn, give me the card back." Neil held his huge hand out across the desk.

Jeremy looked down at the card. "I'll do it."

The transformation was instantaneous and real. An immense smile jumped onto Neil's face. He got up and came around, pounding Jeremy on the back in his excitement. Jeremy choked and concentrated on keeping himself from flying across the room.

"That's the man! Good job. I knew I could count on you. You're going to be very seminal, I just know it. Great."

They spent the next ten minutes discussing Jeremy's progress. Then, Neil advised, "I'll include your name on the list to the magazine. They'll call you at your cell number. Make sure you pick it up, now."

"Yes, sir." Jeremy got to his feet and they shook hands again, their standard good-bye.

Neil checked Jeremy's folder a last time. "Oh, it's your turn to drug test today. You know the drill."

Jeremy nodded and ducked out the door. A few steps down the hall, he heard Neil's call, "Oh uh, Jeremy?" He headed back, stopped in the doorway, eyebrows raised.

Neil rubbed his own chin and pointed at Jeremy's. "The article includes some pictures. How about you make some time to shave, huh?"

Jeremy groaned and nodded. As he made his way to the receptionist's desk for his little white cup, he seriously considered accidentally/purposely losing his cell phone.

All Around the Square knitting pattern

Your free gift from The Green Girl …

This hat was designed for knitters that just don't like working the traditional form of "knitting in the round." The idea is to start with a square, knitting in garter stitch and morph into knitting in the roundafter the square is a specific size. The hat in this pattern is specifically sized for preemies, but is easily sized up for any child. This pattern is a lovely little gift for new babies that need a little extra love and care. Knit up a dozen and take them to your local hospital's newborn nursery. They will be very appreciative. Remember, these babies are a bit fragile - so please do not wash in any detergent with perfume. Use a brand that is considered free and clear or perfumes and dyes.

Peace and joy to you all…
The Green Girl

Materials:

100 yds light weight (size 3) baby soft yarn – you will have a bit of leftover yarn. Yarn must be machine wash and dryable and as soft as you can find. For this example, I used - Bernat *Softee* Baby in the mint color. I find this yarn works very well for the precious little heads that these hats cover.
1 – 5 needle set US 5 double pointed needles
scissors
tapestry needle
1 – stitch marker

Terms:

k – knit stitch
p – purl stitch
M1 – make one invisible increase
dpn – double pointed needle
cast on – CO (long tail cast on is used in the example)
bind off – BOIP (bind off in pattern)
sts - stitches

Gauge – 7sts x 8 rows = 1 inch for stockinette stitch

Sizing – It is easy to adjust the size of the hat for an older baby or child. All you need to do is use a larger needle and adjust to a medium (4) weight yarn for needles US 7 -9. Other than those changes, you follow the pattern as written. The only other change you may want to make is add length by adding more knit rows after the increases – this would allow for folding the brim up, but still being able to cover little ears.

Invisible Increase - Lift the side leg of the stitch below the stitch that is now on your right needle. Knit that loop. (do not lift the bar between the stitches to make this increase.)

Pattern:
CO – ten (10) stitches using a long tail cast on
Knit every stitch and every row for fifteen (15) rows. Slip the first stitch of each row as if to purl and you will have a nice edge that makes for easy stitch pick-up later on.

You will now have a garter stitch square.

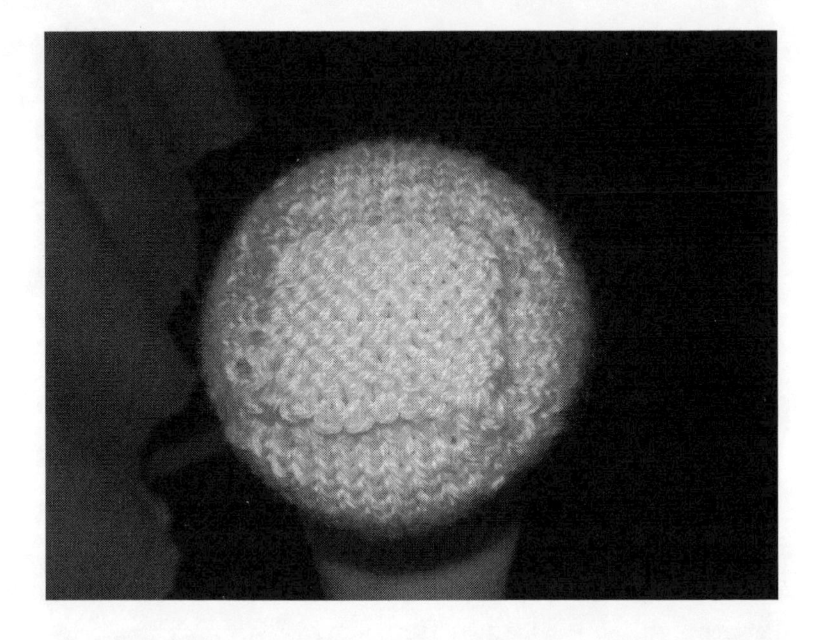

Now you will pick-up stitches around the square to begin the knitting in the round.

You have ten (10) sts on one needle (needle #1)

Now on each side of the square, pick-up six (6) stitches. (needles #2&4)

On the side opposite needle #1 (needle #3) pick-up ten (10) sts.

Now you have one (1) square with a needle on each of the four sides.

Now you begin at needle #1 and start knitting in the round – you are always working on the front side.

Knit one round (knit every stitch on every needle until you are back at needle #1) Place your stitch marker between the last stitch of row #4 and the first stitch of row #1. This will help you keep track of where you are in the process.

Round 1 –*k1, M1, knit to the end of the needle.* Repeat from *-* on all four (4) needles.

Round 2 – knit one complete round on all four (4) needles

Round 3 – *Knit to the last stitch, M1, knit last stitch.* Repeat from *-* on all four (4) needles.

Round 4 - Repeat Round 2 (you should now have 40sts.)

Round 5 – Repeat Round 1

Round 6 – Repeat Round 2

Round 7 – Repeat Round 3 (you should now have 52sts.)

Rounds 8-19 – Repeat Round 2

Brim:

Starting back at needle #1 (do not count needles at this point, but full rounds.)

Round 1: k1, p1 (this is a basic rib stitch)

Rounds 2-5: Follow Round 1 remembering to knit the knit stitches and purl the purl stitches.

BOIP – This bind off is worked in pattern using the basic bind off.

k1, p1 – *then with these two stitches on the right needle, pass the right stitch over the left stitch and off the end of the needle.*

Work the next stitch in pattern and follow from *-*. Work in this manner around all four needles until you have one loop left on one needle. Snip about a 6 inch tail of yarn and pass that yarn through the last loop, pulling it closed.

With your tapestry needle weave in the yarn tails.

Viola! You've made your first hat *All Around the Square*.

A Word About Oz Dust Designs & the Green Girl Studio -

Oz Dust Designs is an online place where people can come and learn new fiber art techniques, find gifts for friends and family, and chat about all things knitty and hooky (a.k.a knit, crochet).

The Green Girl is me, Diana. I've been knitting and crocheting for over forty years because two women (my grandmothers) loved me. They wanted to share their love of the fiber arts with their eldest grandchild.

It is my great joy to instruct others in these art forms and to design items that bring happiness to others. As a cancer survivor, it is my honor to knit and crochet for folks that are recovering from all forms of cancer. I sponsor a local group that knits and crochets for several groups - like new moms and babies at the local hospitals, families in need and others. You will hear all about these events and the people that I meet, the designs that we make and so much more on my blog - The Green Girl Blogs, which can be found at my website.

I hope you all will join me on this journey through the world of fiber arts. It is certainly true that all the stitchers I meet add magic to my life.

I am totally honored that you have taken the time to read this and I hope that you have fun in the land of Oz Dust Designs.

www.ozdustdesigns.com

Other Books by Laurie Larsen

(Books available in all e-book formats and paperback.)

Preacher Man (inspirational romance) *EPIC Award winner!* When Regan moves to Chicago, she's determined to raise her teenage son and adjust to the single life after an ugly divorce. Falling in love with a pastor? Not even on her radar. Yet, as she and Josh grow closer, she knows the secret she's hiding about her past could destroy him.

Hidden Agenda (contemporary romance): A millionaire businessman romances an ambitious advertising executive to get closer to the long-kept secret she holds in her care. When his desire for her trumps his original motives, can love survive her discovery of his hidden agenda?

Break a Leg ***FREE!*** Sequel to *Hidden Agenda*: (contemporary romance) The holidays can be stressful, especially for New York advertising exec Tony White, who just got dumped. Will his Christmas be as dismal as he expects, or will wannabe Rockette Joss McGee dance her way into his heart?

Keeper by Surprise: (contemporary romance/New Adult) College student Keith Hanson cares about grades and girls, not necessarily in that order. But when his parents are killed in a tragic accident, and he becomes guardian to his siblings, life changes drastically.

Inner Diva (contemporary romance) Monica is a modern-day Cinderella who longs to get out from under the expectations of her family and into the spotlight. Carlos is from the wrong side of the tracks with a violent past. Opposites attract, but these two are about as opposite as you can get. And yet, maybe they're just what the other needs to make their dreams come true.